RJ SCOTT

Montana 1

CROOKED
Tree RANCH

Love Lane Books

Crooked Tree Ranch

Montana series, book 1
Copyright ©2015 RJ Scott
Second Edition
Cover design by Meredith Russell
Edited by Sue Adams
Published by Love Lane Books Limited
ISBN 978-151920-477-6

DEDICATION

Thank you, Maria BlackHeart Flores, for naming Jay's cute slow horse, Diablo.

Thank you for Aurore Rose and her advice regarding the horses. Any mistakes that might have slipped through are mine. Thank you to Elin Gregory who re-read and hinted where I should put more – you rock.

A special thank you to my wonderful proofers. Dawn Mayhew, Christina Manole, Rick Mulholland, Hanne, BJ Williams, Catherine Lievens, Kathy Kemp, Susan Kadlec and Tyra Berger.

And always for my family.

CHAPTER ONE

Nate pinched the bridge of his nose and attempted to quell the combination of anger and fear churning inside him. When he'd woken to an absolutely perfect Montana morning, he hadn't expected his day to turn sour so damn quickly. Zach's voice on the end of the phone kept going, the tone a mixture of apology and demand.

"I'm sorry, Nate, if it were up to just me, then I'd let the feed delivery happen, but Dad is getting pissy with it being five months outstanding an' all."

"It's probably an oversight," Nate said quickly. Marcus was the one who looked after the accounts, and they'd never had problems before.

Nate had gone to school with Zach, and it was humiliating for someone Nate had spent much of his childhood around to be telling him this. Hell, Nate hated that people outside Crooked Tree might think they were struggling.

Zach continued. "We spoke to Marcus last week, Nate. He said he was going to make good on the balance when we explained that the account was in arrears. I wasn't going to bother you with this, but the account is still outstanding. I kinda felt I owed you an explanation since the order we got yesterday, isn't going to be filled."

Tension banded Nate's head. This was the third supplier in the last week who had implied Crooked Tree was in arrears. Hell, not *implied*, two of them refused to deal with the ranch at all. Did they all talk to each other? Jeez. When the first supplier stopped their deliveries, Nate considered it was probably an error. He kept meaning to talk to Marcus about it, but never quite got around to it. And this was the second call he'd had to deal with. On the call before this one, when the veterinarian turned around and basically said no to the usual Crooked Tree meds order without citing a reason, Nate was angry but wasn't sure where to place his anger. Things had been up and down with the suppliers over the last few years. One day Marcus was on the ball, the next he'd be wallowing in grief and unable to keep on top of things. It made for uncomfortable relationships with those to whom the ranch owed money.

"I need the feed," Nate said. The door into the kitchen opened and Gabe walked in. Nate turned his back on his brother and spoke more quietly. "Take the money from my private account."

Zach coughed and paused for a few moments. "You'll need to top it up, Nate."

"I'll sort it this morning," he said firmly. "You have my word."

He ended the call and turned to face his brother, expecting to have to explain anything Gabe may have overheard. Instead, he didn't have to worry. Gabe obviously had something on his mind if the concern written on his face was anything to go by.

"You need to come out and see this," Gabe said. He turned and left without further explanation. Nate followed him and pushed the worry about the unpaid accounts to the back of his mind. He'd talk to Marcus as soon as he could.

"What's wrong?" Nate asked worriedly. "Is it the horses? A guest?"

"It's Luke," Gabe said softly. Gabe pushed open the door of the small barn next to the house. Sunlight flooded the dim interior and dust motes danced in the breeze caused by opening the door. It took a few seconds to focus in on what Gabe was pointing at.

Luke, his youngest brother, lay on the floor naked, staring up at the roof and humming softly.

"Fuck, is he drunk?" Nate asked immediately.

Gabe picked up the small bag discarded by the door and handed it to Nate, who sniffed the contents. *Weed.* Nate knew immediately what his little brother, spirited and full of the need to explore his world, had done.

"Jeez," Nate groaned. Then, squaring his shoulders, he crossed to where Luke lay.

"You're not even seventeen yet," Nate snapped at his youngest brother.

"July twenty-eighth today …" Luke slurred. "Hundred and fifty days 'til Christmas an' my birthday. I wan' a bike an' a Barbie an'…" Luke giggled and held a hand in front of his face. He proceeded to examine his hand as if he hadn't seen it before.

Nate despaired at the fact that whatever he said, Luke did what he wanted anyway. Luke looked up at him with a goofy grin and a spaced-out expression on his face. Nate bit back his temper.

"It won't hurt him, Nate," Gabe placated. "We were younger than him when we tried it."

"We were rebelling, Gabe. What's he got to rebel against? He does what he wants anyway. It's not like we stop him." That much was true. Luke was an independent teenager and a good kid—responsible, organized, everything Nate hadn't been at sixteen.

Gabe shrugged, then chuckled. *Great.* Now he had Gabe laughing. Admittedly, finding Luke naked in the middle of their barn, staring up at the roof and talking about his Christmas Day birthday, was kinda funny on the surface. Still, drugs anywhere near his little brother were a dangerous matter and one Nate had to take seriously. Crossing his arms over his chest, Nate widened his stance. Add Luke high on pot to finding out Crooked Tree owed thousands in unpaid feed bills, and Nate was quietly losing his cool.

Gabe copied his stance, but he was still half-smiling. "Seems I remember you were sixteen when Mom found you stretched out in the backyard talking to the sky, and you told her you hadn't been drinking."

Nate heard what Gabe said and instantly recalled the day with the familiar grief of remembering his mom.

"That's beside the point," he said angrily. "You were younger than me when you did it, but *we* never got found out." As he spoke, he knew what he was saying was complete crap and ever so slightly irrational. He also knew Gabe was going to call him on it.

"Mom always knew," Gabe said.

"Luke should have realized."

"What exactly are you angry at?" Gabe asked. "That Luke has pot, or that he was caught with it?"

Nate ignored Gabe pointedly. "You're both my responsibility."

He wasn't lying. He wanted his brothers to have a different life from him, a better life, more choice. Why did they seem to follow what he did and then not listen to him? He wanted them to see that they could take a better path than the one he'd had to follow out of necessity.

Gabe thumped him on the arm. "Jesus, Nate, I stopped being your responsibility the day I turned eighteen."

"I'm still the head of the family," Nate snapped. That was always his final defense, and one he knew wouldn't stand up with his brothers. Ever since their parents had died in 2004, when he was only eighteen, Gabe fourteen, and Luke barely six, he had assumed the mantle of sometimes-parent, even though he was fully aware it was a losing battle. Hell, Gabe had been an easy one, and Luke had been a good kid until he fell in with the Hemsley twins.

"Head of the family," Gabe snorted, then bent at his waist in laughter.

Nate felt affronted, then realized what he had probably sounded like. "Fuck you," he said without heat.

"Head! Family!" Gabe said again. He was evidently unable to stop laughing, and it was contagious.

Finally Nate couldn't help but join in, and soon he was laughing so hard he had tears in his eyes.

"Guys?" Luke interrupted their laughter. A frown marked his youthful features. He clambered to stand, and there was straw sticking out of his hair. Nate considered where else there was probably straw, and that started him off laughing again, his temper long forgotten.

"What do we do now?" Gabe asked with a grin.

Nate looked at Luke with deliberation and, in a smooth movement, had his youngest brother up and over his shoulder. He stalked out of the barn with Luke kicking and yelling. Gabe fell in the side of him and stopped Luke from kicking Nate's stomach and his unprotected balls. In one fluid motion Nate upended his brother into the deep area of the runoff outside the house before standing back, with his hands on his hips, watching Luke flounder in the water. Finally Luke stopped panicking and surfaced with a snarl on his face.

"You fucker!" he snapped at Nate.

"Next time think on smoking that shit," Nate said evenly.

"Next time I'll think on not getting caught," Luke shouted back.

"He has a point," Gabe smirked.

Nate shook his head. His brothers were idiots. With a shove, he pushed Gabe into the same water, then with a whoop, splashed in after them.

"You're freaking crazy!" Luke snapped.

Nate pushed his brother under the water and held him there, then released him. Luke popped up like a cork, spluttering and cursing.

"Mind your mouth," Nate said with a grin.

Gabe lay on his back and floated in the water. He and Nate were dressed in jeans and sleeveless T-shirts and, thank God neither had taken time to pull on boots, both in sneakers. Nate joined his brother in the lazy floating and looked up at the canopy of trees that gave them shade. The water was icy cold after the hot August sun had burned into his skin all day. The latest group of vacationing wannabe cowboys had been hard work and Nate was feeling the ache in his head after another long day. A good ache in his muscles, but he could have done without the enthusiastic yee-hawing from the guests. *Frightening the damn horses.*

"It's been pretty quiet the past month. Do we have bookings for next week?" Gabe asked as he floated close. Crooked Tree was at the height of the summer season, but even then, it wasn't fully booked. They'd all dropped the baton on the place.

"Four families is all." Nate would have shrugged if he'd been sitting, but it was near impossible to do when you were floating in the river.

"That's pretty low. I think we should be worried."

Their dad had owned a third of Crooked Tree, which had passed equally to his sons on his death. The three of them floating here had a stake in making the ranch pay, as well as an emotional connection with it.

"Marcus says we're hitting targets and we're covered 'til the end of the season," Nate explained. He didn't mention the fact the ranch had outstanding accounts with two feed places and the veterinarian. He wasn't going to share with Gabe until he got to the root of it all. "He said we need to think of next year now."

"He said the same thing to me," Gabe admitted.

"You talked to him?"

Gabe huffed. "It's what he always says, that next year will be better. But yeah, he came up this morning with the post, and we got to talking about the future of Crooked Tree. He was kinda deep about it all saying all this stuff about improvement and expansion. He's all worried about the cabins we have empty—says he's thinking of shutting down the Creek Cabins."

Nate had the same idea. They only ever rented out maybe one or two a season and the others stood empty. Meanwhile some of the River Cabins were empty. If they could move the few bookings at the creek to the river, then they could cut down on overheads, like housekeeping, by having them all in one place, and also deliveries.

The ranch covered over twenty-nine thousand acres, bigger than the average Montana ranch. But Crooked Tree was one of those places where the owners were land rich, and cash poor. The actual tourist cabins on the dude ranch were laid out with three miles between them. Some of them fronted the six miles of private access the ranch had to the Blackfoot River, others were in the pine area behind and along the creek. Spread-out places gave people privacy but stretched the ranch some. Upfront costs were spiraling, feed wasn't cheap, and Nate had been lying to himself when he hadn't thought the recession would hit them as much as the next guy. They'd struggled to pay off loans taken out during the boom years when expansion seemed the way forward.

"Yeah," Nate admitted. "Shutting 'em down is probably something we should think on."

"Can I be honest with you about something?" Gabe turned from floating to treading water.

Nate copied, and Luke swam the short distance so that he was in on it as well. Nate didn't want Luke to worry about the ranch at his age—wanted him to have more childhood yet, but he couldn't deny that Luke, even at his young age, owned 11.1 percent of Crooked Tree and had an investment in it surviving.

Laughter was over, and Gabe was deadly serious. "We had two cancelations this week. Two of the larger cabins lost, and I think Marcus is looking for you to get a manager in, someone who can build the business side. I said I'd ask you for him."

"Since when can't Marcus talk to me direct?"

Since everything went to shit nine years ago, that's when. Since Marcus had loosened his control of the ranch and lost himself first in depression, then in denial.

"Maybe he doesn't want you thinking that what you're doing isn't enough. Hell, we all know that without your winnings, we'd be screwed."

Nate bit his lip. He hated that, just because he plowed his bull-riding winnings into the ranch, everyone trod on eggshells around him, looking for him to make decisions and drive things forward. Marcus had carried the ranch for the last nine years, ever since his youngest son, Justin, had vanished, taking Marcus's drive to make Crooked Tree survive with him. And his other son, Ethan? He was never here, lost in the need to find his brother, even after all this time.

"Yeah, and last time he talked to you about a manager, you kinda lost it," Luke interrupted.

"That's what Marcus should be doing," Nate said evenly. He recalled the day Marcus suggested getting in a third party to market the ranch. Looking at the rows of figures that Marcus was showing him was embarrassing. He couldn't make head or tail of overheads, profit and loss, or balance sheets. Numbers eluded him, but then, writing pretty much did as well. You didn't need either to ride the eight-second dream. You lived and rode, or you fell and lost—that was an easy equation.

Nate couldn't admit that to Gabe and Luke... hell, they looked up to him. They assumed his lack of education was due to the fact he left school early to trail the rodeo. He wasn't going to correct them in any way. He'd worked hard at his profession, earned good money, and he was lucky that Gabe and Luke had a place to be when he wasn't around. He owed Marcus for that. The old man had been a surrogate father to Nate's brothers in more ways than one.

"I'll talk to him."

"Tonight?" Gabe asked gently.

"Tonight. In fact, I'm going there next—"

"I don't feel so good," Luke interrupted suddenly. He scrambled to shore before losing whatever was in his stomach to the undergrowth. Gabe made a move to go help, but Nate stopped him.

"He'll be fine," he said. "He'll learn better if we don't fuss. He won't want his brothers around him when he's ill."

Gabe nodded. "When did you get so wise?"

"Since I made the mistake of clearing up your vomit when you were his age. Didn't teach you a thing."

He swam to the edge and heaved himself out, and Gabe followed.

"Bacon sandwich, Luke?" Gabe shouted. When retching sounds echoed from Luke's space, Nate took that as a no.

Juno slowed from the fast run across the wide open space, and Nate enjoyed the lazy meander through the trees on their side of the river and down past the Strachan house. He reined Juno in and slid from the saddle.

"Hang tight," he whispered and scratched Juno behind the ears.

The horse shook her head and butted him. This was a nightly occurrence for the two of them. They raced the long stretches with no restrictions, then trotted down to the second of the three owners' houses.

He walked Juno down to the next place, Marcus's home, and tied his horse on the verandah post. He knocked on the door and waited longer than usual for someone to come and invite him in. Sophie opened the door, her face flushed and her hair in disarray.

"Nate!" she exclaimed.

"Is Marcus around?"

Flustered, she let Nate in and gestured him into the large front room with the stone fireplace and the wall of photos. He sat on the chair closest to the door. "I'll tell him you're here. Would you like beer? Or coffee?"

Nate didn't have to think long. "Beer is good."

"I don't know what he's doing. He's in his office," she mumbled, then left the room.

Nate smiled to himself. From Sophie's flushed face, it was pretty clear what they had been doing. It was public knowledge that Marcus and Sophie were an item and had been for years. They'd just never gone public with it all, not even to friends and family. That was another mystery that Nate had never got his head around.

Marcus came into the room with two beers and handed one to Nate. "Is something wrong?" he asked immediately.

Plenty. Unpaid accounts for a start. Nate wasn't ready to talk money just yet, though, and instead he cut to the chase. "Gabe said you came to see him."

"You, actually. I came to see you."

Nate raised an eyebrow. "At ten in the morning when you knew I'd be out on the roundups with the guests?"

Marcus sighed. He looked older every time Nate saw him. Older, and less of the person he used to be. "It's easier to talk about things like this with Gabe," he admitted.

"I get that. Gabe was always the one with his head straight on his shoulders."

In fact, Gabe had a degree in math and was waiting for a response to a teaching position in a school in Missoula.

"Don't do that," Marcus snapped. "I hate when you play like you're dumb, boy." Nate bristled. He hated when Marcus called him boy or felt he had a say in what Nate should or shouldn't do. It wasn't Nate fucking things up and not paying suppliers. "You're as capable as Gabe when it comes to Crooked Tree. You're just prickly and ornery and difficult to talk to."

Nate placed his beer very deliberately on the coffee table in front of him. On a coaster, of course, else Sophie would kill him. Prickly and ornery was something Marcus had a life's worth of experience in. "I'm not the one who isn't paying the bills. Fuck. Is that what you got me down here to say? 'Cause I got stuff to do even if you get to sit on your ass doing nothing at all."

"I didn't get you down here," Marcus snapped. "Seems like you made your own way down."

"You want to tell me why the feed company blacklisted our account?"

"They've been paid, damn idiots," Marcus said.

Nate could see the lie for what it was, and suddenly he was scared for Crooked Tree. *What the hell's going on?*

"And what about the veterinarian?"

"Him too."

"I can see you're lying, Marcus—"

"For God's sake," Sophie snapped from the door, "will you two grow up? You're like kids arguing about a toy. You both want the ranch to work, so do it together. Marcus, stop lying and tell Nate the truth, and Nate, you sit down and damn well listen to what's happening."

Nate bristled. He always listened. "I do fine running my parts of Crooked Tree." He had responsibility for the livestock, the horses, the tours, and the roundups.

Sophie gripped a hand in her blonde hair in obvious frustration. "Yes, and Marcus says he does his bit as good, which turns out to be not exactly true." She shot a glance at Marcus, but Marcus wasn't looking back at her. In fact, Marcus looked devastated and small. "Unless we get someone who can bridge the difference, Crooked Tree is likely to be lost to us all." She sat on the edge of Marcus's chair. "Tell him," she said softly.

"Tell me what?" Nate demanded.

Marcus looked ill—pale and sweating—and he pressed his clenched fist against his chest over his heart.

Hell, whatever this was had got Marcus in a real state, and the last thing Nate wanted was for the man his brothers looked on as a surrogate father to keel over and die in front of him.

"Marcus?" he prompted more gently.

"It's my fault," Marcus said brokenly. "I'm not... I didn't... I...." He shook his head and leaned into Sophie as she sat on the side of his chair.

"Things have gotten out of hand," she explained for Marcus. "I didn't know until a few days ago. I want you to listen to what Marcus has to say and give him the chance to explain. Can you do that for me?"

Nate looked from Sophie to Marcus. In his heart, he already knew what Marcus was going to tell him. That the ranch was on the decline, that they were hemorrhaging money, and that something needed to be done. "I'm listening," he said with resignation.

Marcus bit his lip, vulnerability etched into his features. He visibly deflated, became less of a strong, imposing man; broken somehow. "I kept trying new things, taking money from one budget to cover another, but the ranch has been running at a break-even point, some months at a loss. We haven't put prices up, we're losing guests, and not because of what we offer, but things are tight out there. Dude ranches are offering luxury, and we're falling behind."

"We offer authenticity," Nate defended. "Well, as much as we can," he added thoughtfully. "We were never setting out to provide hot tubs and fancy designer riding clothes—"

"Two years, maybe less," Marcus interrupted. "It's what we have if we keep going the way we are and if the recession still bites." He pressed his chest again.

Nate opened his mouth to argue, then stopped. "I know," he said. "Can we at least pay the feed company?"

Marcus nodded. "I delay everything as much as I can. I can pay them today—but I wait until they call."

Nate frowned. "So, why haven't I had them on the phone to me before this?"

Marcus closed his eyes briefly, and Nate saw Sophie squeeze his shoulder gently. "Because I always prioritize the areas that affect you," he admitted.

"So I wouldn't know what was happening?" Nate was aware he sounded incredulous. *Jeez, what kind of secret was this to keep?* He couldn't get his head around the enormity of what was being said to him.

"Tell him the rest," Sophie prompted.

Marcus looked up at her with despair carved on his face.

"There's more?" Nate had a growing feeling of dread.

"We had an offer on forty acres of land."

Nate bristled immediately. "We're not selling land. We always said we wouldn't sell the land."

Sophie held up a hand to stop them both. "I didn't mean the land offer, Marcus. Tell him what the doctor said."

"Sophie—"

"Don't Sophie me. You tell him—he deserves to know."

Nate's stomach fell. "Are you ill?" he asked directly.

"Something wrong with my blood," Marcus explained quietly. "Sophie is overreacting. I'm having tests."

"Jeez, Marcus." Nate looked at his old friend—at the man who was like a father to Luke and Gabe when Nate had been out on the road making money for them all. He was torn. Half of him wanted to yell that Marcus had let the ball drop, while the other half wanted to make everything right for the older man. He should have told Nate the enormity of what Crooked Tree was facing, but then, was Nate entirely blameless? He may not be able to read financial reports, but he could see the effect that falling bookings were having on the grass roots of the ranch. He just always imagined that Marcus had things under control. Even after Justin….

Marcus held out a hand in entreaty. "Can you forgive me?"

Nate heard the question but didn't know what Marcus wanted him to say. Forgive him for allowing the mess to get to this point? For not telling Nate he was ill? He gripped Marcus's hand tight and closed his other hand around the connection. Looking directly into Marcus's eyes, he knew the words he said next would be something that was part truth, part lie, but wholly right for the situation he was facing.

"There's nothing to forgive," Nate said gruffly. He released the grip and settled back in the chair. "So what do we do now?"

Sophie reached over and picked up the notebook on the table and opened it. "I've been thinking." She looked at Marcus. "We've been thinking. We need to work on Crooked Tree. We advertise for someone who can help us build a… what do you call it? A brand, that's it. Someone with marketing experience, someone who knows Montana and is maybe good with horses, with vision, who can bridge accommodations and events and make us shine. Build us a website; use those social media things Luke keeps talking about."

"I guess we don't have much money to pay someone." Nate was only speaking the truth. No one with a stake in the place actually took a significant salary, if at all, and now to find how close to the bone Crooked Tree was running? That was the icing on the cake.

"Not a huge budget, but unless we invest, we could lose everything." Marcus's voice was stronger and more determined.

"Where are we going to advertise?" Nate had the idea there wasn't going to be much in the way of people fitting that description who would be willing to work for a small salary. "I want a local like you said—someone who knows Montana."

Inspired, Sophie sat forward on the side of the chair. "We'll offer them the cabin near the staff place included with a small salary; maybe get them some kind of profit-sharing."

Nate blanched. *Profit-sharing on what profits, exactly?* He didn't say that out loud. To do so would undermine the positive focus of this and push Marcus back to clutching his chest and looking like he was going to die at the drop of a hat.

"I suppose if we get them in with that, whoever it is could bring their family," Marcus said.

"Gabe's good with money. I want him to look at the accounts." Nate wasn't arguing about this point. He should have insisted on it ages ago—another thing he'd fallen down on.

Marcus visibly deflated again. There was no fight in his eyes as he nodded. "I want him to." He reached over for his cell. "Call him. Get him to come down, Luke as well. We should talk about this together."

"We should get Ethan here," Nate suggested cautiously. He knew exactly how that would go down. However, Ethan, while not owning any of Crooked Tree, was Marcus's son and involved in this as much as the rest of them.

Marcus immediately stiffened. "Ethan doesn't want any part of Crooked Tree," he said firmly.

Sophie looked sad. "Marcus—"

"No. He made his choice."

An uncomfortable silence fell between them, only broken by Nate when Gabe answered his cell.

Nate didn't mess around. "Gabe, get Luke and bring him down here."

"He's still sick," Gabe said with a chuckle.

"Bring a bucket," Nate said evenly.

Gabe must have heard the tension in Nate's voice. He was good at reading emotions. "Is everything okay?"

Nate glanced at Marcus and Sophie, who sat so close to each other there was no daylight between them. *Too many damn secrets and lies in this place.* "Just get down here." He finished the call and placed the cell back on the table.

"For the person to help us, we should advertise locally to start," Sophie suggested. "Then move it out if we don't get any interest."

"Agreed."

"Agreed."

Nate and Marcus spoke at the same time, and Sophie smiled angelically.

"Finally something you agree on."

CHAPTER TWO

The ad went out at the end of August, and as Nate expected, there wasn't a deluge of responses. They were looking for someone who was a business manager, a marketing guru, an IT guy… all that with little salary and only the promise of a place to live and a horse. Even he couldn't see the benefit in it.

At least Gabe had got a handle on the finances, and they had managed to eke out what was left of their savings and bought themselves some more time. Hell, Nate even had a meeting with the prospective buyers of a small parcel of Crooked Tree land. That meeting had only lasted five minutes when they revealed they wanted to create a rival dude ranch, but he had at least tried.

Summer turned to fall, and before Nate knew it, October was there and he turned twenty-six on a beautiful fall day. His brothers took it in turns to tease him about his age for what felt like the entire twenty-four hours.

Finally, with Gabe snoring on the sofa and Luke crashed out in his bedroom, Nate had the house to himself. It was only 10:00 p.m., and he could be in Missoula by eleven. The last time he'd scratched an itch was more than three months ago, and he was feeling the strain. He couldn't be bothered. He had a nice beer buzz and a decent supply of porn saved to his laptop. He'd lose himself in a fantasy, pretend he was being pushed to feel, ordered to move, and maybe get off to what was in his head. He locked all the doors, checked the lights, and made his way to the large bedroom at the back of the house. It had been his parents' room, and years had passed before he felt comfortable sleeping in there, but when Gabe had wanted to quit sharing with Luke, Nate had moved so Gabe could have his old room.

Nate flicked the lock on the door in case either brother decided to walk in, then crossed to his laptop. Before long he had drapes pulled, was naked on the bed, and had his favorite scene running on the screen. He delayed coming as long as he could, using every trick in the book to keep himself on the edge, coming along with the twink who was being used by two tops. Timing his release was kind of sad really, but he'd had a lot of practice.

Sated, he pushed the laptop under the bed, then lay flat on his back. He wiped the cool mess with his discarded T-shirt and threw it into the laundry pile. Tomorrow would probably be a good day to tack on an extra half hour to get his dirty laundry sorted.

With his arms crossed behind his head, Nate stared up at the ceiling and closed his eyes.

"Happy birthday," he murmured to himself and slept.

November brought snow, and December added a wind chill that froze him through to his bones. It didn't matter, though. Nate could spend time in with the horses because they didn't have guests from November to February. He loved the horses and worked with Luke, who had mirrored Nate's passion. Of course, the passion hadn't entirely skipped Gabe, but the middle Todd brother was more of an academic. Since taking over the accounts for

Crooked Tree, he'd had a kind of epiphany on what he wanted to do with his life. How a brother of his could—or would want to—become an accountant was something Nate would never get his head around. Ever.

Marcus came into the barn and stamped his feet on the floor to clear off the snow. "Freaking cold out there." He had on a thick sheepskin jacket and shrugged it off. It wasn't warm in the barns, but was comfortable to stand around in sweatshirts and jeans. "Thought I'd come in and check on you."

"You did?" Normally Marcus would come in and check on the horses without announcing it. Nate narrowed his gaze. Marcus looked a little nervous, and Nate knew enough to get that Marcus probably had something to say that Nate wouldn't like.

"We haven't had any replies to our ad. Sophie said we should think about getting in a recruitment company or widen the net to out of state."

Nate considered what Marcus had said. A recruitment company cost money, and it had been Nate who had suggested they get in someone who was local. Offering these two options had Nate in the position of choosing the lesser of two evils. "Best advertise as far as we can, then. Stick something on the website if anyone remembers how. Try Luke, he's good with computers. Use a company as a last resort."

"Okay." Marcus turned to leave.

Nate asked the one question he thought about at varying intervals. A question, or statement, with no real answer, but one that Nate had to get out. "Did Ethan say anything about coming home to work with us?"

"No," Marcus said simply.

"No, he said he wouldn't, or no, you didn't ask?"

"I didn't ask." Marcus stared at him pointedly.

They'd begun this conversation so many times but never got any further than this. Ethan was like an open sore for Marcus, and if Nate was honest, he hated asking, but if only Ethan could make the effort to get over what had happened He'd make a good addition to Crooked Tree.

"Did you get your results back yet?"

"Not yet."

"Really?" Nate blurted the word in disbelief. "I thought you had them done a while back now." He wished he could trust Marcus would tell him the truth, but he got the impression Marcus was keeping secrets to not load up any more stress on Nate.

Marcus shrugged with that "what can I say" expression. "I'll place the ad." He grabbed his jacket and walked out into the cold.

A swirl of snow entered the barn as Marcus left, and Nate watched until it melted on the ground.

Christmas passed in a blur, and January was the beginning of making ready for the March opening. Nate was always restless at this time of year. Four inches of snow had fallen over the weekend and covered the ranch in a beautiful fresh crystal blanket, with foot-deep drifts that softened the landscape. Nate had chores, fences to mend, and places to be, but always at the back of his mind he worried they hadn't found someone to help move Crooked Tree into the new year.

He was on the roof, fixing the wood under the shingles on his house. Okay, so a snowy day wasn't the best day, but Nate was suffering, quite literally, from cabin fever. Luke was up there with him, following instructions and making a damn good job of things. Luke had settled to studying, and thankfully there hadn't been any more pot incidents. Well, none that Nate had found out about, anyway.

"You thinking about college at all?" Nate asked as Luke passed him nails.

"What makes you ask that?"

"Saw some brochures on the table."

"Maybe." Luke refused to meet his eye.

Nate didn't push. The worst thing he could do with Luke was push him. Each of the brothers had a pot of money in trust for education that reverted to them at age thirty if they hadn't used it. It wouldn't be enough to cover Luke's whole time at university, but it was enough to get a start. Nate's own money was likely to go straight to the ranch, but he had three years left yet to get to it. He waited to see if Luke would add any more. His brother's face was screwed up in concentration and a million thoughts were telegraphing in his green eyes. Taking a deep breath and exhaling noisily, he finally looked directly at Nate.

"Thought maybe if I studied marketing or something like that, I could come back and help Crooked Tree," Luke offered. "Like Gabe will on the accounts."

"Uh-huh. Is that what you want to do?"

"Help Crooked Tree?"

Nate guessed his brother was being deliberately obtuse. "Study marketing and business. What about your photography and your art?"

Luke ducked his head. "Shit like that doesn't pay the bills."

Nate cuffed his brother around the head. They'd had this conversation before about Luke resigning his talent to the bin all the time. Nate knew Luke didn't do it because he was looking for praise; the young idiot genuinely thought his talent wasn't useful.

"Not everything is about money," Nate reminded him gently.

Luke huffed a laugh. "Everything *is* about money. Did you actually want to leave Gabe and me when we were kids to go earn money on the circuit? No, it was 'cause we needed the money."

"That's different. I loved what I did."

"That wasn't what I said. You're lucky you made it out after three years with all your bits intact, but you had to choose money over staying here with us." Luke wasn't accusing. He looked deadly serious, though.

Nate recalled Luke at nine, crying with nightmares, and Gabe, dry-eyed and solemn. "I guess I did." Crooked Tree couldn't support them then, not until their parents' life insurance paid out two years after they died, not without extra income. "I was there as much as I could be."

Luke grinned at him. "Of course you were. I love you, big brother," he said.

Nate smiled back. "I love you too, kid. Now pass me another nail." Luke gave him the nail, and only after a few minutes did Nate add the last point. "Study what you love. Don't be unhappy."

Luke looked to be thinking of a reply but was interrupted by Marcus calling up from below.

"Someone called about the job," Marcus yelled.

"Someone qualified?" Nate shouted down.

Marcus shrugged, "I didn't ask."

"And?"

"He said he'd call back when he'd thought about it."

With that, Marcus hurried away. "This could be good news," Luke said with enthusiasm.

"Yeah," Nate answered with a little less animation. He looked Luke in the eye. "Fingers crossed."

CHAPTER THREE

Jay Sullivan knew something was wrong as soon as he stepped in through the swinging doors fresh from his meeting at a new tech company on Fifth. The New York office was quiet. Too quiet. Desks were empty of people, and the normal level of noise accompanying the work at Drayton Partin Marketing was gone. Hell, it hadn't been this quiet since two weeks before Christmas when they lost three accounts in one week. He spotted Roger from Accounts slumped in a far corner and made his way over to him.

"What the hell's happened?" he asked quickly.

Roger shook his head. "Taking everyone in one by one," he began, He visibly straightened in his chair. "I'm still here, but Jean's been let go, Adam, Emma. I'm the only one. They're downsizing and telling us all today."

"They're cutting Accounts down to one person?"

"Me and two interns on piss-poor money."

"I'm sorry, man," Jay offered. He liked Roger. In fact, he liked the whole team. It was a shame that everything had to come to this.

"Don't be sorry for me. I kept my job, and despite a downgrade in pay, I'm luckier than others."

Jay cast a glance at the empty desks. Accounts butted up to the desks the marketing executives like him used. Where was Colin? Lisa? He knew. With sudden and sickening clarity, he knew.

"Us too?" he asked. "They're cutting posts on the marketing teams?"

Roger nodded but looked confused. "Everyone is down in the canteen, and they're being taken out one by one, but you know that. You're here, so you made the cut, right?"

"I was out at a breakfast meeting. I didn't know anything…"

Jay dropped his laptop bag on his desk and inhaled sharply when he saw the Post-it note in Colin's handwriting.

We're fucked. Canteen now.

Jay closed his eyes momentarily. He loved this job, and Drayton Partin was a big company to get into at the ground level. Hired straight from his degree in business and marketing, he'd spent four years with this team, and they'd pulled in some impressive clients. He was only a junior still, but he had a good salary, and the cut-throat marketing arena was his version of heaven.

Losing accounts like they had was hard, but Drayton Partin had seen worse, greater, losses when the dot-com bubble burst. Surely this was just a blip? Drayton Partin wouldn't get rid of their best assets? Would they?

He grabbed his bag, squared his shoulders, and headed for the stairwell.

"Good luck," Roger called as Jay reached the door marked "Fire Exit and Stairs."

Jay looked back and was struck by the expression of complete isolation and desolation on Roger's face. *Fuck.* What if Colin was made redundant? or Lisa? How would he look them in the eye if he still had his job? The three of them had some really good clients, and they worked so well as a team. What if it was him they were cutting, which was more than likely? What about medical insurance? What about Ashley and the kids? What about the rent? Despair pulled in his stomach as the world began closing in on him.

Jay reached the canteen and stood for a moment outside the door. He could see through the circle of glass, and everyone was sitting quietly in the hard plastic dining chairs. He couldn't see Colin, but that didn't mean he wasn't in there somewhere—Drayton Partin had over sixty of their staff in that room, packed into rows.

Steeling himself against everyone looking at him, Jay pushed open the door. As he suspected, every single eye turned to him, and he saw panic, and shock, and resignation in different expressions. Lisa immediately stood and crossed to him, hugging him briefly. He returned the hug but looked over her shoulder for Colin.

"He's inside," she murmured. "They're not letting anyone back in after they've spoken to them."

"I saw Roger upstairs."

"Who else?" she asked quickly.

"No one. Just Roger. He said the others were all let go."

Lisa's whole body sagged in defeat. "That's what I thought. Roger has twenty years here, the rest of Accounts less than that."

If Roger's length of time at the company was the litmus test, then Colin was ten years older than Jay and had been at Drayton Partin for twelve years. Lisa had ten years under her belt. He was the baby of the team. The newbie.

"So it's last in, first out?" Jay asked. He couldn't help the fear that colored his words. Being out looking for a job at this time, with the recession tightening everyone's belts, was a scary, if not terrifying, proposition.

"No one knows," Lisa said.

She went back to sit in the chair at the end of one aisles, and for a second Jay didn't know what to do. He should sit and wait like everyone else. He was in the same boat; he was nothing special. Although he worked hard, covered his hours with the correct levels of income, he was low down on the ladder. In his head, he began summarizing his résumé. A business and marketing degree from NYU—not Harvard, or one of the other Ivy Leagues. Smart and presentable, but not anything sharp in a thousand-dollar suit. With a feeling of absolute submission, he took the seat in front of Lisa. No one talked to him. Not one person said hello, and it wasn't as if he started conversations. Every single one of them in this room was in a kill-or-be-killed position.

The door opened.

"Lisa McAllen, please," a voice demanded.

There wasn't a body that Jay could see, but he recognized the voice as that of the CEO's personal assistant. She was obviously trying to keep a barrier between her and the masses awaiting their fate. She didn't need to worry, no one here looked like they hadn't been expecting this. Job-loss statistics, even in the city of New York, were steadily reported each night on the news.

Lisa stood up, and Jay sent her a reassuring smile. She pursed her lips, and her eyes looked bright with tears.

Try not to cry, Lisa, Jay thought.

He wondered how long each interview took, but when the next name was called in three minutes, he realized this wasn't an exit interview where the person got to convince management they could stay. No, this was a simple apology about being let go and maybe a leaflet on what happened next. Final. Absolute.

Ten others had gone in before him, and each time he had the sense they were walking to the gallows. No wonder people weren't talking, if they all felt like Jay.

"Jay Sullivan, please."

Jay stumbled upright, gripping hard to his bag, and walked in the direction of the voice and through the door. He knew what was behind there: the old smoker's room, which had a door leading to where he had come from and another going straight to the corridor and the exit on this level. The room had been redecorated since all smoking had been banned in the building, but it still had the scent of its former use. Jay pushed open the door and watched bemused as Irene, the PA, closed it behind him. A desk had been placed to one side, and on its front were two boxes. Two women he didn't recognize were manning the desk. The first had a sheet of paper from the pile to her side, and the other a list of printed names that she had a finger on—probably on his name.

They didn't waste time.

"I'm sorry to keep you waiting, Mr. Sullivan. Bad news, I'm afraid. Drayton Partin is having to make some dramatic cuts to support continued growth and stability.

Unfortunately some hard decisions had to be made, and that included looking at personnel requirements. Your job no longer exists."

"Okay," Jay said blankly. He had lost his job. In a few words, his career was stalled.

"If you could return your pass...."

Jay fumbled in his pocket and pulled out the card with the magnetic strip. He glanced down at it as he handed it over. The smiling Jay he saw on the front was a slap in the face. The second woman took it from him and placed it in the left box along with a substantial pile of other cards. From the other box, she pulled out a business card.

"Wilton's Personnel is handling this transition," she said pleasantly enough. "There will be more information through the far door." She indicated a door behind her marked with a temporary sign—"Wilton's"—and Jay realized there was another exit he'd forgotten, one that opened to a loop back to the stairs. Evidently successful people were being sent back to the office. "If you could also leave your laptop with us." She indicated a pile of bags in the corner of the room.

He recognized Lisa's bright pink bag immediately.

"I have some personal photos—" he began, then shut his mouth. What were they going to say to him? It was not like they'd tell him it was okay to fiddle on his laptop when this was the end of the line.

"Your desk contents will be boxed and anything personal will be sent on to you. Any personal files on your IT equipment will be forwarded. Please take a card."

He took the card without thinking and the corner of it poked into his thumb. "Thank you." It was all he could say—words escaped him.

Irene ushered him out of the "Wilton's" door and closed it behind him. The corridor he went into widened into a small seating area, and there was Lisa, ashen-faced and in tears. Next to her, with a similar expression of shock, was Colin. So it had been three for three. Wordlessly, Jay slumped down on the sofa next to Colin. They were the only ones there.

"We waited for you," Colin said carefully.

Jay didn't know what to think. Colin had expected him. He guessed once Colin lost his role, then Lisa and Jay would be sure to be on the same list.

"I'm sorry," Jay said softly. "You and Lisa don't deserve this."

A bleak look filled Colin's eyes. "Nor do you. But—" He sighed heavily. "—that is what life is like now. One day you have a job, the next—" He snapped his fingers. "—it's gone." Colin stood. "Come on, let's go join the others."

Jay followed them down the corridor and heard the noise before he saw the people. He walked into chaos.

Some who had lost their jobs were vocal, shouting the odds and demanding answers. Others simply stood with vacant expressions of shock and watched the bedlam around them.

I have a family, you don't get it!
Twelve years and this is what I get!
And the partners get brand new cars!
We'd already taken a pay cut!

Words spun around Jay's head: voices he recognized, some he didn't, which belonged to people he had never met. Administrators, canteen staff, marketing people like him. He recognized Jean, who was crying, and Adam, who was shouting—both from Accounts.

Several members of Wilton's Personnel tried to answer questions, but no one was listening. Jay stayed with Colin and Lisa and waited his turn. Soon he became aware he had probably slipped into shock. When he left the building for the last time, he had two weeks' pay in his account and a thank-you letter for his hard work.

Feeling like a failure and letting his family down was the freebie on the side.

The journey home was completed in silence. Lisa joined him for the first part of it, but her stop was four before his. He had a full ten minutes on his own in the crowded, tourist-filled train. He had a five block walk from his stop, but that was at least a way to give him time to think. When he pushed his way into the apartment, he was met with the scent of cookies, and he smiled to himself for the first time today. Ashley was in a baking mood, which meant perfect cookies: crumbly, gooey in the middle, and filled to bursting with chocolate. His sister was an expert in the chocolate goodness.

Jay crossed behind her and reached around to steal a cookie. She spun in shock, then pushed him away from her with a huffed laugh. He juggled the hot snack between his hands and retreated far enough away from her to not have the chocolate heaven stolen from him.

"You'll make yourself sick," she admonished.

"No, I won't."

"You'll singe your mouth."

Jay took a big bite of the cookie and cursed silently as the melted chocolate burned his tongue. "No. I won't," he lied around the mouthful.

"You want coffee with that?" she asked.

"God, yes," he said quickly. "Strong, very strong."

She glanced at the clock on the wall. "You're home early."

"Working from home," he said immediately. And yes, that was a lie, but he wasn't ready to dump everything on Ashley—she'd only just started to smile properly again. Not the smile she used for the world, but the smile he remembered from his childhood when he had doted on his big sister. When it was them against the world. She'd pulled up her long hair in a bun on top of her head and fastened it somehow so that it stayed. The laws of physics did not seem to apply to Ashley and her gorgeous hair. He was the one whose hair played him up every day—all cowlicks and curls. He kept it short so he didn't have to worry about it. Both had thick blond hair, one of the benefits of their somewhat confused heritage of Irish, Norwegian, Greek, and whatever else they had in their blood.

He set up his home laptop on the table. Funnily enough, it had been the personnel firm taking back his work laptop that had been one of the hardest things to handle. He had spreadsheets on there from his very first day, with milestones recording his journey at Drayton Partin. To lose those had hurt. They wouldn't be considered as personal files.

Jay turned his old machine on and waited for it to boot. He dug into the small plate of cooling cookies that Ashley placed next to him, along with some dark strong coffee.

She dropped a kiss on the top of his head. "You look tired."

"Just a lot of work," he offered in defense.

"You need cake." She laughed. "Lemon Drizzle or Chocolate Layer cake?"

Jay looked up with a soft smile. He loved Ashley so much, loved her kids. This was the small unit of people for whom he had to make things right. "You need to ask?"

She shook her head. "Why are you not overweight?"

The question was one she asked all the time, and he had a standard answer. Ashley was as slim as he was, but he loved to tease her. "You got the looks, big sis. I got the fast metabolism."

And her reply, as familiar as breathing. "And I hate you for that, little brother."

Jay concentrated back on his laptop and angled it so that Ashley couldn't catch a look at what he was searching for. He pulled up websites for all the major marketing players and lost himself in searching, with a background of the scents and sounds of Ashley baking.

No one was hiring. Some, in fact nearly all, advertised graduate positions at half his salary. Other than that? Nothing. Next stop, recruitment agencies. He had no doubt about his skills and was confident in approaching the biggest firms.

The first one he rang from the privacy of his bedroom said in no uncertain terms that he was the twelfth person from Drayton Partin to phone today. They agreed to see his résumé and that they would file it for future reference, but they didn't want to see him, which stung.

The second biggest didn't mention people phoning but wanted to see a résumé before they even continued the conversation. He emailed it over as they instructed. He heard nothing back immediately, but they were busy people... right?

The third and fourth offered appointments for a chat, tomorrow.

"Uncle Jay!"

Josh's voice was at his door, and Jay shut his laptop and pushed it to one side. He clambered off the bed and opened the door, and his six-year-old nephew launched himself at him with a whoop. Jay caught him and held him close.

"Mom made me chocolate cake!" Josh shouted happily.

"That's my cake," Jay joked.

Josh wriggled to be let down and scampered over to the kitchen. "Not if I get there first!"

Work search forgotten, Jay, Josh, and Ashley enjoyed cake, juice, and some pretty normal family time. In those moments, as rare as they were, Jay felt truly at peace.

Interview one was a bust. They had him filed under administration posts that weren't in the marketing department. Their reason for this was that there was nothing in the way of jobs at his level in the marketing field. They suggested leaving New York, finding another city where jobs were available. They thanked him. He left.

Interview two didn't last ten minutes. Jay had a speech prepared to sell himself to the agency so they would find him a job, but he never got the chance. A fire alarm broke into the interview, and when outside in the parking lot, the woman he had been talking to confided that actually they had nothing on their books and essentially hadn't for maybe two months.

She suggested looking outside the city. Seemed like a common theme.

Dinner that night at home was a solemn affair. Jay was quiet, and he knew it. The thing was, this unit of theirs sometimes depended on him and Josh keeping the conversation going. Especially when his sister was having a "down day" like today, and it wasn't as if his niece, Kirsten, was the most verbose of teenagers.

The problem was, tonight, even Josh was subdued. He picked at his spaghetti and pulled the rest apart on his plate. Josh was never quiet—he was life and laughter and a bundle of positive energy normally.

"What's on your mind, buddy?" Jay asked softly.

Josh raised his gaze to Jay. "Something happened at school," he began.

"What?"

Josh was happy at his school; he had a couple of friends and was enjoying playing mini basketball with them on every possible break. It didn't help he was the shortest among his friends, but he still had fun.

"Derek told me some stuff and I told him it wasn't true, but he said he'd read it."

"What about?"

"You, and being momosecshal."

"Homosexual," Jay corrected instinctively.

"Yeah, that."

"What did he say?"

"That the Bible said you shouldn't want to kiss another boy and that if I ever tried to kiss him, he would thump me."

Ah. So it had happened. Jay wasn't in the closet, but he didn't make a song and dance about his sexuality either. Josh had met Jay's last boyfriend, Mark. Hell, the two of them had even gotten along and Josh hadn't said anything that suggested he thought it was odd, or different. So he considered his nephew and the fact that Josh was six. What did Jay need to say to be able to handle this one? "Some people think that," he began diplomatically.

"Bigots," Kirsten interrupted.

While he loved that Kirsten was so at ease with the world and the whole issue of equality, "bigots" probably wasn't the right word to explain to Josh how people could be. Jay shot her a discouraging look. She very deliberately put the buds of her MP3 headphones in her ears and pointedly stared in the opposite direction.

He continued. "Anyway, some people think that, but I don't agree. I think God wants you to love who you love."

"So, if one day you loved a girl, that would be okay with you?" Josh asked curiously.

"If that happened," Jay said. *When hell freezes over.* "It's not going to happen, though. I like men."

"I like Melanie in the next class. She smells nice and has really cool lunches. I don't wanna kiss Derek. He picked his nose in assembly and everyone saw it." Josh wrinkled his own nose. "So, yeah, can I have more water?"

With that, the conversation was over. Josh accepted what Jay said and took it all in his stride. Jay had to admire the little guy—he was being raised by a goth teenage sister, a depressed mother, and a gay uncle.

Yay for the American nuclear family.

CHAPTER FOUR

Jay's optimism on finding a position he was trained for waned by week two. He'd had to come clean with Ashley, but all she'd done was hug him close and tell him everything would be okay. He wished he believed her. Her small income from waiting tables for the lunch rush at the nearby diner wasn't enough to pay the rent on this place for a day, let alone a week. Jay had savings, but they were dwindling rapidly. He was left with two options: find a job outside the city, or find another career altogether. Today he was finally going to give in and look for anything within commuting distance.

At least he'd told the family, so he didn't have to hide in his room to search the available vacancies. There were three possible positions in Boston—that wasn't too far. Maybe he could get a place there to rent if the money was good enough; move the kids and Ashley out of the city to something cheaper and better. Hell, he should think about getting all four of them out of the city. He'd lived and worked all his life around New York, but—

A news item appeared on Jay's Facebook feed. He clicked it to read the article in the *Advocate*: two sickeningly happy guys married in Texas and fighting for same-sex adoption. That was another cloud on his horizon, the lack of a love life. Jay wanted happy, and he missed Mark sometimes. Not all the time—after all, the man was a two-timing ass—but the quiet times when they had cuddled and slept in the same bed; those times, he missed. Articles like this gave him hope for one day marrying a man he loved, but, at the same time, made him look at his barren love life with regret. Maybe one day he would find someone he wanted to stay with for longer than a few months. Someone who stole his breath and made him believe in forever.

He huffed a laugh. Mark had disappeared to Florida on a work exchange for six months to "find himself" and to escape Jay's "emotional unavailability."

"You spend too much time worrying about your family" had been the parting shot from his frustrated lover. Of course, that had been after Jay found Mark bending over an intern in their bedroom, his cock quite firmly in said intern's ass. Mark was good at that. Not fucking—he had always been distinctly average in that respect. No, Mark was good at deflecting blame onto other people.

That had been nearly a year ago, and Jay had heard through the grapevine that Mark was back and working in a rival marketing firm. Since Mark walked out the door, Jay's sex life had been as empty and quiet as the job market. Apart from a few casual hookups, his entire social life was barren.

What if Mark had been right about the "emotional availability" thing? Jay could argue he had reasons for being the way he was. He couldn't just up and leave for a weekend at a hotel, or be out for dinner at two in the morning. He had a family to think about. Jay wasn't unemotional, but completely the opposite—he was permanently freaking worried. He worried that Josh was never allowed out to play because their apartment building was right on the main street, he hated that Kirsten had yet another piercing and was falling in with the wrong crowd, and not to mention poor Ashley and her unlucky choices in men who used her as a punching bag.

One link led to another on the site, and Jay spent a good hour reading through posts on a gay support forum looking for one person—just one—who was the same as him, with a family to support and care for and no job. Of course, he didn't find a single person exactly like him. Seemed he was unique. A link to gay-friendly holidays came up, and he clicked it out of curiosity that in this day and age they even had a label for gay-friendly.

The first on the list was a ranch of some kind. In Texas. Deep in thought, he scrolled through pictures of horses and cityscapes and lost himself in dreams of hot days and even hotter cowboys. The thought of going back to the days when no one needed marketing guys to sell things, back to horses and a six-shooter and a simple way of life, was compelling. Then reality kicked in. Josh had English homework he was struggling with—he was behind his class in reading and the teacher had commented that Josh may well have some kind of word-blindness.

Jay searched for "dyslexia" on another screen, and while a PDF downloaded, he went back to have a better look at the ranch. There was a link to more ranch holidays. He scrolled past Double Ds and other cliché-type ranch names. Round about page five he was going to give up because the PDF was 85 percent downloaded, but a name caught his eye: Crooked Tree Dude Ranch. That was a cool name, and the ranch was in Montana. The website was pretty poor—white on black with low-resolution pictures and navigation that didn't always work. He could do better just using free web tools on the Internet.

"Whatcha looking at?" Josh asked from behind him.

Jay quickly minimized the PDF that reached 100 percent as Josh spoke. He maximized the crappy website for... he peered closely at the cursive script that wound its way across the top of the screen to remind himself of the name—Crooked Tree Dude Ranch.

"Horses," he said quickly, "on a ranch in Montana."

Josh clambered on his lap and Jay huffed as the full weight of the small boy landed awkwardly on his knees. Josh wriggled to get comfortable and pushed Jay's hand out of the way.

"Look," he exclaimed. "Horses, and lots of 'em."

Josh had a thing for horses. He collected posters and told stories involving them. Jay always promised that one day, when they weren't in an apartment building, Josh could get a pet. Of course, he had to point out it was likely to be a hamster or a cat, not a horse, but one day...

Something caught his eye as Josh rapidly clicked through pages.

"Go back a page," Jay said.

Josh did, and at last, after some fumbling as an error page came up, there it was, an ad for a job. It took some looking at before it made any sense, but the heading was clear enough.

Business Manager with experience in marketing, websites, and computers.

Salary on request, accommodations and horse included.

Call for more information.

There was a number below, Jay looked at it, then back at the wording. Marketing, yes, he could do that with his eyes closed. Websites? Easy. Computers, he knew enough, and there was software he could use. Business management? He contemplated what that meant? Running an office? Dealing with staff—maybe dealing with a few cowboys?

But… living in Bumfuck, Montana? That was a deal-breaker. He needed to remember he had a degree in business and marketing—that was what he wanted to do with his life, what he had trained for. Cutting-edge marketing in the middle of the most vibrant city on earth. This job wouldn't be pure marketing. It sounded more like they wanted a bit of everything. Still, maybe he should call them, test the waters—what did he have to lose? In the economy today, maybe this was the way to go. Think laterally and use all the skills he had instead of focusing on one. The accommodations sounded good, as did the word "family," but of course it was likely that the salary would be way low down. As to the horse? That was probably a typo.

Jay pushed down the feeling of anxiety curling in his stomach. Ashley would never go for it. Leaving New York was leaving her comfort zone. Kirsten would definitely not agree to go. He wasn't exactly sold on it—except it seemed like the easy way out.

"I wish we lived on a ranch," Josh said wistfully. "Then I could have a horse, and a dog." He clambered down and went over to the TV. One out of four wasn't bad, Jay supposed. He dialed the number, and a woman answered immediately.

"Hello?" She sounded out of breath as if she had run for the phone.

Jay sure as hell hoped the ranch place had a better phone-answering system for bookings than a woman with chronic breathing problems.

"I'm calling about the ad on your website."

"Oh," she gasped. "I'll, um, hang on...."

Jay heard the receiver knock against the wall, or the desk, or the floor, or wherever it was situated, then the sound of shouting, which he could make out easily.

"Marcus! Phone for you!"

"Who is it?"

"Someone about the job!"

"Tell 'em I'll be right down."

"Hello?" the woman said into the phone.

"Hi," Jay replied to let her know he was still there.

"You'll be speaking to Marcus Allen," she said. "He'll be able to help you."

"Thank you." Jay waited until the noises down the line indicated the receiver was being passed over.

"This is Marcus Allen. You're calling about the vacancy?" Marcus sounded more than a little hopeful.

"I don't want to waste your time," Jay began carefully. "I have a few questions."

"Shoot," Marcus said enthusiastically.

"The ad is a little sparse," he began tactfully. "You don't mention a salary or detail any career progression."

"Um…." Marcus said.

That was it. That was all he said.

There was a silence as Jay waited for more. Then Jay realized Marcus was expecting him to say something next. "So, the position itself?" Jay encouraged.

This is awkward. At that point, Jay wasn't sure why he was on the phone. Stupid spur-of-the-moment phone call was his idea of hell. He hated hesitation—he worked much better on absolutes and direct information.

"Salary is negotiable," Marcus said grandly. He added quickly, "Within reason and budgets. There's a four-bedroom cabin that comes with the job. We want someone who… hang on—" Again it went quiet. "—okay, this is what Gabe and Luke wrote for me. We need someone who can move the ranch forward. We want to increase bookings, look at a new website, and social networking, and brochures. We need someone to start immediately, and we're looking at a year's contract, but to start there'd be a trial for three months and the person could leave, no harm done."

"Three months?" Jay asked incredulously. Marketing campaigns took longer than three months to get off the ground. What was this ranch playing at, getting someone in for so little time? What were they expecting? Three months wasn't long enough to write a freaking marketing plan, let alone guide implementation.

"Is that too much?" Marcus said quickly. "Two months, then."

Jay sighed. "I'm not exactly sure what you're looking for."

"Someone to help us out. Nate is working every hour he gets, and the horses take up a lot of his time. Not only that, but he has the hands and the forestry to control. Gabe is lost in accounts and his books, and he's looking for a job in town. Luke is only good at Facebook and that tweetering stuff. My son Ethan is a cop in Missoula, y'know, but he's not here on the ranch, and Nate and I know nothing about any of this."

While it was interesting to be supplied with a long list of totally irrelevant names, Jay couldn't see the point of being told any of it. So Nate and Ethan, something, and whoever the hell else, weren't interested in marketing, and another guy knew Facebook. He pinched the bridge of his nose between his fingers then pressed them to his temple where a headache threatened.

"Can I summarize for you?" Jay asked, then continued without waiting for a reply. "What you need is someone to come in and do everything that no one else wants to do." To Jay, it sounded like there were a lot of people doing a lot of things, all of them probably pushing the business side away, then most likely squabbling over what needed undertaking. Whoever took this on would need to be diplomatic, firm, and hard-assed.

"More or less got that right," Marcus agreed.

"And in return that person gets…."

Marcus coughed. "A house, some money, and the use of a horse."

A horse? So it isn't a typo? Of course there's a horse included. Every job should have a horse included!

An email arrived in his inbox and Jay clicked on it as he listened to Marcus expound on the beauty of Montana, the stunning mountains, and the promise of a new life. What he read made him smile. He cut Marcus off mid-flow.

"Thank you. I will call you back when I've had time to consider everything." He ended the call and with a grin, he spun in his chair.

He had an interview with Deeks Hyland! Jay fist-pumped the air. He could consign the awkward conversation with the Marcus guy to the bin. Euphoria had him dancing awkwardly in a circle.

Then reality hit him. It was only an interview, and Mark worked at Deeks, and he'd have to spend time avoiding him, but yes—he had a goddamn interview.

New York 1, Montana 0.

CHAPTER FIVE

The interview was long and tedious, but Jay felt he'd done well. They asked him all the right questions, and to his mind he gave all the right answers. The panel of three—two men and a woman—seemed keen on his ideas and nodded in all the right places. The salary they offered was way less than he had been paid at Drayton Partin, but that would only be for the first year.

The kind of work we'd be having you do for the first couple of years is at intern level with the appropriate salary point, but this is a chance to learn Deeks Hyland from the ground up.

We have a team that we could slot someone of your caliber into immediately.

You have a very impressive skill set that we feel would benefit Deeks Hyland.

Incidentally, do you have any clients you could bring with you from Drayton Partin?

Finally the interview finished. "If you could wait in the other room, we'll have a think on this and call you back in."

Jay left the room with a grin, and it stayed with him for a solid ten minutes. Okay, so he needed to make concessions, but he'd have paid employment, not to mention healthcare and other benefits.

The other door into this breakout room opened and he looked up instinctively. Mark. Ex Mark, in a dark suit, with a scarlet tie, and a grin on his face that smacked of confidence.

"Hello, Jay," Mark said quickly.

The last time they met, they'd punched each other in the face, Mark had ended up on the floor, and Jay had threatened to punch him again. Given all that, Mark's hello was kind of confident. Actually, considering the last time had ended in punches but started by Jay finding Mark with his cock in someone else's ass, Mark was fairly smug and superior. This didn't bode well. "Mark."

"How'd it go?"

"How did what go?" Jay asked, feeling a little stupid.

"The interview?"

"You knew about the interview?"

"Knew about it? I said they should snatch you up from Drayton Partin. I told them you'd been let go. Will has just been promoted, and I have a junior vacancy on my team. I told them I wanted you and you alone."

Shock hit Jay front and center. The interview wasn't because he'd sent in a beautifully formatted and detailed résumé? It was because of Mark.

Wait…. On Mark's team? Mark had a *team*? He'd be reporting to Mark? *No fucking way.*

"Will's been promoted?" Will, the guy whose ass Mark had been using in their bedroom?

Mark had the grace to look a little uncomfortable. "Yes, but that's all water under the bridge." He pasted a cajoling smile on his face. "The three of us will make an awesome team. With your artistic vision and my skills in the bullshit, we'll be unbeatable. I can't wait until I have you back under me," Mark raised his eyebrows then winked. "I've missed your ass in my life."

The facts mixed and muddled in Jay's head. He'd be reporting to his cheating, lying, bastard ex; he'd be working with Will—was Mark still fucking Will? and who cared?—he would be taking home thousands of dollars less than he was used to, working in a position where he was starting at the bottom. Jay didn't see the win here.

"I haven't decided if I want it," he said in summary.

Mark's smile left his perfectly smooth face. "Don't be fucking stupid. Of course you want it. I set it all up for you."

Jay stood and brushed the seat of his pants to give himself time to think. He needed to handle this diplomatically. The job might not be ideal, but it was a job, right? He was twenty-nine, he had years ahead of him, and he could bite his tongue about what a complete asshole Mark was. He could even avoid Will in the office if he had to. "What's in it for you?" He stepped closer to Mark until there were only a few feet between them.

Mark moved closer too, until Jay could have reached out his hand and touched his shoulder. Having Mark this close was unsettling. The scent of him, expensive and cloyingly sweet, was so familiar. But the memories it brought back were less of love and more of feeling like he was some kind of weak-spined idiot to have stayed with him for as long as he did.

"I *have* missed you," Mark said quietly. Jay considered if that was the first honest thing Mark had ever said in his presence. "Things didn't really work out well with Will, and I know why. It's because he wasn't you."

Jay stared directly into Mark's eyes and quickly saw he was lying.

"Did he kick you out as well?" he asked abruptly. "Did you punch him, then tell him he was emotionally unavailable and fucking useless in bed?"

Mark frowned. "Will was nothing to me."

The door to the interview room opened.

"We're ready for you, Mr. Sullivan."

"Go," Mark encouraged.

Jay looked from the door to the room, to the exit, then to Mark. This was wrong. All wrong. He faced the interviewer standing in the doorway, who had a frown marring his face and looked a little confused, his gaze flicking from Mark to Jay and back again.

"I'm sorry to waste your time, sir," Jay said formally, then, before anyone could say a thing, he left.

What have I done? He stumbled out into the cold drizzly day and found himself surrounded by everyone who had jobs to go to—men and women with coffees and phones, the chaos and confusion of a city day parting to move around him and continue on its way. Everyone had a purpose except him.

Home. I need to go home. I need to remind myself of the responsibilities I have to my family, then I need to go back in and apologize at Deeks Hyland. Swallow my pride. I need that job.

Arriving home, he found Kirsten sitting in front of the TV with a game controller in her hand. Again. The images he had in his head of providing for his family were forgotten as he took in his niece killing zombies and cursing at the screen. She ignored his entrance, probably hadn't heard him come through the door.

"Why aren't you at school?" he asked immediately. She ignored him and concentrated on killing whoever the hell was on the screen. "Kirsten, I asked you a question."

With a huff, she paused the game and looked up at him. Her expression was mutinous. Actually, her expression was permanently rebellious these days.

"I'm ill," she said with the air of the put-upon.

"You don't look ill," Jay observed. "If you're ill, how come you can play video games?"

"It's women things," Kirsten said irritably. "It doesn't affect my hands."

When did she turn from being the niece who loved nothing more than sitting on his lap and listening to him read *Harry Potter* to her? What had happened to the gorgeous blonde kid who loved her uncle Jay? He closed his eyes briefly. He was in a losing battle with the whole time-of-the-month argument, and he knew it. Maybe Ashley could get her to see sense.

"Where's your mom?" Jay hadn't seen his sister before leaving for the interview this morning. They needed to talk about Kirsten and the time missing school. If Kirsten really was ill, why were her eyes ringed in the customary thick black liner, her lips a pouty scarlet and her dark pink hair straightened like she was going out clubbing?

"In bed. She says she's ill too, a migraine I think 'cause she's lying in the dark. It's okay, though, I got

Josh ready for school." She looked at Jay expectantly, as if her getting Josh ready for school negated the fact that she had decided not to go in herself. Jay fought the instinct to say thank you. If Ashley was ill and he wasn't in the house, Kirsten taking the initiative was a mark in the plus column, but he was still pissed at the fact she was skipping another school day. When Jay said nothing, she sighed loudly. "What are you doing here anyway? I thought you had an interview?" she asked.

It sounded like an accusation and she narrowed her gaze at him.

Jay was immediately on the defensive. "I turned it down," he lied. Who knew if they were actually going to offer him the damn position anyway. "I'm researching from home." He indicated the dining table that straddled the space between the open kitchen and their small living area. At the moment it was covered in homework and reading books and some kind of half-finished art project that Josh demanded be left where it was.

"Well, I'm playing games," she said quickly. "I was here first."

Jay opened his mouth to argue, but shut it again. He used to be so close to Kirsten, but recently the fifteen-year-old had become hostile and belligerent, prone to quick temper and quicker cutting sarcasm. He couldn't face a fight today, not with the headache that banded his skull.

"Turn it down and we'll be okay," he said instead.

She huffed again and restarted the game, turned the sound down one notch. The jarring noise of guns and engines and screams was serving to make Jay's headache worse.

He made coffee and drank a whole cup before he poked his head around the corner of Ashley's door. He needed the caffeine to give him a bit of a high before he admitted to her what had happened. They'd spoken with hope about this interview today, like it was the answer to every problem they had. If he got the job, Kirsten might be happy overnight. If he got the job, Josh might not show signs of dyslexia. If he got the job, maybe Ashley could get counseling and set up her freelance cake-decorating service as she wanted. Hell, if Jay got the job, maybe he could spend time away from everything here and get a touch of a life of his own.

Guilt consumed him. That was not what he thought at all. He wanted to provide for his small, dysfunctional family as much as the next guy.

"Hey, sis," he said softly into the gloom.

The curtains were drawn, but there was enough faint light to see that Ashley appeared to be sitting upright in bed with her arms around her knees. He made out that much, but couldn't see her face clearly. "Kirsten said you weren't well."

"I'm fine," Ashley said. "Go away, Jay."

Jay ignored her. He was good at that. She might be older than him by three years, with a teenage daughter and a young son, but she was not strong enough for him to feel like he needed to follow her orders. He crossed to the drapes and pulled them open, letting light into the room.

"Jesus Christ, Jay," she shouted hoarsely.

He turned abruptly to face her and inhaled sharply.

"What the fuck, Ash?" He crossed to her side and clambered onto the wide double bed before gripping her hands and pulling them from where she was attempting to hide her face.

She winced and let out a yelp of pain. A dark mark marred her cheekbone and mascara ran from wet eyes. She wriggled free of his hold, and he let her go.

"What the hell happened?"

"Leave me alone," she sobbed.

"Tell me. Who did this to you?"

"Lewis," she said brokenly.

Jay couldn't believe what she was saying. Lewis Kaplan, her ex, had done this? "What the hell, Ashley? He's still serving time, isn't he?"

"He got out last week," she replied woodenly. "Early release."

"How did I not know this? Why didn't you tell me? Jeez, did you go to see him? Ash? Talk to me!"

"I had to! He's Josh's dad, he wanted to talk custody—"

"The fucking bastard lost that chance when we won in court. He abused you and scared Josh." Jay shook his sister and she yelped. He immediately let her go. Why didn't she see what she was doing? "Why did you see him without me?"

"I knew you'd be angry with me. I make everyone angry," she sobbed. "I told him not to worry about Josh, that when he was in prison you looked after us, that you were like Josh's dad, and he said some disgusting stuff about you and slapped me. I told you... I made him angry." She raised her gaze to his and scrubbed furiously at the tears.

Deflated, Jay sat back and away. He could only focus on one of the things she'd said. "Why would you say something like that?" His sister had gone from one bad relationship to another. Pregnant at fifteen, she'd been through a succession of losers. Jay couldn't be there all the time, but he thought they'd put Lewis behind them. "You didn't make him angry."

The counseling she'd done some time ago had begun to help her, and Jay felt helpless that she'd somehow drifted back into connecting with her ex.

"Was this the date you told me you had last night?" He'd babysat for Josh and watched twelve *Tom and Jerry* cartoons back-to-back with his nephew. And all that time Ashley was meeting the man who had nearly destroyed her?

Ashley placed a hand square on his chest, and he winced at the touch. "He was so nice to me, Jay. Bought me dinner, told me he was sorry, that he wanted to try again.... Why did this happen?"

Jay couldn't decipher what his sister was asking. Was she railing at the world, asking why everything in her life had happened? Or was she asking him to explain why Lewis was an asshole who abused women? He didn't have an answer to either. Instead, he pulled her into a close hug and held her gently. She cried into his shirt.

At least he had his mind made up.

Montana was thousands of miles away, but the words that Marcus Allen had said had been filed away in Jay's head: *a new start*—for him and Ashley, for Kirsten and Josh. There had to be good schools there.

"Jesus, fuck." He rested his head on hers.

Now things were different, now it was Montana 1, New York 1.

CHAPTER SIX

"I hate you," Kirsten said. Again. She hated Jay as much as she hated the fact they were heading for Montana.

Jay was numb to the constant histrionics by then. Kirsten had loathed him when he told her he was relocating, and she told him to fuck off when he explained all four of them were going. She had packed her bags to go and stay with her boyfriend of the week—Stan, or something—and Jay patiently unpacked twice before she got the hint.

"All my friends are texting me, saying they miss me, and offering me beds to stay in," she muttered from the plane seat next to him.

Jay had drawn the short straw. Ashley got to sit next to Josh, who was visibly vibrating with excitement. To him, Montana meant cowboys and adventure. But Jay got Miss Miserable, who, if she was to be believed, had just had her entire life destroyed by her uncle.

"You'll find new friends," he suggested helpfully.

The look of mixed disbelief and disdain she sent him was enough to have him wincing.

"I don't want new friends!" she shouted. That was the first sign her anger was overtaking her sulking again. "I want Stan. I love him, and he loves me."

"You've only known him a few weeks." Jay attempted patience. He was the last person to sniff at first love, and he didn't want to belittle Kirsten's emotions, but Stan was an idiot who smoked and couldn't really afford it. Not only that, he could only speak in words of one syllable.

"He's getting my name tattooed on his neck. He loves me."

Simple teenage logic. Thank God she had yet to succumb to tattooing—she appeared to be satisfied with changing the color of her hair each week.

Jay was caught between rolling his eyes at the drama and imagining poor Stan in ten years' time with Kirsten's name on his neck but hitched to another woman. In the end, the vision of Stan—who was only sixteen—at the age of twenty-six with ten different names on his skin made Jay laugh. He couldn't help the smirk that made its way to his face.

"Don't laugh at me!" Kirsten shouted. She sounded like turning hysterical was only a few steps away.

"I wasn't," Jay lied.

Shit, he hadn't meant to show that to Kirsten. He had no idea how to handle this version of his niece. Teasing each other had been replaced by bitterness and stress. He didn't recall being such an ass to his parents when he was her age. Maybe he had been, though.

"I hate you," she said in a softer voice.

If she was hoping Jay wouldn't hear, then she was wrong.

"Well, I love you, and I always will," he said just as quietly.

She shot him a quick look that he could see in his peripheral vision, then she quickly stared down at her Kindle and ignored him.

Jay shuffled in his seat. This part of the journey was the short part. They'd been stuck at Minneapolis-St. Paul International for three and a half hours on a layover, but all the waiting around made him worry about what exactly he'd gotten them into.

He'd phoned Marcus back, accepted the position, sorted out some details, then broke the news to the family. They were all coming with him because he was providing for them and he hadn't left any room for negotiation. He was doing this for Ashley and the kids as much as for himself, but one thing he did know was that no one was going to be immediately happy, except maybe Josh.

Kirsten was the most vocal of her dismay as Jay had expected, but after Josh contemplated leaving his friends, he had quickly decided that Montana sounded fun.

Oh, to be six again.

Jay spoke to Ashley separately. She had made such a thing of Lewis being around for Josh that Jay had expected her to want to stay in New York. He couldn't actually make any of them go with him, but he was willing to argue his side: new opportunities, a fresh start, being a family.

He had all the arguments ready to go, but Ashley surprised the hell out of him. What he hadn't expected was that she would be so eager to leave the little job she had and the man she said she loved. He wondered if it had anything to do with the new bruises he had seen on her face this morning. She'd covered them with makeup, but it wasn't enough to hide the marks or the sadness in her eyes.

Jay hated that he had nothing he could do to help his sister. She had been trapped in a cycle of abuse and low self-esteem, and it didn't matter what he said, she had been adamant that there *was* hope for Lewis and that he *had* needed her.

Hadn't Jay felt the same way about Mark and hoped that one day Mark would wake up less of an entitled asshole? At least Jay had punched back. Ashley had been overwhelmed.

He opened his laptop and clicked on the Dropbox folder he was collecting all his information in. He'd spent the last week putting everything he owned into storage and researching Crooked Tree and Montana. He had a couple of websites that he thought made a really good job of promoting what they offered, but he needed to know a lot more about what a dude ranch actually did before he could begin sketching ideas. The rest of the flight was quiet, and all too soon the four of them were collecting their cases and making their way out of the building to wait expectantly.

"They're not even here," Kirsten said. "Shows how much they want your ass on their ranch."

Jay bit his lip. He was the grown-up in the situation. He would not rise to the sarcasm nor start to worry when no one from Crooked Tree arrived to pick them up.

"What time did they say they would be here?" Ashley asked.

"For when we landed."

"And you gave them the right time?"

"I'm sure I did. Give them ten minutes, and I'll call them."

Privately he hoped this wasn't what prospective guests were presented with when they arrived in Helena. He knew that the ranch had a pickup service, and he hoped to hell it was normally on time for the people that mattered.

"Jay Sullivan?" a voice said behind them.

Jay spun on his heel and immediately shook the extended hand of the guy standing dressed in head-to-toe denim with a hat on his head. *A Stetson—it's a Stetson.* He was tall and slim and very pretty, despite the denim. Jay curbed his assessment of pretty—the last place he wanted to be seen perving over a cowboy was in cowboy country itself.

"Gabriel Todd," Stetson wearer and insult to fashion in general said with a smile. "Middle brother. Sorry I'm late. Nate got called away, and I left as soon as I could."

Jay waved away the apology. "No worry."

Josh held out his hand. "I'm Josh," he said formally.

Gabriel inclined his head in hello and shook the proffered hand. "Hello, Josh. Welcome to Montana."

Then Gabe turned to the girls. Ashley was perched on her case and Kirsten sat on the floor cross-legged and still looking mutinous. "And these pretty girls must be Kirsten and Ashley?" Gabe asked with a cheeky wink.

Jay held back an audible sigh. Kirsten was going to eat him for breakfast.

Kirsten scrambled to stand. "Pretending we look the same age isn't gonna get you face time with my mom," she said firmly. She stood between Gabe and Ashley, and crossed her arms over her chest.

Gabe smiled. He had dimples—pits of cute—but Jay could see he was looking past Kirsten and focusing on Ashley. Seemed like tall, dark, and pretty wasn't playing for Jay's team. Good job too. Jay wasn't here to mix business with pleasure.

Gabe held out his hand to shake Kirsten's. Finally she relented and they shook. Gabe then reached around Kirsten and offered a hand to Ashley. Instead of shaking hands, he used the grip to pull her to her feet. She thanked him and looked around herself—anywhere except at him. Jay saw the exact moment Gabe noticed the bruising on her face.

Gabe tightened his jaw and thinned his lips. "You okay, ma'am?" he asked softly.

"Tired," she said, then shrugged free of his light clasp and took hold of her case. "Let's get to our new home." She walked in the direction Gabe had come from and sidestepped as he attempted to take her bags. Jay felt a swell of pride in his sister, then focused on himself and the kids. Finally all the bags were in the navy van emblazoned with the words *Crooked Tree Dude Ranch* in pale blue and comic sans with a picture of a cartoon horse next to the name. Did the place not have a real logo? Jay had imagined the cartoon horse on the twelve-page, rambling, nonsense-filled website was some kind of placeholder, but hell, it *was* their logo? And comic sans *was* their font? That would be the first to go.

Jay sat up front with Gabe and was relieved when the guy turned out to be the talkative sort, which meant Jay didn't have to think of things to say. As they moved north toward the ranch, Gabe gave a running commentary on the things they saw. One hundred miles of driving on good roads and bad, and two hours after their flight landed, the Sullivan family arrived at the turnoff to the ranch.

"Can you stop the car?" Jay asked.

Gabe glanced at him. "You okay?"

"I want to remember this," he murmured. He climbed out of the van, and when he jumped to the ground, a puff of soil left the road. *Cold.* Montana in February was cold. Turning three-sixty he saw mountains and snow, with green poking through the snow at this elevation. An icy wind made him turn up the collar of his coat. He cataloged what he assumed was pastureland and a long dirt road. Sometimes, when companies had him assess their marketing, they cleared up, changed things, altered the starting point. This seemed raw and real, and Jay wanted to be able to recall every image for when he began planning.

He climbed back in, shut the door, and placed his hands on the heater, which to be fair wasn't throwing out that much heat.

"Ready?" Gabe looked curious and probably had a million questions, but Jay wanted to be selfish and hold tight to his first opinions.

"Uh-huh," he answered. "Let's go."

The road widened and ran under a large sign, the kind of thing he recognized from ranches on the TV and in films: a large wood-and-iron structure with the words "Crooked Tree" formed in metal and suspended over the entrance. The road then narrowed, and they drove over a bridge onto the commercial ranch area proper. A collection of buildings lay off to the left, and along to the right, a sign proclaiming "Store" along with a large restaurant called "Branches."

"Was told to take you straight to your place, let you get settled in," Gabe said as he turned left to the buildings Jay had first seen. "This is the staff area, but it's kind of empty, so it'll be private down here." He pulled up outside a cabin that looked like it had seen better days. "It's on the plan to make good on the exterior," Gabe explained, "but the interior's comfortable. Sophie came down and changed all the bedding for you."

Gabe helped the four of them with their cases and opened the door with a flourish.

Jay was shocked. He wasn't easily shocked, but this place was huge compared to the size of his apartment. An open-plan kitchen-dining area, living room, another room for an office, he guessed, and then four doors led off from the main corridor at the rear to what he assumed were bedrooms and bathrooms.

"Each bedroom has its own half bath, from when staff shared the place. Marcus said about inviting you up to dinner, but I thought maybe tonight you'd want your space. I'll come down to collect you for breakfast at seven."

"Seven. Okay." Jay didn't expect to sleep much tonight—he was wired.

"There's food in the cupboards, and Sophie put dinners in your fridge—just heat 'em in the microwave. See you tomorrow morning."

Gabe left after replacing his hat and tilting it at Ashley. For her part, she blushed and looked away again. *Jeez.*

After their taxi service had left, it was suddenly just the four of them in a loose huddle in the living room. "Josh, Kirsten, you two take first pick of the rooms."

Josh sprinted for the nearest door and opened it before running out and into the next one. He'd looked in all four before Kirsten moved an inch. Nate thought he could see a spark of enthusiasm in her expression, but she was hiding it damn well beneath an air of indifference.

"This one!" Josh announced. "It has two beds and it's so cool!" He dragged his case on its wheels into the room and began to unpack without prompting.

"I'll have this one," Kirsten said. She'd chosen the one next to her brother.

"Your turn," Jay said to Ashley.

"Let's both look." Ashley gently entwined her fingers with his.

Together they looked in all four. Josh's and Kirsten's were at the back of the property, and when they went into the third room on one side, Nate knew it would be perfect for Ashley. Light streamed in through the window and the room had all those feminine touches, like a fringed lampshade over the bulb, and curtains with those tieback things. When the fourth room revealed itself to be decorated in a neutral sage green with an enormous and solid king-size bed, the decision was made.

He hauled in his two cases, then shut the door on everyone else and sat on the edge of his bed. They'd made it here. He'd be lucky if Kirsten lasted a week, but everyone was safe, and he could do what he did best without barriers in the way.

He could take care of his family.

CHAPTER SEVEN

Nate and Juno moved at a slow pace away from the house, making their way through the deep snow. Gabe had told a lot of stories at dinner, and Nate hadn't failed to notice that he spoke an awful amount about Ashley, the new marketing guy's sister. He said she was skittish, sported a bruise on her face, and by the end of dinner he'd guessed at reasons why the blonde—because, yes she was blonde—carried such marks on her.

Nate wanted to know about this Jay guy. He was still on the edge of being pissed that Marcus had hired him without general consensus. He, Gabe, and Luke deserved a vote. Come to think of it, the Strachan family, wherever they were, were eligible to have a say-so.

Nate and Juno emerged from the trees by the creek and walked smoothly among the empty Creek Cabins. Nate still hadn't made a decision about whether they were opening them come March. That was in the hands of the new business and marketing guy, and the not knowing was driving Nate screwy. He'd worked with Gabe and Luke on the remedial work that needed to be done but had focused on the River and Forest Cabins. They really needed new staff, but Nate wasn't sure where the money would come from to pay for them.

He gave Juno her head and they flew across the familiar landscape, the mountains lost in the darkness and the sky glittering with stars. He reined her in at the top of

Ember Bluff and sat there for a while, simply breathing in the fresh air. In daylight he would have been able to see the layout of the commercial side of the ranch, behind him was the roundup canyon, in front of him the accommodation for the people who came here for the genuine pretend-cowboy experience.

This was his life, and he wanted it to carry on, to weather the storms and survive so that Gabe's and Luke's kids would have something to inherit in the future. Nate resolved to be patient with the new guy and open to new ideas. He would forget that Jay Sullivan and his sister and her kids were "city." It didn't mean the man wouldn't slot into the Crooked Tree just fine and bring new ideas to the table.

He turned Juno around. They took the return a little more slowly. The air was icy cold. What would probably be the last snowfall before spring was threatening to fall tonight. They broke into a canter when they reached the flat plain toward the river, then splashed through a shallower part that Juno knew well.

With a nudge, Nate encouraged her up the bank on the other side, and with a burst of speed, they jumped the small ridge to the pathway—straight into a flashing, glaring light and loud yelling. Juno reared and instinct kicked in for Nate.

"It's okay," he crooned as he settled her.

The yelling was still going on, and Juno wasn't that impressed as she shied away and shook her head. Nate slid from the saddle, taking the time to settle Juno before tying the horse off loosely. Juno was a solid horse, not prone to spooking, but Nate wasn't taking any chance.

He stalked to where the yelling was coming from. A figure lay prone in the snow with their hands over their face and curses dropping from their lips. A male voice. A flashlight on a dropped phone sent up a beacon into the dark night. Nate blinked with the sudden blindness, then kicked the phone over so it was dark.

"What the fuck are you doing?" the owner of the voice that had dripped with curses spluttered. "You could have killed me."

"I could ask you the same thing, you idiot," Nate snapped back.

The man cursed loudly, "I'm the idiot? Fuck. I was walking, and suddenly your devil horse mowed me down."

Nate looked pointedly at Juno, who, in the light thrown by the moon, was standing still and docile by a tree. "You're the idiot, 'cause you don't go crawling around in the dark on a freaking ranch."

"I'm on a cleared path, and there should be lighting here."

"Jeez, get your ass off the ground," Nate snapped. He didn't have all night to be talking to whom he guessed was the guy from the city himself, Jay *freaking* Sullivan.

"Help me up," Jay ordered quickly.

"Get yourself up," Nate offered in return. "You fall over, you get yourself up and standing. The rule of the ranch."

"The ranch with no freaking lights. There should be a rule about *that*. Where's my damn phone?"

Nate's eyes had gotten used to the dark again after being blinded by the blue-white light of Jay's phone. He kicked the phone closer to Jay's hand, and Jay fell on it like a starving man. He pressed buttons and the damn flashlight shot a beam of bright light into the trees above them. What the light illuminated was an image Nate was going to remember for a long time. This guy—the new man who was going to whip the ranch business into shape—was all slim and blond and sexy and ruffled. Covered in Montana snow, he was messed up, but he wore the damp well. Nate's body fought warring emotions: instant appraisal of a fine piece of meat, and abject horror that Jay Sullivan was a complete moron. *A shivering moron.*

"Turn off the light, you idiot." Nate grabbed the phone from Jay's hand and turned it over, wondering how the hell he was going to turn the light off. When he couldn't immediately work it out, he pocketed the cell.

"What the hell, asshole? Give me back my phone."

"No," Nate said steadily.

Jay stumbled quickly to stand toe-to-toe with Nate. "Give me my damn phone."

Turned out Nate's first assessment of the guy being shorter than him was right. A good three or four inches less and skinny to boot. He looked strong enough if you liked the soft, gentle curves of a man stuck behind a desk. Nate found himself contemplating what color Jay's eyes were, then caught himself, and immediately stopped thinking of anything inappropriate.

Jay lunged for the phone and Nate sidestepped the move, catching Jay's arm and preventing him from face-planting in the snow. With temper in his stance, Jay shrugged off the grip and rounded on Nate.

"My. Phone," he bit out.

"I'm keeping the phone," Nate said perversely. He realized he was enjoying having five ten of slim, sexy man, all roiled up and temper driven, standing in front of him. It had been far too long since he'd seen temper this unbridled in anyone.

"You're an asshole," Jay snapped and lunged again.

This time, Nate didn't move. Instead, he allowed Jay to fall into him and enjoyed the feeling of a male form pressed against him. Shame it was all about the temper.

Nate pushed Jay away; he was enjoying this teasing play far too much. Jay clearly wasn't seeing it as teasing or playing—he was spitting mad. "I'm not the idiot making himself blind by staring into a light," Nate said. "We deliberately don't have lights this side of the river, so you'd best get used to using the moon."

"I'm not a fucking idiot. I value my life, Cowboy, and a no-light situation is stupid."

Nate ignored the whole "fucking idiot" and "cowboy" reference. "What's stupid is stumbling around in the dark on your first night here with no idea of where you're going."

Nate watched as Jay purposefully brushed himself down and appeared to take the time to get himself together. Again Nate wished he could see Jay's expression clearly, but his eyes were still adjusting after being blinded by the damn light. Seemed as if Mr. City was calming himself down and consigning Nate to some kind of group of people he had to deal with in a special kind of patient way.

Finally Jay held out a hand. "Jay Sullivan." Nate took the hand. "And you are?"

"Nate Todd."

"One of the Todds. Gabe's brother."

"Big brother."

"The horse guy?"

Nate raised a single eyebrow. That was what he was being labeled as? "The horse guy," he confirmed.

They released the grip, and Jay held out his hand again. "My phone," he said very deliberately. "Please," he added firmly.

Some stubborn streak in Nate had him contemplating throwing the space-age junk in the river. That would stop Jay from frightening horses. Then common sense prevailed. Juno was fine, he was fine, and thankfully no one had died. He held out the phone but snatched it back just as Jay's hand reached it.

"What the fuck," Jay cursed.

Some small part of Nate loved that Jay's practiced civility had dropped and the cursing was back.

"No more sneaking around until you know the ranch."

Nate could see well enough by then to notice Jay's mouth opening and shutting like a damn trout. Then the guy pulled himself straight and upright. "I wasn't sneaking around. I was learning the place."

Nate released the phone to Jay. "This side of the place isn't yours to know," he said simply. "You stick to your side of the river and away from the private cabins."

"I didn't realize there *was* a private side."

Nate ignored the sarcasm in Jay's tone. Clicking his tongue to get Juno's attention, he clasped her reins and led her away.

But not before he left with a parting shot. "Well, now you know. See you at breakfast."

Nate fumed all the way back home, and it took him one hell of a long time to calm down. Not only had his cock stood to attention, he hadn't been able to stop the damn thing. He was in need of getting some action, and soon. So instead he focused intently on the emotion he could handle—temper.

His anger, which began with Jay crawling about with a flashlight—albeit on a phone—and scaring Juno, began to morph into anger toward Gabe. His brother should have explained that the Sullivans must stay put until they'd had the proper guided tour and that the three houses up on this side of the river were private property.

By the time Nate had stabled Juno and made his way indoors, he was itching for a fight. He'd asked Gabe to do one thing, and one thing only—get the Sullivans and hole them away in the old staff cabin until the meet-and-greet tomorrow.

The inside of the house was dark. Gabe and Luke were asleep, but that didn't stop Nate from shoving Gabe's door open. The noise of it crashing on the wall had Gabe upright in his bed in fright. The book he'd fallen asleep reading fell to the floor with a *crack*.

"What's wrong?" Gabe said immediately. "Is it Luke?"

Remorse broke into a little of Nate's anger but not enough to stop him. He hadn't meant to make Gabe think the worst. "Next time I tell you to do something, for God's sake do it right," he shouted.

"What?" Gabe flicked on his bedside lamp. He looked dazed and unfocused. "What's wrong?"

"I only found Jay Sullivan creeping around in the snow near the Strachan place! Damn fool flashed a light at Juno and near got me thrown."

"Okay," Gabe began. "That's my fault how?"

"You should have told him everything beyond the stables is off limits."

Gabe sighed and rolled onto his side to reach across and shut off the lamp. "Go to bed, Nate."

"We need to talk about this."

"No. You don't want to talk, you want a fight, and I'm asleep. So go away."

"Gabe—"

"Jesus, Nate, will you go and get laid and work out some of this testosterone! You're freaking Luke and me out with all this arguing shit."

"Gabe—"

"Just fuck off."

Nate felt oddly drained and deflated. He hated it when he and Gabe or Luke argued. Hell, he had to face it, what had happened hadn't been an argument because his freaking brother hadn't risen to the challenge. Just spouted some shit about getting laid. Grabbing his keys, Nate decided that his brother might well be right. Ever since he'd confronted the fact that the ranch was heading toward meltdown and accepted his part in it, he'd been frustrated and antsy. Months of no sex and tension mixed with worry left him with a hair trigger. He was in his truck and off Crooked Tree in less than five minutes.

Before he could really settle into driving, he had reached town and continued through. He pulled up outside Carter's, a biker's bar in the back of beyond, and parked. He was out of the truck before he could change his mind.

Pickings for a man with his appetites were pretty slim in town—no such thing as a gay bar there—but at least here he could get some easy sex without repercussions. He pushed open the door and was greeted by a wall of sound. No one turned and looked at the door; no one in here cared who he was or what he wanted. The place was heaving with men and women alike, a good proportion of them bikers from various towns this side of the mountains.

A mix of needs walked side by side in this place: gay, lesbian, bi, het, ménage, rooms where the doors shut and no one asked questions. He didn't see familiar faces—hell, he wasn't really looking—and he made his way to the bar. Holding a bottle, he turned to face the crowd and leaned back against the bar. Nate crossed his legs at the ankle and waited. He didn't have to wait long. The first couple of advances were girls, and he dealt with them politely and firmly and waited for word to filter out to their friends.

He had his eye on a couple of guys old enough to be legal, and soon enough one of them approached him. No words were spoken, but they moved through the crowd and into the corridor behind the bar. Paying a cover charge had them legitimately hiring a room, and the blue-eyed blond assumed the position as soon as the door shut. He pushed down his jeans, laid a condom and lube on the table, then tilted his ass in the air with his hands on the bed. This wasn't about foreplay; this was about stretching the guy out enough to fuck him through the mattress.

No emotions involved, but Nate felt the familiar wash of peace flowing through him. He needed this. Gabe was right, and wouldn't his brother be crowing about it tomorrow? *Fucker.*

Nate spent some time stretching the man, but everything was clinical and quick. When he was balls-deep and fucking Anonymous Guy into the mattress, he gripped the guy's hair and turned his head so he could see the expressions on his lay's face. Need, lust, and greed took their turns flowing across the guy's face.

"Tighter," the guy said. "Grip it tighter."

Pushy bottom, but Nate didn't hesitate. He pulled at the guy's hair and held tight. His rhythm became erratic as an orgasm built inside him. He bottomed out with each shove of his cock into this warm and willing body. "Use your hand," he ordered.

The pushy bottom complied. Nate guessed he was fisting himself by the keening noise he made and his shouts as he came on the bed. Nate followed him over and grunted as he lost it.

He didn't hang around. As soon as the last pulse of come left him and he softened, he held on to the condom and pulled out.

"Fuck, that was hot," Anonymous Guy said. "I'm Liam—"

"No names," Nate said firmly. "Thanks for the fuck."

Without a backward glance, he left the room, made his way back out of the bar, and headed immediately to his truck. In seconds he was back on the road, but as soon as he rounded the bend before the main road, he pulled the truck to the side and cut the engine.

Sitting in the dark, Nate crossed his hands on the steering wheel and buried his head in them.

What kind of life was he living here? That Liam guy had been cute. Nate didn't have to be so fucking closed off. He could go back, see if Liam wanted more—a drink maybe, or a chat? Just because he was gay didn't mean he couldn't have a lover, a real one. Add to that the worries he'd allowed into his head about Crooked Tree and suddenly he was exhausted.

How long he sat there, he didn't know. His only thought was that Gabe was right. No wonder Gabe had told him to get his head straight. He was fucked.

CHAPTER EIGHT

Jay woke to sunlight pouring in through open drapes. A quick look at his cell phone showed him it was only 5:00 a.m. At some point after he'd stumbled home, with snow melting in his pants and temper in his head, he must have slept. He peered closer at his Samsung—the screen had a crack in it. Great. That freaking cowboy broke his damn phone kicking it about in the piles of snow. Not exactly a brilliant start to a working relationship.

He showered in his small bathroom and dressed in near-black jeans and a white shirt. He considered a tie, but dismissed it and instead left the top button of his shirt open. In the mirror the glint of his thin gold chain caught his eye, and he fished it out. On it hung his parents' wedding rings, which he held close to his heart. One day they would go to Kirsten and Josh, but today they were still his. He pushed the chain back down under the shirt and slipped on polished black leather shoes.

It was still only six, but he knocked on everyone's door to let them know they were being picked up in an hour. Jay made coffee and sat out on the veranda at the back of the large cabin, appreciating its spectacular view of the mountains.

Josh was the first to appear. In thick PJs and with severe bed hair, Josh curled up in Jay's lap for cuddles. "Will they be nice here?" he asked quietly.

"Of course they will be."

"Do I have to do my hair?"

"Probably. You want to brush your teeth as well."

"I already did that."

"For how long ?"

Josh was quiet for a long time. "I don't know," he said. "I forget a lot."

Jay cuddled him close and laughed. "Go, wet your hair, and brush your teeth. I'll come find you when Gabe gets here."

Josh ran into the house, and Ashley was the next to appear. Her long blonde hair was drawn up in a ponytail and he saw she'd used makeup again to hide the bruise. She had her own mug of coffee and slipped into the chair next to him.

"I don't think I've slept that well in years," she said with a smile. "It's so quiet here."

"That's a good thing, sis," Jay said, returning her smile. "We could all do with more sleep. Did you hear if Kirsten was up yet?"

"I heard noises. You know it takes her half an hour just to get her makeup on." Ashley shook her head wryly.

"Now you know what I have to put up with having you as my sister."

She punched him on the shoulder. "Actually, little brother, you're not looking too bad this morning." Ashley smirked and lifted an eyebrow. "Making an effort for Gabe?"

Jay near choked on his coffee. "No, I'm not. This is work for me. Not all of us are on holiday. Anyway, Gabe wasn't staring at me." He threw a look her way and she glanced away. She was blushing, and it was nice to see, then she grew serious.

"I don't want anyone looking at me, Jay. I don't see this as a holiday either." She curled her legs under her and sipped on her coffee. "I see this as a fresh start for all of us. Lewis knows where we are and could come make trouble for me, but for a while we can build something strong here, so when he does come, I'm ready for him and not so damn needy."

Lewis. Everything always came back to Lewis and the cloud he cast over Ashley's life. He'd lost the right to have access to Josh when he'd been jailed for hurting Ashley and rendering Josh unconscious when he was little more than a baby. Josh remembered nothing of that day, but Jay remembered every single detail of the frantic call from his sister and what he found when he got to her place: Ashley bleeding, Kirsten crying hysterically, and Josh limp in Ashley's arms.

That day Jay could have killed Lewis. He still wanted to; he just kept it hidden.

"Yes, he could follow us after he's off the tight leash the justice system has him on. He's a lawyer and he knows his way around the system. Neither of us is stupid. He'll come and try to contact Josh. He'll try to win you back, but you know what, Ash? We'll be ready for him."

Ashley held out her hand and Jay squeezed it. Linked that way, they both looked up at the mountains, lost in thought.

"He's here," Kirsten said from the back door.

Jay stood and threw the remains of his coffee onto the ground over the side of the porch. Catching sight of his niece's face, he sighed inwardly. She looked like something out of a music video shoot. Thick black lined her eyes, but she'd added a flick to each side which made them look odd. The bold design didn't stop there. Slashing scarlet lipstick covered her mouth and her dark pink hair had new streaks of blue-black in it. She wore black jeans, a black tee, heavy black boots, and had the expression of someone who'd lost a winning lottery ticket. They were due to look at schools in a few days in an effort to get Kirsten back on track, and he hoped to hell, the much smaller than they were used to, local high school was forgiving. Otherwise that would be another reason for the list of things Kirsten hated to grow by one.

"Mornin'," Gabe said as they walked back into the house.

"Morning, Gabe," Jay answered immediately.

Ashley didn't say a word, but she did smile, which was a step in the right direction.

"Hear you went walking," Gabe added. "Met my brother."

Jay groaned. He'd been an idiot wandering about like that in a place he didn't know and had asked for trouble. Still, make no bones about it, tall, dark, and rugged Nate Todd—or Nathaniel, as the job offer was signed off—was a stuck-up, opinionated prick who needed a dose of manners. One that Jay determined to give him today. Last night he'd pushed the late-night meeting to one side and managed to compartmentalize it enough to get at least some sleep, but everything was rushing back as he stood looking at Gabe. Yes, he knew he'd probably gone about things the wrong way, but he was collecting information for himself. Nate didn't have to near kill him with a horse.

He looked at Gabe closely. Was this what Nate looked like? Did he have the same emerald-green eyes? The same wavy hair? Did they look alike? Nate had appeared bigger than Gabe last night, but then, Jay *had* been lying on the ground, so his perspective had been a little skewed. Except, of course, for the part when he wasn't on the ground but up-close and personal with the man who smelled of the night and horses. Then the height difference and the build of the tall cowboy had been damn obvious.

"Yeah, we met" was how he summarized it. Gabe and he exchanged a quick, easy smile, and the weight of what he imagined Gabe thought of him lifted a little. He was a city slicker, so sue him for not knowing the rules of the range or whatever they had out here.

"It's not far. We can walk." Gabe peered down at Jay's shoes and winced. "You may want to think about getting boots," he said. "Pretty snowy in winter, then dusty in summer around here for leather like that."

"I'll get something," Jay said.

The family shrugged on heavy jackets and made their way out into the snow-covered landscape. The path was cleared, but the banks were maybe four foot deep. The white was stunning.

They made their way across the bridge over the river that Jay had walked over last night. The Blackfoot was wide at this point and shallow enough that Jay could see stones through the clear water. The sound was soothing, the sight spectacular. Jay stopped and framed a virtual photo in his head—from here, the water, the snowy banks, the mountains—a perfect sales shot.

"You coming, Uncle Jay?" Josh shouted from ahead.

Jay blinked. He'd fallen behind and lost himself in collecting images. Jogging, he caught up with the small group, and a few minutes later they were walking past a sign displaying the big word Private. Damn, he'd missed that last night.

"Up here there are three houses. The one at the top is where I live with Nate and my little brother Luke."

"You have a little brother?" Josh interrupted. "Can he play with me?"

Gabe chuckled. "He's seventeen, but I can tell you he plays some mean video games."

Josh frowned at the age, then smiled at "video games." "Does he have a PS3, or what?"

"I have no idea," Gabe said with a shrug. "You can ask him at breakfast. The first house is where we're having it." Gabe pointed at the house settled low on the side of the mountain just where the terrain began to rise away from the river. "Belongs to the Allens. Well, Marcus anyway. He has a housekeeper called Sophia who is like a goddess of cooking. She sure beats anything the three of us can come up with, anyway."

They reached the house and climbed the steps. Gabe knocked, then walked in, and Jay indicated that Ashley and the kids could go in next.

"We're here," Gabe called unnecessarily as an older woman appeared around a corner with a spatula in her hand.

"Come in, come in," she said. She pulled Josh in for a quick hug, then Kirsten. Josh loved it; Kirsten struggled a little and smudged some of her makeup on the woman's skin. "I'm Sophia," she said as she embraced Ashley, then Jay in turn. "I'm so pleased you all made it safely. Come into the kitchen and meet Marcus."

They all followed her into a wide-open space that clearly worked as the very heart of the house—a large range, with appliances and bowls and tins, and Sophia at the center with a grin on her face. A man who could only be Marcus stood, and he and Jay shook hands. He had steel-gray hair and dark eyes, and he was grinning ear to ear.

"So good to finally meet you," he said. His voice was deep and gruff and had less of a drawl than Gabe's did.

"This here is Luke," Gabe said by way of introduction.

A young man stood from the table. He was definitely related to Gabe—he had the same green eyes and the look of his brother. Luke politely shook hands, with Kirsten, who was faced with something new—a boy near her age with manners. All of them took seats at the large table, and Jay wondered where Nate was.

"Nate'll be here in a minute or two," Luke said as if he could read Jay's mind. "He's with Juno, and he's running late."

"Juno?"

"His horse. The one you met last night."

The door opened, and the noise of boots on the wooden floor heralded Nate's arrival. He kissed Sophia on the cheek, then slid into the empty chair between Gabe and Luke. That put all three Todd brothers in a row, and boy, they packed a punch. Getting his first proper look at Nate was a huge shock for Jay. He had this image of a shadowed man, big and hulking and all kinds of intimidating. He wasn't wrong on some of those points. Nate definitely looked like someone you didn't mess with. His features were harder than Gabe's, his worry lines more pronounced, but the grin was the same as his brothers' and his eyes a similar startling green. He was half a head taller than Jay's own five ten—six two, maybe? Height appeared to have skipped Gabe, who maybe had an inch on Jay, but it looked like Luke was going to be tall, the same as his oldest brother.

There was a harnessed energy in Nate, and Jay watched unnoticed, Nate ran big hands through his dark hair that was pressed flat, probably by a hat—*a Stetson*. His hands were big and the back of one them was scraped raw. Had he done that last night? Was Jay scaring the horse something that caused that scabbing on the man's skin?

As if sensing the scrutiny, Nate looked directly at Jay, his piercing eyes devoid of welcome despite the fact he had been grinning when he sat at the table. Jay could feel the ice from here. Thankfully Nate didn't hold the look; he simply concentrated on coffee and breakfast, which meant Jay got a short time to stare uninterrupted.

The Todd brothers were different. Gabe was pretty—really pretty; there was a softness about him that spoke of romance. Luke was young and relaxed and gave the impression he was easy in his own skin. Nate, on the other hand, was hardness personified: in the way he held himself, the way he sat silent, the fact that his flinty eyes were cold. Shame he had the looks but was icy with it. There was something about him that piqued Jay's interest even though the big man was a client, his employer, and Jay should remember that.

Jay sat eating breakfast, and an uncomfortable conclusion came from thinking about what had happened last night. He hated it, but really he owed the man an apology. He shouldn't have let his creative mind demand that he go and walk to get a better feel for the place. As soon as he'd left the bridge over the river, he'd become lost in the dark. After breakfast, maybe?

Shit, he needed to do it right then.

"About last night," Jay started.

Nate looked right at him again, and this time there was a spark of something in his eyes. Anger? Resentment? Or was he laughing? Fuck if Jay could tell with the accompanying inscrutable expression on the other man's face.

"Yeah, Nate, what exactly happened last night?" Gabe asked. "You came into my room like war had been declared, ranting about—" He stopped with an *ooof* as Nate elbowed him.

Jay took the interruption as his cue. "I just wanted to say it's my fault. I was walking around, and I met Nate and his horse out on the path up here. My apologies for coming onto private land." He included everyone in that. Manning up and apologizing when all he wanted to do was rail at Nate for scaring the shit out of him was his first step in building friendly relations.

Nate looked directly at him. "I overreacted," he said gruffly, then concentrated on forking eggs into his mouth, and Jay realized Nate was done talking. Well, to him, anyway.

"Sorry," Jay heard Nate say to Gabe between mouthfuls.

They fist-bumped, then dug into eating. What that was about was clearly not going to be explained. Some brother thing, Jay guessed.

"This is lovely food, Sophia," Jay offered.

The rest of his family agreed, and they began talking about schools and settling in.

"Luke is at the local high school," Gabe said when the subject of Kirsten's school came up. "He can tell you what you need for school."

"Happy to," Luke said immediately.

He was smiling at Kirsten, but Jay could see she wasn't in a happy place, and she simply scowled at the boy. *Great start.*

"Not sure I'm going to school," she announced airily. Everyone fell silent.

"You're going to school, Kirsten," Jay said firmly.

"'S not like they can teach me anything. Stan says it doesn't matter what I do, we've got nothing we need to learn," she said in response.

Again silence.

"What is it you've decided you want to do as a career, Kirsten?" Sophia asked her carefully.

Kirsten shrugged. "Things that don't need school," she said rudely.

"Kirsten, mind your manners," Ashley warned.

Jay groaned inwardly. This was not a good time for Ashley to reprimand Kirsten, though she was right to do so. He could almost script what happened next, and he was right.

Kirsten pushed herself up and out of her seat and made to leave.

"Sit down, Kirsten," Jay ordered.

"Why?" she began belligerently. "I don't want to be here. Why are you making me sit with them?"

"Kirsten—"

"I'm leaving." And she did.

"I apologize," Jay started as soon as she left. Ashley made to get up and go after her, but Jay stopped her with a hand on her arm. "Leave her be." Ashley looked at him, and he could see her eyes were filled with pain. "It will be okay."

An awkward silence fell at the table, and Jay felt the pressure of failure pressing down on him.

"Gabe, do you remember when you ran away 'cause you didn't want to go into eighth grade?" Marcus asked.

Jay's attention moved from Ashley, and he was damn glad of the distraction. Gabe gave Marcus a death glare.

Marcus continued without apparent concern. "I remember. It was because Mary in your science class was bullying you."

Gabe sighed noisily, but there was no anger in his expression. If anything, this was a scene that had played out before at the table—the good old embarrassing-story section that guaranteed family laughs.

"She was bullying me," Gabe protested. "She kept poking me with a pen when we were teamed up on that project about the environment. I was scared. I didn't know it was because she was into me."

"You ran away?" Josh asked, wide-eyed. He sat upright in his chair and was absolutely mesmerized with whatever Gabe said.

Jay wasn't stupid—he could see a serious case of hero worship from Josh toward the laid-back Gabe.

"Got as far as Ember Bluff as I remember," Marcus said thoughtfully.

If anything, Josh's eyes grew wider. "Is that a long way?"

"Fifteen minutes by horse," Marcus said quickly. "Pity you fell off."

"Lightning was spooked," Gabe said with the start of a grin on his face. "She threw me."

"Spooked by what?" Jay didn't like the idea of snakes, but he knew he'd face them out there in the stretches of plain up to the mountains.

Marcus huffed a laugh. "A thunderstorm. Lightning— the irony."

"She's a good horse," Gabe reminisced. "Fifteen hands and solid as a rock."

Jay listened to the byplay between Gabe and Marcus, watched Luke grinning at Gabe, and saw the start of a smile on Nate's face, all at the same time as shoveling in bacon and eggs like he was never going to eat again. The food was damn good, and Jay's body clock was telling him he was a few hours past breakfast.

"Thought we could get started after breakfast," Marcus said. "If that's okay with you, Jay."

"I'll take Ashley and Josh on a tour if you like?" Gabe said quickly.

"Don't forget the cabin," Nate reminded him.

Gabe narrowed his eyes and looked pointedly at Nate. "I have a list," he said simply. "So, Ashley, Josh, you want to get out of here and see what we got?"

"Is that okay?" Ashley asked. Jay waited for someone to answer, then realized she was talking to him. Wait… she was asking his permission? Why?

"Of course it is," he said with a smile. They needed to talk—Ashley didn't answer to him. He looked away and caught Nate looking at him with a distinct scowl on his face.

Now what have I done?

CHAPTER NINE

Nate helped clear the table, and all the while he thought about what he had just seen. Jay really wasn't all that effective as the head of his family. The teenager was out of control and rude, and the sister appeared unable to deal with her own daughter. Only Josh acted normal, but then how bad could a six-year-old be? The more he saw of the city guy, the less he was inclined to be charitable in his assessments of him.

Jay was shorter and slimmer than Nate, and had the look about him of a man more comfortable in a suit and tie. His hair color was a darker blond than his sister's, but that was probably due to whatever gunk he put in it to keep it in that "just got out of bed" look. His brown eyes held a wary expression, and he didn't appear to be that comfortable sitting at the table. He was quiet, ineffective and had scared the shit out of Juno last night. Three marks against him already.

Nate knew they should have got someone who actually knew the terrain, and he wasn't just talking the ranch, but Montana, horses, and the reasons why a working ranch had been changed to a dude ranch catering to rich tourists. Did the city guy know how hard it was out here? Nate sighed inwardly. This wasn't what he had been hoping for, and he hadn't heard the guy speak yet.

With the table cleared and dealt with, he, Marcus, and Jay sat down.

"So," Marcus began. "Where do we start?" He sounded excited, like Jay was going to have all the answers.

"Brand," Jay said simply. He placed a notepad on the flat surface and wrote "Brand" in the middle, then circled it dramatically. "Like Coke, or Snickers, or Nike. We need to identify a brand for the ranch."

Marcus sat forward in his chair and nodded. "Can you explain what you need?"

"Well, at its most basic, a brand exists or is created to differentiate between competing but similar products or services. Brand meanings can be tangible, with real characteristics, or intangible, like the emotions or symbolism associated with them. I'd like to carry out a brand audit." Nate watched as Jay scribbled "Brand Audit" in the middle of the page. "The purpose of carrying out a brand audit is to understand how a brand has evolved and what can be done to it so that it becomes more attractive to an audience."

Jay looked at Nate, then at Marcus. "Essentially I need to know why Crooked Tree exists and what you do here. Then I can assess brand equity."

"What the hell is that?" Nate snapped.

"How much the brand is worth to your bottom line, and the core values that define your brand."

Nate refused to ask another question and nodded like that all made complete sense.

Jay continued, "I'll look at seasonal trends, market shares, and statistical analysis, then come up with a real-time solution."

Nate's stomach fell. He was a fish out of water in this room. He knew what worked, but he didn't know shit about brands. The only brands he knew were on cattle and horses. Hell, he *knew* horses, animals, the ranch, and the people who worked with him. He knew that whatever Crooked Tree was doing wasn't enough, but what made a brand just seemed like a bucket of horseshit to him. For all they knew, Jay was making this crap up as he went along. Did anyone check he'd been to a university? His application cited he was twenty-nine, but he could have forged evidence and actually be someone who went around to unsuspecting family ranches, ripping them off.

"Can you give me an example?" Marcus asked.

"Like Coca-Cola. People have trust in the brand, the logo means something, and in most parts speaks of quality."

"So what you're going to do is create us a logo. Is that it?" Nate was irritable. "Hell, Luke can draw—he'll make us something—we don't need long words to describe that."

"It's a lot more than a logo," Jay began patiently, which only served to irritate Nate.

Nate cursed his reactions silently. What was wrong with him anyway? He wasn't normally this much of an idiot when it came to the ranch.

Jay continued. "What we need to do isn't just a brand. It's about a focused image of what you're trying to do here. Having a plan for making this place sell starts simply and will grow quickly. So I need to give you both questionnaires that I devised." He passed a thick sheaf of papers to Nate and Marcus. "If you could fill in the gaps and maybe summarize what is happening here, that would be good."

Nate stood and pushed his chair back in sudden horror. "Marcus can do that. Nothing I can do here really," he said abruptly. There was no way he could sit here and attempt to read the questions, let alone formulate answers. Fear coiled inside him, accompanied by a very real panic.

"Nate, you don't need to fill them in. Listen… sit down," Marcus pleaded.

Nate ignored him. The last thing he wanted was for Marcus to go all understanding on him and make him a laughing stock in front of Jay. "I haven't got time for this. I need to see to the horses."

"Mr. Todd," Jay said quickly. "Give me three words that mean Crooked Tree to you."

Nate stopped and turned on his heel. Was this some kind of trick? Jay looked so damn serious.

Jay explained. "No writing it down and no thinking. Give me three words."

"Family. Sky. Horses."

Nate watched as Jay scribbled that down with an intense look of concentration. He asked the same question to Marcus. "What about you?"

Marcus didn't hesitate. "Family. Mountains. River."

Nate decided to give Jay a few more seconds.

"So, look at that, Jay announced with a flourish. "Consensus on family. Your family, or other families?"

"Our family," Nate said.

"Others as well—the people who come here," Marcus added.

"And the river, the sky… what about the mountains, the sounds and smells of the ranch? They carry evocative imagery." Jay waved his hands in a wide gesture, then stood to give himself more room. He began to pace. "Crooked Tree, the place under the sky, the mountains and the sky, the history of the river, a journey, journey's end, the wide expanse." His voice was getting louder as he walked, He stopped directly in front of Nate with an animated expression. Nate was taken aback and not sure where to look. "The horses, Nate. Tell me about the horses. Do you breed them? Do you have a family history, provenance, or whatever you call it with livestock? Do you consider them livestock? Why was Gabe's horse called Lightning? Why is Juno called that? Who looks after them? How much do you love your horses?"

He stopped as suddenly as he had begun, his face flushed and a spark of excitement in his eyes.

"Bloodlines," Nate said, "if that's what you mean by who was born to whom. It's called a bloodline. Lightning was born to a beautiful mare called Storm, who belonged to my dad, hence her name. Gabe got her on his fourteenth birthday, and she's still here."

"History," Jay said firmly. "Family and history, stability, forever. We can use that."

"What about the website?" Marcus asked from the table.

Jay rounded on him. "You can't do a website until you have the passion inside you to sell what you are. I can give you the technical expertise, but until I understand your ties to Crooked Tree, I can't give you an effective plan."

Nate thought he was following this. Jay was basically saying that it didn't matter what words he used, he needed to see the ranch and understand why it had to survive. There really was only one way to do that—by horse.

"Come with me," he said.

Jay retrieved his notebook and pen. "Where are we going?"

"I want you to meet someone."

Jay followed him out of the house, and they walked the narrow trail from the back of Marcus's house to the stables. Nate couldn't fail to notice that Jay slowed down as they got closer, until he'd fallen behind. Nate stopped and turned to face him.

"What's wrong?"

"Is this a horse thing?" Jay asked quickly.

Nate considered what to say to the flighty man who had apprehension painted across his face. Where had the spark-eyed, enthusiastic ideas man gone? Jay had known this was a dude ranch with horse riding, horse trails, and in fact all-around horse. In the end, Nate didn't criticize. The ad they'd placed didn't specify that their business guy should ride.

"Keep up," he snapped instead.

Jay caught up with him. "I don't need to see the horses."

"You said you wanted to understand what we are."

"You could just tell me."

"I thought you liked hands-on. You were the one skulking in the bushes for inspiration."

"I was not skulking. I was researching."

They reached the large barn doors. Nate opened the door and indicated Jay should go through first. "I need to turn them out." Jay looked at him nervously and Nate could see the pinprick of blood where Jay had worried at his lip. "Stay here," he said firmly.

Jay didn't argue. He leaned against the wall and watched as Nate dealt with getting some of the horses out into the enclosed paddock through the other doors at the rear of the barn. Jay pulled out his phone and took photos, or at least Nate assumed he was taking photos.

"Are they allowed out in the snow?" Jay asked.

"They're quarter horses, built hardy. They're not out for long and we manage the paddock."

Jay wanted to ask what that meant, but he didn't really need to know that at this point. He wanted numbers and names. "How many do you have?"

"Enough," he said. "Plus Juno, Lightning, Ricky, and Diablo, who are our horses."

"Juno is your horse, I remember, and Lightning is Gabe's."

"Ricky is Luke's."

"And Diablo?"

"Your horse for the time you're here."

"Even if I wanted a horse, which I kind of don't, you think it's a good idea to give me a horse with a name that means 'devil'?" Jay stiffened and moved away from the wall.

"Part of your wages here," Nate answered. He ignored the whole Diablo-devil thing and gestured Jay over.

"I don't know anything about horses," Jay said. He stepped closer, placed his notebook and pen in his pocket. "And I'm honestly more than happy to forgo having a horse. I'll walk everywhere."

Nate shook his head in disbelief. "You do know that Crooked Tree is twenty-nine thousand acres with over sixty miles of trails?"

"Don't you have one of those four-wheel buggy things?"

"Not unless you brought one in your suitcase," Nate deadpanned. What did Jay expect? The ranch was running on empty, 4 wheelers were not on the to-buy list.

"Ha-freaking-ha." Jay moved closer and peered over the stall half-door.

Nate tapped his fingers on the door. "This here is Diablo. He's a paint quarter horse gelding. His registered name is Detail for Devil, but we like Diablo."

Diablo snorted and stepped forward, snuffling Nate's outstretched hand.

Jay sighed. "I don't suppose you have a horse called Angel, or Cutie, or Slowpoke, or something sweet."

That would have been funny, had it not been for the very real edge of fear in Jay's voice. Concerns rose again at how the hell they had managed to hire someone who had no idea how to ride a horse, let alone how to sell a ranch.

Nate couldn't help the irritation that slipped into his tone. "Have you ever actually ridden a horse?"

Jay gave a nervous chuckle. "Do carousels count?"

Why did Nate want to bang his head against the nearest wall? This city guy with his stumbling around in the dark and not knowing how to ride, was scratching at his last nerve. He'd seen worse, he'd taught worse, but this idiot was supposed to be working on the ranch and he couldn't ride. Nate didn't have time for this shit.

"What did you think you were going to be able to do for us?" he snapped.

Jay looked startled at his change in tone from irritable yet patient to plain old annoyed.

"What do you mean? You mean here as a job? I'm here to create a marketing plan for you—"

"Do you even know what we do?"

Jay blinked up at him with confusion pasted on his smooth, pale face. "Isn't that what you're going to show me now?" he asked.

"You may be able to sell your overpriced drinks, or condoms, or washing powder, but this is real life." Nate shook his head. "Horses are a big part of what we do here—"

"Constipation," Jay interrupted loudly.

Nate narrowed his eyes. "Excuse me?"

"I've never really suffered from it, apart from one night after—never mind that. Look, I ran a whole marketing initiative for a company that manufactures meds for constipation. After implementation of the plan, their market share increased by 5 percent, and instead of laying people off, they recruited their own small marketing team to keep up the work."

"What does that have to do with horses?"

"I learn fast. I learned what the meds did, and I made a plan that supported their marketing. I can learn horses if I try hard enough. So get on with the showing and less of the disapproving."

Dumbstruck, Nate wasn't entirely sure what to say. "You do know who you're talking to, right?" He stepped right up into Jay's face as anger roiled inside him.

"Yep," Jay drawled, all trace of his East Coast tone gone. "You're the guy who needs my help and is a stubborn bastard who won't fill in forms."

Nate's mouth dropped open in shock. "I pay your salary."

"You hired me."

"Marcus hired you."

Jay crossed his arms over his chest, pressing his lips in a tight line. "You could always stop trying to provoke an argument and instead show me the damn horses."

"I could tell you to pack your bags and fuck off back to the city."

"Happy to leave." Jay raised his eyebrows. "Given I would earn more working in a McDonald's, I assume you have other applicants willing to move to the middle of nowhere for next to no money and a horse?"

Despite the anger that Nate suspected threatened to break Jay's even tone, Jay's smooth talking was irritating. At that single moment in time, Nate wanted to punch the man with his big words and his frustrating arguments.

"And a house," Nate pointed out.

"There is that. It's a nice house," Jay said with a tight smile.

"If we're doing this, then you need to listen to me," Nate ordered.

Jay indicated his notepad and pen. "Can I take notes?"

"No."

"No?"

"No. Come with me. This is Juno, she's fifteen hands and a quarter horse, same as Diablo. Watch and learn."

Jay followed him into Juno's stall, but his expression was fearful and he looked like he was being dragged into hell. Nate spent a short time fussing with Juno to settle his thoughts, and to give Jay a few moments to settle being this near to Juno. There was something about Jay that had him getting his back up. Part of it he knew had to be because he'd been put on the spot with that whole form-filling thing. He'd come across the situation before, but it had never been an issue he couldn't handle. The other part was because they hadn't pulled in anyone local. He needed to add in the fact he wasn't getting laid enough and Jay—gay, straight, or bi—was kind of nice to look at. A combination of slim and blond, with those brown eyes that had him recalling Mr. Austin, the art teacher who had been Nate's first crush at fifteen.

Pulling himself out of his thoughts, he concentrated on what he had to tell Jay. "You have to groom your horse before you put a saddle on. Although maybe you don't know what a saddle is or what grooming means." Nate meant that as a veiled insult but regretted saying it as soon as the words left his mouth. He picked up the curry comb and waved it under Jay's nose. He continued before Jay could say anything. "This is a rubber curry comb; it massages the horse's muscles. This should be done before and after riding. Then you use a stiffer brush and brush the way the hair grows, not against it."

"Got it. Curry comb, stiffer brush, not against the hair."

"Watch me," Nate ordered. "With a flick of your wrist at the end of each brush, any dirt the rubber one brought to the surface is moved away."

"Flick," Jay repeated. Nate looked at him to see if he was taking it all seriously, because if he wasn't, Nate had words coiled inside ready to unleash. Jay seemed to be concentrating, though, and was worrying his lip again. "Will they kick at you?"

"I'd like to say no, but just be careful what you are doing when the horse can't see you."

"Doing what? Like standing behind them?"

"Always make sure they can see you. Then you check the hooves, like this." Nate demonstrated what needed to be done. "This is to make sure there aren't any rocks or caked-on dirt that could hurt the horse and cause damage."

"You do this every day to the horse?"

"Every new ride. The horse isn't some car you can abuse; these are living, breathing friends. Next is tack up your horse. Put the blanket on, covering the horse's withers—this bit here—completely."

"The ridge between the shoulder blades, that's the withers. Got it," Jay confirmed with a nod.

"Make sure the horse's hair is flat then put the saddle on." Juno moved a couple of steps and Nate wished he had thought to demonstrate this in the place he would normally be tacking her—outside in the corral behind the barn. "The girth comes next, that's the thing that goes around the horse to make sure the saddle stays on."

"Got it. How tight do you do it?"

"You'll learn what's best by touch. But you have to remember that when you put this on, you have to walk Diablo around a few steps and check it again. Juno here likes to inhale when you touch her so you have to make sure it's tight enough or not too tight. Then comes the mouthpiece. Put the reins over the head—you can do all this in the stall, but it's easier if you walk them out of the stall and into a corral using a halter."

"A halter. Okay. You didn't use one of those on Juno, though."

Nate chuckled. "Juno is used to me now and stands where I leave her. Diablo is the same."

"So, getting up there?" Jay thoughtfully examined the stirrup and touched it. Juno danced away a step and Jay backed off. "It's a hell of a long way up."

"Always mount from the left side, though I've known people who do it from the right after having had a stroke. But if you're right-handed, it's safer on the left."

"Why?"

"Most people are right-handed. In order to leave the right hand free for roping, opening gates, and anything else, the reins are held in the left hand. Okay?"

"Okay, but I still don't…"

Nate stifled his sigh. He'd explained this to his new riders before, why then was he cutting short the explanation?

He continued, this time with extra patience. "See, if a rider were to mount from the right, he'd have to switch the reins from the right hand to the left, momentarily losing solid control at the very time a horse is most likely to act up."

Jay nodded. "I get it."

"So, left foot in the stirrup and swing up and over. Anyway, you saw me saddle up Juno—let's see what you can do with Diablo."

CHAPTER TEN

Jay's heart skipped a beat. Nate led him to Diablo's stall, and suddenly Jay was faced with the irrational fear that stalked him every time he went near Central Park. Horses were not his friends. They were big and unwieldy and scared the life out of him. Luckily, unlike Ashley's fear of spiders, it was unlikely he'd ever find a horse in his bath. Still, he hadn't needed to confront his fears until then.

"He's well behaved and extremely friendly," Nate was saying. Jay attempted to listen carefully—he needed all the reassurance he could get. "He's a good trail horse with plenty of experience riding alone and also with larger groups. He's been trained for a rider to open gates while on horseback."

Nate opened the gate to the stall, and they slipped inside. Jay couldn't help himself—he half hid behind Nate. Nate clearly wasn't having any of that and moved so that Jay was abruptly face to face with a million tons of horse. Diablo snorted and shook his head. Jay stepped backward and only stopped when he heard Nate chuckle. *The fucker.* Squaring his shoulders, he held out a hand and, at the last minute, remembered to turn it over so that the horse could sniff his palm. He'd watched the TV shows. He should have an apple or something.

"Juno is a black quarter horse mare. She stays jet black even during the hottest time of the summer. She was foaled 1994." Nate continued talking. "Diablo here is a paint. He was foaled in 1997 and is what we call a gelding."

"Oh, you poor guy," Jay murmured. He might not like horses, but he knew what the horse had lost to be a gelding. He was talking nonsense, but at least it was centering his thoughts. He continued, "Never mind, it's not like I ever see any action either." He stepped to the right of Diablo and scratched behind his ears. The horse seemed to like that and butted his hand. More confident, Jay accepted the rubber brush thing that Nate passed to him and began to rub in the way the hair lay in a rhythmic movement. Diablo stood impassively, apart from every so often pressing his nose to Jay's arm. Nate disappeared out of the stall, and Jay felt tense at being alone with the stunningly gorgeous, tall, dangerous, maybe-killer horse.

Covering his nerves was easy. He did what he would do in any situation where he felt uncomfortable—he talked. Softly he leaned in and whispered, "You are a beautiful horse, aren't you? I guess you're used to this, but I thought I'd just get it out there. Please don't let me fall off, and please no crushing me against the walls of the stall. Oh, and I have no idea what I'm doing, so be good to me. I'll bring apples, or carrots, or sugar."

"He prefers carrots," Nate said from the doorway.

Jay groaned. Had Nate heard what he'd been whispering? Still, it wasn't anything that Nate didn't already know, right? With a little prompting, he managed the other stages of tacking up. The flick to get rid of the dust, the hoof checking, the blanket over the withers, the tightening of the cinch. He looked pointedly at Nate, who moved out of the way, and Jay managed to recall that he needed to walk Diablo a little to ensure the horse hadn't been breathing in, or out, or whatever, when he tightened the girth.

He was proud of himself when finally the horse was ready to go.

"Done!" he said triumphantly.

"Not bad, City," Nate answered.

Jay sighed inwardly. "Don't you think it's a bit cliché to be calling me 'City'? Just because I'm from New York?"

Nate shook his head. "No more cliché than you calling me 'Cowboy.'"

"But you are a cowboy." Jay knew he sounded bemused.

"And you, Jay Sullivan, are all city."

Jay wasn't entirely sure what to say to that. Seemed like he had a nickname, and he didn't really like it. He didn't have time to argue, though, because Nate was assessing Jay's feet critically.

"You can't ride in those." Nate said and passed over a pair of worn boots. He looked down at Jay's feet again. "I wasn't sure what size but these are some of the spares we keep. I chose these, but we do have others."

With much swearing and a lot of help from Nate—who smelled of soap and deodorant—Jay had his boots on. They pinched a little, but nothing to complain about after it took five minutes to get the damn things on. Although five minutes, with Nate holding on to him and leaning over so Jay got a good look at his firm, muscled butt, was nowhere near long enough. Then Jay caught himself thinking that and shuffled back and away from Nate, which ended up with him falling off the block he'd been sitting on and ending up ass first on the ground.

For a second, he sat in shock. Nate stared down at him in total disbelief, and suddenly Jay was very much on the defensive.

"The block moved," he lied quickly.

Nate toed the block with a foot and raised a single eyebrow to indicate he was calling Jay on the bullshit excuse. He held out a hand. Jay took it and was pulled to his feet as if he weighed nothing. This brought them up together, and again Jay found himself having inappropriate thoughts about the cowboy gripping his hand. The last time his gaydar had pinged liked this was a long time ago.

Hell, his gaydar was faulty at best. Nate was a cowboy, all yee-haw and campfires and macho crap. It was unlikely there would be any Brokeback action anywhere near Crooked Tree. Jay shook himself free of his thoughts. Nate equaled "the boss" in a manner of speaking. Jay knew he reported to Marcus, but he was aware Nate had a holding in Crooked Tree. *Time to concentrate.*

"So, what next?" he asked to pull himself out of his thoughts.

"Next we get you on the horse."

Jay swallowed his apprehension and looked up at Diablo, who stared back at him placidly. "How tall is he?"

"Just a bit shy of fifteen hands," Nate explained.

"What is that in feet and inches?"

"Five feet give or take."

Jay grimaced. "That's a long way to fall."

Nate led Diablo out into the open air and stopped next to another box. "Get on the damn horse."

Jay looked at Diablo and recalled what Nate had said—something about getting on using the left side, foot in stirrup and swinging up and over. Easy. He'd seen this on TV as well. He'd also seen films where the guys fell off, with a foot caught in the stirrup, being dragged to their death. Concentrating on where his foot was going, Jay used every ounce of his gym-fit muscles to heave himself up and over. In shock, he realized he was sitting atop Diablo and looking down at Nate, who had a look of something on his face that Jay wasn't convinced was real. He almost looked like he was proud of Jay's move.

In a few minutes, Nate explained the position of the reins and that Diablo would mostly be happy to follow Juno. "You'll need these and this."

Jay took the proffered gloves and hat gratefully. He could imagine he'd need both if the Montana wind had its wicked way with his city-soft skin. Nate crossed to Juno, and in a smooth move, was up on the horse's back. With one hand on the reins, he guided Juno next to where Diablo stood. Jeez. Jay thought it was sexy when he saw cowboys on the screen, but having one this close, all scruff and leather and confident sassy horseback riding, Jay was finding it hard to keep it in his pants. *Tonight I must find cowboy porn.*

True to Nate's word, Juno led and Diablo followed, and when they were out of the gate to the paddock,

Diablo was content to trot, or walk, or whatever it was he was doing, enough so that Jay could settle himself into the saddle and not feel like he was falling off. He stared hard at how Nate was sitting, how he held the reins, how he used his feet, what he was saying, and tried to copy as best he could.

Jay's face was cold, but he wasn't ready to release his death grip on the leather in order to tilt up his collar, so he sucked up the fact that the ever-present Montana wind was pricking his skin with icy fingers. They moved down to the bridge over the river and stopped for a second.

"The Blackfoot is a snow and spring-fed river. Some places it's really deep, like at the end of Crooked Tree, and some places it's shallow. It's why the ranch is here. When the friends bought the land, they had plans for a ranch. That'd be my great-granddad, Marcus's granddad, and another guy—all of who made it back from the Second World War hoping for more. In the seventies, the decision was made to expand into dude ranching; something my dad was really involved in. As the dude ranch grew, the cattle side was cut down."

"But dude ranching doesn't pay as much now," Jay surmised.

Nate stared out over the flowing water, his hands resting loose and his weatherworn face creased in a frown. "There's a dude ranch up the river, huge and successful, but they're backed by external funding, some actor who wanted to invest. For us to get to that level? Hell, we don't have the money."

Jay began to form a response in his head about money or lack of it but decided against it when he saw the sadness etched into Nate's expression.

Nate changed the subject anyway. "The restaurant will begin getting ready to open in the next few weeks. That's Sophie's domain. It's called Branches as a play on words from the fact we're Crooked Tree Ranch."

"I like that," Jay said. "Good name."

"It seats sixty and is used mainly by the guests where we offer breakfast first thing, then lunches. We open to the public for dinner, and outside visitors account for some good income, so I hear."

"It's a busy place?"

"Good home-cooked food—our chef is a local guy, Samuel Walters, who works for us mid-February to Christmas Day. I'll introduce you when he arrives. If you need to know more, you'll have to speak to Sophie, although she doesn't know what menus Sam has in mind, I guess."

They crossed the bridge and carried on past the house that was Jay's for the duration, and entered a stand of trees that thickened, then opened into small pockets of space. Each space had a cabin that sat firmly in the landscape and looked well-tended and comfortable.

"These are what we call the Forest Cabins. There are six of them." He waved behind them. "Two miles that way are the River Cabins. They sit on the bend of the river, hence the name. There are six of those as well. We'll see them on our way back."

"So you have twelve cabins you can rent out." Jay shifted in the saddle and turned to look the way Nate had pointed. Why he did that, he didn't know. After all, not only were they two miles away, but he couldn't see past the trees that formed a natural privacy barrier.

"We actually have twenty-one potentials. But the Creek Cabins have been put in mothballs—they're not being filled, so we put all of our efforts in Forest and River."

"Okay, I'll need to look at that," Jay said thoughtfully. What if they needed to use the cabins? What was the turnaround on getting them ready for guests? His head spun with the questions he needed to ask, and he wished to hell Nate had let him bring his damn notebook. He should have got his cell out and recorded the questions, but the phone was in his ass pocket and he was sitting on it, and there was no way he was rummaging for anything this high off the ground. Instead, he focused on more questions. "What is the occupation rate like?"

Nate frowned back at him. "Wasn't that in the pack of information Gabe sent you?"

Jay quirked a lip. "He glossed over that point."

"I'm sorry," Nate said. "I don't get involved in that."

Juno moved off and Diablo dutifully followed. It took Jay a while to get himself seated in the saddle properly, and his death grip on the reins had Diablo lifting his head and snorting. Jay relaxed his hold and hoped to hell Nate didn't see what a crap horseman he was proving to be.

"Tell me what you do get involved in, then," he asked as he drew level again.

"You're cold," Nate replied instantly. He leaned over to Jay and tugged at the thick sheepskin collar that stood upright when pulled. The barrier to the cold covered

Jay's ears and half of his face, and he was never more pleased to have something stopping the damn frigid wind.

"Thanks," he muttered against the material.

They set off again, and Jay contemplated asking Nate what his full role was at the ranch, besides something to do with the horses. He had to interview everyone to get an idea of how this place worked. Nate hadn't forgotten the question, though—he simply waited until they had moved out from under the trees and made their way up a shallow incline.

"We have five staff working here," he began. "Three of them for me: Henry, Bud, and Amy, all working with the horses. I'll introduce them another time. I manage them, the horses, customer excursions, the mock roundups we do, and I look out for the river and the conservation concerns."

"More than just a cowboy," Jay summarized.

Nate glanced at him. "No man who works a ranch now is *just* a cowboy," he answered quickly. There was irritation in every syllable, and Jay felt instantly that he should be apologizing for his stupid throwaway line. "Not in this day and age anyway," Nate added. He sighed. "People come here to live a cowboy's way of life, but they want to be safe. They want everything sanitized, including hot tubs, and a five-star restaurant. There are ordinances to follow, health and safety rules, insurances...." He stopped talking and shrugged. "I like it best when it's only the horses and me."

"You sound like you don't enjoy working with the people who visit the ranch." If that was the case, Jay had a big problem. The idea of working at making Crooked Tree a saleable, marketable asset was a big ask if the people who owned it weren't happy.

Nate chuckled. The deep, throaty noise sent a shiver of interest through Jay, and he quickly shook it away as Nate began talking.

"I love what I do, Mr. Sullivan—"

"Jay."

Nate inclined his head. "I love this ranch. It was my parents' legacy for me, Gabe, and Luke, and I want it to be here for my brothers' kids one day."

Jay picked up on that. His gaydar wasn't good, it never had been, but there was something about Nate, about the way he held Jay's gaze that made Jay think Nate wasn't as straight a cowboy as Jay had first imagined.

"You don't want kids?" he asked.

Nate frowned, but he didn't answer, and instead carried on with the explanation. "For every person who comes here that causes grief or hates it, there are ten more who go away feeling like they could channel John Wayne, and I love every minute of working with them."

"Or the Lone Ranger," Jay added.

They exchanged smiles, and Jay was kind of stunned by how Nate's face changed when he smiled. He'd seen it at breakfast, but not close enough to see the way the amusement sparked in Nate's eyes.

"No, definitely John Wayne."

They reached the top of the incline, and Nate maneuvered Juno so that the two men could turn and look back on where they had come from. Jay concentrated on the puffs of breath he could make in the cold air and not the fact that Diablo was circling and slipping on the snow. Horses should have snowshoes, he decided. Finally, Jay could see the vista that was Crooked Tree and it was one of the most breathtaking sights he'd ever seen. Nate dismounted, Helped Jay down, which was the cue for all sorts of inappropriate thoughts about sinuously rubbing himself down the other man. *I don't do cowboys... I don't do cowboys....*

Forcing himself to concentrate, he looked down at what lay before them. They weren't really high up here, but there was enough elevation for Jay to make out the river clearly enough, and the bridge. He identified three deliberate and managed clusters of forest area which he assumed were the cabins' placements. If he squinted hard, he could see the roof of his new home. Beyond the ranch, the mountains formed a backdrop that most artists would die for—solid and a slash of white, blue, and mauve against the absolutely still sky of the cold February day. The sun was behind them and Jay wished he had his camera with him to capture the great vastness of the view, and the image of his and Nate's shadows in the snow. Instead, he pulled out his phone, and with sausage fingers because of his gloves, he managed to snap a few shots of what he could see.

"Stunning," he summarized. "Like a film set."

"We own acres to the west and north that we use for trail riding, and we also have our very own sheltered canyon where we can corral the herd we use for the roundups. We share the space, so that is some income to cover the wrangler we have up there, Duncan."

"Can I see that as well?"

"Another day. Your ass won't thank me for making you sit in the saddle too long today. So tell me what you are going to do."

"Do?" Jay looked squarely at Nate. "About my ass?" he added, curious as to what Nate meant.

"Despite me wanting to talk about your ass, that isn't what I meant." Nate chuckled again. He went scarlet. Somehow the gruff cowboy had slipped into teasing and evidently it didn't sit well with him. "What are your plans for Crooked Tree?"

Jay sighed inwardly. Clients always did this. Put him on the spot wanting to know what he was going to fix and when. The thing was, he'd never had a client so intimately involved in the product he was trying to work on. He could sit here and talk about the brand, which had clearly gone down like a ton of bricks this morning in the meeting. Or maybe he should ramble on about search engines and image and profit margins, and insert as much management bullshit into it as he could. Nate didn't deserve any of that, and Jay wasn't ready to serve up the crap with a side of false assurances.

"I'll get a report to you all as soon as I can," he evaded.

Nate rounded on him instantly and gripped his upper arms. "Promise me you know what you're doing. Never lie to me that everything is going to be okay. I want the truth on a daily basis so I can see if we need to think about other options."

Jay opened and closed his mouth a couple of times. The words were on the tip of his tongue, covered in management-speak about achievable targets. He tensed up when Nate gently shook him. "Jay?"

Clients didn't shake him. They didn't demand honesty with a mixed expression of hope and disbelief. None of them had ever had such intense and clear green eyes.

"I promise," Jay said. "Every day I will tell you the truth."

Nate released his hold a little and Jay relaxed. "Start now," Nate ordered firmly.

Start now? With what? Telling the truth? That he could think of nothing better than being shaken by Nate again? That he wanted to taste Nate's skin and that his employer's eyes were the perfect shade? No. That wasn't what Nate wanted.

"I'm here to do a job, and I will do it to the best of my ability, but I'm scared I won't be able to help you change a thing," Jay blurted out. *Fuck. Where did that come from?* He began to explain away his own insecurities and the fact that he'd specialized in marketing and not carried on the business side of his degree so much, but Nate cut him dead.

"Good," he said brusquely. He released his hold completely. "That's honesty I can get behind. I may not have the degrees, but I know Crooked Tree better than you ever will. I've buried my head in the sand. I know what we have to do is huge, and I'm just as scared."

The exchange of honesty was verging on brutal. There was fight in Nate, and Jay felt the same way. This career shift might not have been in the cards, he might well have compromised on what he wanted in order to be here, but he was damned if he was going to fail.

Jay stumbled back a step and straight into Diablo, who didn't move or complain, unless his snort of what Jay imagined as surprise was actually a horse curse word. He wrinkled his nose as Diablo snorted at him again. "I'm not sure he likes me."

Nate chuckled. "If he didn't like you, he would have taken a bite out of your hand by now."

Jay pocketed his hands immediately. "He does that?"

Nate shrugged. "We never did find the rest of the last marketing guy we had out here. Just his left foot and some of a boot."

Jay's heart stopped as horror flowed through him too quick for him to stop it, then almost immediately realized he was the butt of Nate's apparent dry sense of humor. He knew horses didn't eat people, for God's sake. *I'm seriously losing it out here*. Not to mention his thighs hurt and his ass ached—and he'd only been in the saddle for twenty minutes.

He threw a dirty look at Nate and managed to get up on Diablo's back with only one false start. There was no way he was going to rise to the man-eating horse crap. *I am a professional and I don't joke around on the job.*

"So what ideas do you have so far?" Nate asked conversationally as they made their way back down to the cabins and onto the bridge.

"Nothing set in stone," Jay said immediately. "But it helped to see this. Am I okay walking the place in daylight?"

Nate cast a look at Jay. "You can take Diablo out whenever you'd like to. If I'm not around, then Gabe or Luke can go with you."

"I'm happy walking," Jay said airily.

Nate chuckled.

Fucker.

CHAPTER ELEVEN

They'd stabled the horses, with Nate showing Jay the reverse procedure to getting a horse saddled. He'd done okay, then waited for Nate to pull in the other horses. Jay decided there and then that he needed to know more about why the horses under Nate's care weren't running about the open fields like he'd seen in the movies. He filed it away as a later question.

"How much will my butt ache after this?" Jay asked.

Nate simply looked at him and raised his eyebrows. That didn't bode well. Jay supposed it was like any new exercise—forty-eight hours later and he'd probably be crippled. He didn't push for an answer because right then Nate was showing him his office, and Jay felt excited to see where he would be working. He'd only ever had a cubicle, never an entire room that would be just his.

The building sat squarely next to Branches and the small on-site shop that looked empty inside. At first glance, Jay's new office seemed to be a temporary structure that someone had added as an afterthought. It was squat and square and Jay could see two front-facing windows. He'd always had a rat hole in a maze of similar desks, and the thought of having his own space outweighed the obvious ramshackle exterior of his new place.

Nate pushed open the door with a flourish and indicated Jay should enter first. Jay did so with trepidation. What he saw inside pretty much echoed the outside. The interior rocked the "wood on the walls and floor" effect, and it was warm enough, with two small oil heaters.

"We're looking to connect it into the restaurant heating and to tidy up the outside before opening. But the inside isn't high on priority at the moment, I'm afraid. We'll probably get to it after we open and when we have the time."

Jay did a three-sixty, then nodded in agreement. "The inside is fine, I'll work with it. But the outside is another untidy reminder that investment in the place has dipped. Imagine someone comes to the restaurant, which at first glance looks kind of cool, and they spot this. We should paint the outside, dig over the ground, and maybe put some gravel down to make it more welcoming. You could change it into an information center after I've gone. Don't worry about labor. I'll get Kirsten, Josh, and Ashley on it."

"Okay." Nate sounded doubtful, but at least he didn't look pissed at Jay's frank assessment of one of the ranch's current problems.

"I need to go to the nearest stationery and office furniture place, if you could give me an address."

"Missoula. It's an hour from here. I can take you now."

"Don't you have other things you need to do?"

"Nope, my day is yours, all penciled in on the schedule and everything."

Jay's gaze flicked to the sexy cowboy, who stood with his thumbs in his pockets and stared around the small office, assessing the interior as much as Jay had done. The way the other man stood screamed alpha male, hot and heavy, and Jay forced himself not to concentrate on that. Nate had given no clear indication he was gay, apart from the no kids thing and the fact he wanted to talk about Jay's ass. But Jay had noticed Nate's gaze wandering south. Jay was not going to waste precious time lusting after the tall, muscled, green-eyed, dark-haired, sex-on-legs cowboy, though.

Using his five-ten height as a gauge, Jay mentally figured out the kind of space he had to work with—looking to be eight-by-ten-foot square at its base and about eight foot high. Finally he left the room and waited for Nate to follow him out.

They walked to a large black Jeep, and Nate clicked the key fob to open the doors. The Wrangler was far from new and more than a little beat-up. Not only that, but it wasn't what Jay had been expecting Nate to drive.

"I thought cowboys drove trucks," Jay commented dryly as he buckled himself in.

"Maybe I'm the exception to the rule," Nate drawled. "What do you drive? Doesn't everyone in the city drive Porsches and Ferraris?"

Jay chuckled. "Touché. I don't own a car. You don't need one in New York, but if I had one, then of course it would be a silver Porsche—wouldn't want to step too far away from the stereotype."

They drove off Crooked Tree and joined the main road, and there was no more talking. Nate turned on the radio to a local station that was mostly talking and ads, and Jay stared out the window at the passing landscape.

He was thinking hard about what he'd seen this morning. Potential. Yes, the cabins were a little dilapidated, but the beauty of this place was staggering. Pastures white with snow led to the base of mountains that created a stunning backdrop for the ranch. The trees clustered around the cabins gave privacy, and as for the river.... The Blackfoot was beautiful—a tumbling, hissing mess of white water at one end of the cabins and a smooth, shallow path of clear beauty at the other.

The horses were like they were supposed to be— pretty, sturdy, and Nate clearly had a handle on what he was doing. Jay hadn't talked to Marcus yet, not properly, but he would make time to do that, and also to Luke and Gabe. Which only left the silent partners in the ranch, some guy called Strachan who, according to Marcus, had little say in how Crooked Tree ran. He guessed there was drama there in the way Marcus's lips thinned when he mentioned Strachan's name. Jay would find out one way or another what had happened, and if it would impact on any suggestions he might come up with as part of the plan.

They reached Missoula in under the hour and stopped outside a huge Staples. Anticipation rose inside Jay. He would never admit it to anyone else, but he loved places that sold stationery.

"You can stay here if you want," Jay said. "I won't be long."

"I need to pay," Nate said.

"You could meet me at the end."

"Nope." He was in the middle of taking his seat belt off, and he didn't stop. He appeared intent on following

Jay around. That meant Jay couldn't spend time admiring notebooks, which was a bit of a disappointment, but at least he'd have Nate helping him to carry things. He focused on the desk and chair and decided on ones they could take home. Nate went off to load the car, and that gave Jay time to collect up noticeboards and everything else he wanted. He had a definite vision of what his new space was going to look like.

Next, they stopped at a DIY store and bought paint for the outside of the office, a sage green shade that Jay thought would help the building merge into the background. They left Missoula for Crooked Tree.

They got home just after lunch and agreed to meet at the office half an hour later. Nate strode up the hill toward where Jay imagined Nate's home was, and for a short while, Jay watched the easy stride of a man who knew exactly where he was going. Every flex of thick thighs was enough to have Jay nearly salivating. Shaking himself free of the infatuation with the way Nate walked, he let himself into his house and found Ashley in the kitchen, singing and baking. His heart filled with love for his sister, happy that she was relaxed enough to sing where just about anyone could see her.

"Hey you." Jay kissed her neck and stole a muffin when she was distracted. She smacked at him with a spoon but missed.

"How did it go?" she asked. "I saw you driving off with the big brother."

"We went shopping for stuff for my office."

Very deliberately she turned from the bowl of pink frosting she was carefully adding to the top of a tray of small cakes and faced him. "You have an office?"

Jay grinned. "It's more of a shed, really," he admitted, "and I could do with volunteers to help me paint the outside."

"Count me out for that one," Kirsten grumbled from behind them.

She helped herself to a muffin, and Jay was amazed to see streaks of orange next to the pink in her hair. Fashion statements he could handle, but he was pretty certain there was nothing written anywhere that said fire orange and cerise pink matched. His single gay fashion gene was offended.

"When I said 'volunteer,' I actually meant all three of you will be helping me. Tomorrow."

"I have stuff to do tomorrow," Kirsten said abruptly.

"Like what?" Jay asked just as quickly.

Ashley glanced at him, and the warning in her eyes was clear. *Don't poke the ant's nest.*

Well, fuck it, Kirsten was sixteen in the summer and Jay was getting a bit tired of the affected misery that enveloped her in a cloud.

"Stuff," she answered.

There was a challenge in Kirsten's eyes. She wanted an argument because they always ended up with Jay shouting and Kirsten slamming into her room. The upshot was that Kirsten got out of the things Jay wanted her to do, like studying or helping her mom, and Jay just got a headache. She played on him coming home from work and being tired. This time, that wasn't happening. Jay inhaled and exhaled deeply.

"I'm not arguing," he stated as simply as he could. "Nine sharp and I want you up and in your old clothes at the shed."

"But—"

"Enough," Jay warned. Mutiny was in her expression again and her thick-lined brown eyes started to glisten with tears. He knew she was frustrated—hell, he'd been a teenager himself once—but he had a responsibility to be the father she didn't have.

"You're not my dad. You can't order me around!" she shouted before turning to Ashley. The tears were for real then and tracked black down her face. This was normal as well—the moment Ashley backed down and Jay was left twisting in the wind.

Instead, Ashley turned back to her frosting, and in a few simple words Jay was shocked to hear, Ashley closed the whole thing down. "Wear the black jeans with the holes and the Kasabian T-shirt," she said. "It's too small for you anyway."

Kirsten stood for a few seconds, spun on her heel and walked out of the kitchen—but not before issuing a parting shot. "I hate you both, and I hate this place."

"I love you," Ashley called out. It was what she always did.

When the slam of the door indicated Kirsten was locked in her room, she glanced out of the window. There was a wistful smile on her face, "and I love this place."

Nate waited outside the shack-shed thing for Jay, and not for the first time questioned the science behind suggesting this would make a good office. Originally a storage shed, Marcus had proposed the new use when they'd received Jay's "yes" to the job offer. It was strong and sturdy but not exactly the prettiest place on earth for a man to get ideas on how to sell Crooked Tree to the public.

Nate heard footsteps and watched from under the brim of his hat as Jay joined him at the office. Jay had a wide grin and looked like the cat who'd swallowed the cream. He was still smiling when he pushed his way inside the shed and stood for a few seconds with his hands on his hips. Nate had brought in the desk and an extension lead that he'd rigged to give temporary electricity to the two old lamps Sophie had dug out of Marcus's junk room.

"Desk first, if that's okay," Jay suggested.

Together the two of them affixed the legs and set it up the correct way. After a few false starts, they positioned it so Jay had a clear, if small, view of the far mountains. They placed all the stationery on the desk, which left the noticeboards. Nate counted ten of them, and he considered the amount of wall space they had available was maybe not enough to hold all the boards.

"Okay...." Jay began.

Nate turned to look at him and did a double take. Jay was peering at instructions for the hanging of the noticeboards, and he was wearing glasses. Add to that he was worrying at his hair with his spare hand—carding his fingers through the short length and creating an image of a confused and delightfully rumpled mess. Was that Jay's bed hair? A mess of cowlicks and crazy angles? Did he wear his glasses to read? Why hadn't Nate seen him in them before?

"You wear glasses," he blurted out. *What the fuck is wrong with me?*

"Only for reading," Jay replied before looking back down at the instructions.

Glasses. Scruffy-sleep bed head hair. Slim. Brown eyes. Who the fuck was messing with him by dumping Jay in his lap? *Shit.*

Don't think of laps or Jay sitting on you.

Too late...

...fuck! Inappropriate erection.

"So, if I measure and mark, will you bang the nail in? Then we need to thread the wire."

I can probably bang it in with my freaking dick.

Jay pulled on his lower lip with his teeth as he read, and that was it, Nate was done. He grabbed the first board and held it in front of his groin. Jeez, he needed another trip to Carter's pretty damn soon. Nate imagined anything he could think of to get his head away from where it was at and actually help fix the inside of this place. By the time they had the boards hung in a ring around the entirety of the room, they'd exhausted football, politics, and ranching. Seemed like Jay knew a lot about politics and football, and it was Nate who covered ranching. Between them, the afternoon went quickly, and they stood to admire the work for a few minutes.

"I'll plan on that one"—Jay pointed to the board closest to the door—"then work my way around with ideas. I need some photos of the ranch."

"Luke is a really good photographer," Nate said proudly. "He has photos from all around the ranch, and he'd also be your best guide to the small areas others might miss."

Jay smiled up at him from the piles of stationery he was sorting through. "Like you? Do you see all the small stuff as well?"

"I know every inch of Crooked Tree," Nate said softly.

"Maybe you could show me sometime?"

Nate was startled. There was a definite edge of flirting in Jay's voice and warmth in his eyes.

"If I get time," Nate replied gruffly.

"Thank you for helping."

Nate suddenly felt very uncomfortable with Jay's scrutiny, he really needed to leave before he got yet another erection from the glasses and the hair and the smart-assed, crooked smile.

He left with a wave and didn't stop walking until he was in the barn leaning on Juno's gate, looking in at her.

"Jeez, Nate, didn't you hear me calling?" Gabe asked from behind him. "You walked up that hill like your pants were on fire."

This was the perfect moment for Nate to share with Gabe that he'd met Jay only yesterday but had passed directly into lust with an attached inappropriate-erection phase. He looked sideways at his brother, who appeared grumpy and sweaty. Maybe now wasn't the time for a heart-to-heart. "What's up?" he asked instead.

"Rotting fence up at the Nine," Gabe reported. "I fixed it up as good as I could, but it'll need us hauling some wood up there."

"Okay, we'll get up there tomorrow morning," Nate answered easily. The Nine was at the eastern point of Crooked Tree, and as such it wasn't a huge priority to go there now. He calculated that was a morning gone and there were only three more weeks to the first day of March and opening. "How many bookings in for the first?"

Gabe knew what he was asking and rolled out the statistics in a list. "Four, all in the River Cabins. The next week we have five, again all in River. We only get Forest from the end of April."

"That gives us another month." As he considered, Nate bowed his head to stare at the toe of his boot on the bottom support of the gate. "We'll prioritize working on River, and we'll be absolutely fine."

"Henry was causing trouble this morning."

Nate sighed. Henry, in one way or another, was always causing trouble. Just him breathing caused an issue among the staff. To be honest, Nate and his brothers were sheltered from most of his crap, but Nate was nearing the end of his tether with the guy.

"What now?"

"He told Amy she should think on, and I quote, 'Pushing babies out and leaving men to look after her.'"

Nate felt like banging his head on the fence. The damn dinosaur was going to be the death of him. One more year—that was all they had to put up with him. Marcus refused to get rid of the one person who had been a constant at Crooked Tree for the last thirty years. Something about continuity or some such shit. Personally, Nate thought Marcus was fishing for any excuse that meant he didn't need to deal with Henry.

"One more season," he said softly.

CHAPTER TWELVE

Nate stopped by the office on the way out. Dropping in on Jay was a daily occurrence. Every day at six, he would wander by with questions. Since Jay had set up the office, the walls had filled with photos—of the horses, the landscape around Crooked Tree, the cabins, the hands who reported to Nate. There were informal shots of him and Gabe from last week's debacle at the Nine with the rotting fence posts. Somehow this room, in the two weeks Jay had been here, had become the nerve center for this mythical plan he was working on.

Nothing had changed yet that affected the ranch directly. There was still no new website, although Jay promised something by the end of February. Given they opened soon, they would lose out on whoever booked through the site—although to be fair, no one booked through the existing site. So there was no real loss.

"Hey." Nate announced himself at the door.

Jay glanced up at him, and not for the first time, Nate thought he looked adorably rumpled. His hair was messy from the way he constantly ran his hands through it as he worked and his glasses were askew on his head, probably from all the hair pulling. He looked adorably cute—and that wasn't a thought that crossed Nate's mind often. Jay stared back down at the sheets in front of him, then, with an almost immediate second glance, he looked right at

Nate. He frowned and checked Nate from head to foot. "Did I miss the invite?"

"I have a meeting," Nate said quickly. He wasn't going into the whys and wherefores of what he was doing tonight.

"Looking good, Cowboy," Jay teased.

Nate ignored the comment. "So tell me what's happened today."

They'd taken the whole telling-the-truth thing to the point where every single day Jay summarized what had happened with the ongoing projects.

"Luke was in earlier. I talked to him about some photography, and he drew this for me." Jay turned the paper around so Nate could see it, but Nate had to walk to the table to peer at the half-page drawing. He smiled as he looked at a simple pencil sketch of Juno. In a few strokes with some shading, Luke had pulled together the broad nose and intelligent eyes of Nate's horse. Nate swelled a little with pride—Gabe was a genius with numbers, and Luke could take whatever he looked at and condense it into a simple pencil drawing. Nate couldn't be prouder of his little brothers.

"He's very good," Jay said softly.

"That he is." Nate gently touched the edge of the paper. "What made him draw this?"

"I asked him about a logo for the ranch, and he was talking and sketching at the same time. A simple outline of the head of your horse would make a good eye-catching logo. He's going to work on it some."

"He's talking about studying business at college, coming back to Crooked Tree to run the ranch."

Jay leaned back in his chair and twirled a pen in his hands. "Taking my job, you mean," he said with a smile.

Crap. Nate hadn't meant it that way. He'd meant to start a conversation about Luke's art versus business and marketing. He could feel the familiar embarrassment rise in him, along with his damn cock, which was permanently interested around Jay. In two weeks Jay had never indicated anything about his sexuality—or indeed anything about what he wanted while he was here at Crooked Tree. Both things left Nate feeling antsy. One minute he could swear Jay's searching gaze held interest, the next they were back to colleagues at the ranch. It didn't help that the scent of Jay filled this room—a mix of aromas both natural and manufactured: aftershave, deodorant, the wood of the walls, and the smell of ink. Nate wondered if Jay tasted as good as this room smelled.

"Earth to Nate?" Jay said with laughter in his voice.

Nate snapped out of his reverie. "Sorry, bad day. Did you get to talk to Henry?"

Jay had asked to talk to the hands and any other staff, of which there weren't many as it was off-season. In a couple of days, the quiet ranch would become something else—the week before opening was always hectic and time-consuming. Nate himself had repairs to do in the barns and was working with Gabe on scheduling and figuring out when to bring down the horses, hence he felt tired. It wasn't the physical that did him in, but the mental of sitting and attempting to get his head around the color-coded chart Gabe had created.

The smile left Jay's face. "Henry wasn't around, so not yet."

"I told him you wanted to see him." Nate was confused not only at the fact that Henry hadn't been by to talk to Jay, but also that Jay's expression had changed from happy and relaxed to tense in a few seconds.

"I did some more calls today," Jay began carefully.

"The ones to the people who'd stayed here?"

"Those ones. The usual. They loved the accommodation, although the comments about interiors looking tired still concern me. Everyone scored the horses, and you and Gabe, ten out of ten. One woman I spoke to said you both deserved elevens and did I know if either of you were single." Jay looked down at a notebook. "A Marjorie Aston? Know her?"

Nate snorted a laugh. "Know her? I still have bruises on my ass."

Jay lifted a single eyebrow in question.

"Hell, not like that. She kept pinching my ass, and her husband was damn well watching. She propositioned me and Gabe. Turns out they liked threesomes and would we join them for a foursome. Husband was hot, but she scared me."

That damn eyebrow didn't drop, and Nate belatedly realized what he had said. Not that it bothered him, but he suspected Jay was interested in him and blatantly saying he found men hot to Jay's face left Nate very exposed.

Jay stood from his chair and walked around his desk to lean on it opposite Nate.

"I knew it. Ashley told me she'd ask Gabe, but I knew it anyway. Didn't use to think cowboys could be anything but hetero. Are you gay? Or bi?"

Nate looked down at the highly polished boots he kept for best. If he said he was gay, was Jay going to stalk the rest of the way over to him? "You first," he said softly.

"Oh, gay," Jay admitted with a smile. "All the way gay."

"Gay," Nate offered in return.

Jay nodded. "So the gay porn with the cowboys I've seen on the Net wasn't a lie." He stepped away from the desk and Nate tensed. Was this it? Was this where Jay told him that he wanted to fuck, and Nate had to find a way to turn him down because he never mixed business with pleasure? Would Jay listen? Would Nate actually listen to himself? Jay was damn sexy and pretty and all smooth and polished, and Nate longed to get his hands on him. Jay came to a stop in front of Nate, and no more than two or three feet separated them. This was it. This was do or die.

Jay leaned in and whispered, "So, between you and me, can you tell me where the nearest gay bar is?"

Nate reared back. That wasn't what he'd been expecting. "Uhm," he began, "through town, Carter's. It's a biker bar for want of another description. You can't miss it."

Jay rocked on the soles of his feet. "Mmm, bikers," he said with heat.

Nate left before he made a fool of himself, his stupid brain imagining all kinds of things that weren't going to happen. Just because they were both gay didn't mean they had to assume the position and fuck each other into the floor. Not that Nate wanted to do that. No fucking. On the floor. Or in the office. *None.*

As he left Jay's office and stalked up the hill to home, his freaking erection caught in a twist of underwear and denim and he rearranged it forcefully. Nope. Fucking Jay was a big no-no. A definite no. If only his damn cock would get the message.

Gabe met him, coming down the hill with Luke trailing behind.

"Thought we were meeting at Marcus's," Gabe said.

"We were," Nate snapped. "I changed the plans. You were late, so I came to find you."

Luke jogged to catch Gabe, and the three walked back down past Marcus's house, Jay's office, and the restaurant, to the parking area for ranch vehicles. Nate threw the keys to Gabe.

"Designated driver," he snapped.

Gabe gave him the raised-eyebrow look that Jay seemed to have perfected as well. "You don't drink on weeknights."

"I have to sit through a parent-teacher conference, I need a beer." Too late Nate realized what he'd said. Damn it, he was fucking everything up tonight.

"You don't have to go," Luke snapped. "Gabe can be the parent tonight if you like." His little brother yanked open the door and clambered inside, then slammed it shut behind him.

"Not cool, bro," Gabe drawled.

"Fuck it," Nate kicked the tire then knocked on the window where Luke sat. For a few seconds, Luke ignored the tapping, but in the end he gave in and opened the door again.

"What the hell, Nate?" Luke's voice showed he wasn't pissed so much as hurt. Nate never resented being the parent figure, and he didn't know why it had happened today that he thought to say something that would hurt Luke.

"I'm sorry," Nate said. He opened the door and pulled Luke out of the car into a hug. "I wouldn't miss this for the world. I'm just in a bad mood."

"Okay." Nate's shoulder muffled Luke's answer. Luke always was quick to forgive Nate for any lack in parenting skills. "Did you see what I drew for Jay?"

"Juno... and it was beautiful. Proves to me you could make a living from art."

Luke shrugged, then pulled back. "See what the teachers say tonight."

They climbed into the car, and Nate took the keys back. He didn't want a beer, really; he wanted the heat of a confrontation with Gabe. Instead, he got nothing but an upset with his baby brother. Damn hormones.

He slowed to let Kirsten walk in front of the car. She was a weird kid. Sullen, head-to-toe in black, and with long hair hanging around her face, she cut an odd picture about the ranch. Added to that, she never said a word to anyone.

"I can't see how Ashley and Kirsten are related," Gabe said in a low voice. "They're so different."

"She's a teenager," Nate commented as he waved at her and received nothing in return. "They're all at odds with the world."

"I'm not," Luke piped up. Nate glanced in the mirror to see Luke staring out at Kirsten. Luke continued, "I worry about her, though. She's starting school next week, and they're going eat her alive."

"It's up to you to look out for her," Nate said needlessly. Luke was one of the good guys. "But you already planned to do that, didn't you?"

Luke nodded, and as they pulled off the ranch heading for the high school, he said, "I'll see what I can do about getting her to try and fit in more."

Gabe and Nate exchanged looks. All Kirsten talked about was leaving on the next bus out of town and back to New York. Ashley was skittish. Jay was buried in work. Josh was the only one who showed any life in him.

"Good luck with that," Gabe said dryly. "The Sullivan women are tightly closed up. I try talking to Ashley, and she shuts me down every time."

Nate glanced over at Gabe, who was focusing on something on his phone. "You like her?"

Gabe shrugged—the universal Todd way of not wanting to talk. "She has a way of getting under my skin," he admitted. "All that hair, and her beautiful eyes. She had awful bruises when she got here, and she seems scared of something or someone, maybe an ex?"

"And you want to protect her," Nate summarized.

"Nah, big brother wants to get handsy and heavy with her," Luke said dryly from the backseat.

"Fuck you, asshole," Gabe said without heat.

The two of them bickered, and that allowed Nate to settle his thoughts about Jay. Sexy and attractive the guy might be, but if he was like Nate and wanted to keep business and pleasure separate, then Nate could do that. He would offer to take Jay to Carter's and not entertain any more notions in his goddamn head about a short-term affair while Jay was here.

That settled, he turned from the main road into the school parking lot and pulled up alongside a truck he recognized as belonging to one of his hands with a kid in Luke's class.

Engine off, all three climbed out of the Jeep and made their way inside.

The high school wasn't the biggest, but it was a good school, and Gabe and Luke had both done well here. Luckily there were no teachers here from Nate's less-than-impressive time. He'd skipped most days for one reason or other and spent the rest of the time rebelling as a way of hiding that he couldn't make heads or tails of half of what he was reading. Less than half, if he was entirely honest. He couldn't help feeling a certain amount of nerves every time he entered the damn school.

They shuffled around and spoke to as many teachers as they could, until finally they only had the art teacher left. The queue wasn't long—seemed like not many students took art. The teacher rose as soon as they approached.

"Luke," she said warmly. She held out a hand to Gabe, then to Nate. "I'm Mrs. Reuben, Luke's art teacher for this semester. You must be Gabe and Nate. I've heard a lot about you and recognize you from Luke's drawings."

She gestured for them to sit, then pulled out two large sketch pads that Nate recognized from the stationery run they'd made when school began. Mrs. Reuben flicked to a page, turned it around so Nate could see it.

In stunning and intricate detail, Luke had captured his brothers leaning against a paddock fence. Each with one foot on the bottom rail, dressed in jeans and jackets with their hats on their heads, they looked like two cowboys shooting the breeze. Luke had colored them with gentle tones and left the background stark in blacks and grays.

"That's amazing," Gabe said. "Jeez, you really did get all the artistic genes from Mom."

Nate hugged Luke from the side, then settled back for the report. This was one he always liked to hear. Mrs. Reuben spoke for ages about potential and further coursework, and had Luke thought about college for Fine Art? Luke took it all in his stride. Nate was a little jealous—Luke had everything spread out in front of him, a whole future he could shape for himself. Not that Nate resented the hand he'd been given in life. He was happy and loved what he did. He didn't want more or need more—

Until Jay and his come-to-bed eyes had walked into his life.

"So, if he were to apply, I would support him in the work he needs to do to create the correct portfolio for them to see."

Nate blinked at Mrs. Reuben, and nodded as if he had been listening all the way along and not distracted by imagining Luke's future life and recalling memories of Jay's eyes.

Damn fool, you're losing it here.

They said their goodbyes and ended up back at the school parking lot. Luke stopped by the car door and scuffed his feet.

"I could do that?" he asked softly. "I could go to college and study art?"

Gabe by this time had clambered into the passenger side of the Jeep, so it was Nate who heard what Luke said. The words dripped with the incredulous knowledge of what he could do.

With a brief brotherly hug, Nate climbed into the driver's seat. "Luke, you can do anything you want."

CHAPTER THIRTEEN

Jay made some final notes and stretched in his chair. He had forgotten to talk to Nate about Henry—about how concerned he was at what he was hearing and how he didn't know where to start to put it right. The one thing he meant to cover and it had flown from his head. *Talk about my cock ruling my brain.*

He'd been damn pleased to hear the word 'gay' coming from Nate's mouth, and hell, he'd just *known* that Nate was checking him out. There was a lot of Nate that Jay wanted to check out in return. From the tip of his leather boots to the cowlicks in his wavy hair, Nate was all man. All cowboy. Two weeks since that horseback ride—fourteen days—and he had managed to look his fill of Nate at every occasion he could without getting caught for a single one of them. Apart from Ashley, who called him on it last night. Jay had managed to avoid a conversation when—*thankfully*—Josh asked him to take down a box of cereal, but Jay knew the subject would not be dropped.

"Hey, little brother," Ashley said from the door.

Talk of the devil....

"Hey."

"You finished in here now?"

"Just." He closed the folder with his findings. Tomorrow he would catch Nate, or maybe Gabe, and ask them about Henry. The hand was an old-timer, just short of sixty-three, and was mentioned more than once in the phone conversations he had made today. He could be a fly in the ointment that was Crooked Tree.

"Can we talk?" Ashley sounded hesitant, but that wasn't a new thing. Though she had Jay's unconditional support, she still worried about discussing anything with him.

He pushed his chair from the desk and picked up the folder. He'd check through all the notes when he was in bed. "Sure."

They left the office, and Jay pulled the door shut. The sharp Montana wind, icy and cutting, swirled around them as they walked outside. Jay pulled up the collar of his jacket and cursed the fact that the office was too warm to wear thermals, because he damn well needed them out here. He let Ashley decide where they were walking, and she led them over the bridge and into the stand of trees that hid their place from the private houses.

"Is it Kirsten?" Jay asked as soon as they stopped. Ashley shook her head, then scuffed her feet. "Josh?"

"Josh. Me. Lewis," she said wearily.

Concern knifed through him as keenly as the cold air affecting his skin beneath the material of his jacket. He focused solely on Lewis's name. "Did that bastard contact you?" He'd been expecting a call. It wasn't as if they were hiding, and Lewis had contact details for Josh—not that he had ever used them when he was inside.

"No," she said firmly. "Nothing from him."

Jay had played this scene before. He was the little brother, but he was also the one thing Ashley had to be her crutch. He had a certain set of questions he asked whenever Lewis came up in conversation. If she fancied herself still in love with Lewis, then it wasn't Jay's place to say she shouldn't be. He was there to facilitate her understanding of where she was in life and how she was handling things. Or so the family counseling woman had said. He hadn't thought to ask if Lewis was even allowed out of the city? Did he get parole? Was he tagged? Was Ashley sad that Lewis had taken no action to find her or Josh?

"How does that make you feel?"

She shrugged. "Like he's a long way away, and I can breathe."

"That's a good thing, then." Jay had never heard Ashley consign Lewis to the distance. He had always been so prevalent in her life.

"Yes and no—I'll have to see him one day, birthdays, graduation, you name it—it's not fair to expect Josh to miss out on having a daddy."

Jay said nothing. He didn't agree at all. He wanted Lewis gone permanently so that Ashley could move forward. Instead, he focused on the other name she'd thrown out.

"What about Josh?"

She chuckled. "Just that he was born to live here. Have you seen? He's around the horses whenever he can, and he's got one of Luke's old hats. I've not seen him this happy in a while. I don't want to take him away from here when your contract is up."

"We always said we'd left New York permanently," Jay said softly. "We're not going back. And as for Josh?

He's always been a good kid, Ash, we'll see how it goes when he gets to school." Jay had accompanied Ashley to both of the kids' schools. Kirsten had sulked most of the time, but the principal didn't seem fazed at all by it. That was a plus point.

Kirsten didn't argue when she was told that only one piercing was allowed in each ear although her expression was mutinous as she listened. Josh's teacher was a bundle of sunshine, or that was how Jay described her in his head. Short, blonde, vivacious, she had teaching experience in special needs and decided there and then that Josh was going to be a little star in her class. Jay could almost see Josh fall in love with her on the spot.

"Then there's Gabe," Ashley added quietly.

"What about Gabe?" Jay left the statement open-ended. He kind of knew what the issue was but needed to hear it from Ashley.

"He asked me out to dinner," she said carefully.

"He did? That's great. I like him, Ash. I'd have to murder him in his sleep if he hurts you." He was joking and at first couldn't understand the sudden pain that flitted across his sister's face. He realized what he had said, and he hated his careless use of words. He didn't want to put any link to Lewis against Gabe's name.

"That's the thing," she said. "I like him. He's good with Josh, and he tried to talk to Kirsten."

"But there's a problem? You don't want to go? You're worried he's like Lewis? I don't know him or his brothers that well, but seems to me he and Lewis are as different as night and day."

"How can you tell that, Jay? We've only been with the family two weeks and already you say you *know* what Gabe is like?"

Jay immediately decided he wasn't rising to that line of questioning. The last thing he wanted to do was bring up the fact that the first time he'd met Lewis, the man had been stoned. Gabe was all sincerity and manners, and he was friendly and welcoming. "It's easy, Ash. You like him, right?"

"But what could come of it?" She hugged herself around her middle and shifted a little closer to the shelter of the nearest tree and out of the wind.

"Dinner," Jay said firmly. "A nice steak, maybe some wine, embarrassing silences. The usual. Maybe you'll have fun."

"You make it sound so easy."

Jay stepped forward and pulled his sister into a close embrace. "It can be easy if we want it to be. We have to go with the flow." She chuckled in his hold and burrowed into his jacket.

"I love you, Jay."

"I love you too, sis," Jay said quietly.

They stood that way for a while until she was the one to pull back.

"Your turn. Tell me about Nate."

Jay snorted a laugh. "What is this? A Todd brothers appreciation night?"

She pushed him in the chest. "Have you found out yet what team he's on? Is he gay like you thought? Is there a chance?"

"When is my gaydar ever wrong?"

"Are we counting you hitting on our postman, who was married with three kids?"

"Marriage and kids does not a straight man make," Jay deadpanned. "Actually, I've not long found out for sure with Nate."

She tilted her head in question. "And?"

"And what?" He could play deliberately obtuse if it gave him more thinking time.

"What next?"

That was a leading question. What next...? He'd been drooling over the rough-and-ready cowboy for two weeks, which was bad enough. To then add in the man all polished up? That wasn't fair on his libido.

"I wound him up tonight. Got all close, then asked where the nearest gay club was. You should have seen him fly after that. He's definitely interested in something, and it would be cool to have someone to keep me warm at nights."

Ashley smacked him on the chest again. "It's not like you to do that; wind a guy up then laugh about it."

Jay winced. She was right, he was never the one who played games. Straight down the middle, anyone he was with always knew exactly what he wanted. "I just ruffled him up a bit. To see what's what. You know I didn't push him too far, because he's the guy who writes the checks."

"I get it, you're playing around. Just be careful," she warned.

"I was joking." Jay was suddenly serious. "Just... I don't know... there's something about Nate that makes me want to do things I've never done before."

Like kissing. A lot of kissing. And talking. And sex with my boss... lots of sex.

"Like?"

"Sit in the dark with a campfire? I don't know what, just... things."

"I know what you mean." Ashley sighed and gripped his hand in hers. "Gabe has that effect on me."

"Imagine if we ended up with brothers," Jay teased. "Is that kind of weird?"

Ashley laughed and together they walked toward the place Jay thought of as home. A Jeep pulled in the parking area on the other side of the bridge, and the Todd brothers piled out. Gabe and Luke were laughing and joking and generally acting like hyper siblings. Nate looked more serious—more so when, with his arms crossed over his chest, he stared over at Jay.

Damn cowboy was making a statement there and then; drawing a line in the dirt with his heated looks and his stubborn sexiness. Jay deliberately lifted a hand and waved, and in response Nate turned on his heel and walked up the path to the private houses. Gabe waved back though, a grin slashing his face. Luke said something, and whatever he said had Gabe cuffing his little brother around the ear. Then they followed Nate, and all too soon Jay and Ashley were in their own place with the door shut against the world.

"Got to love those cowboys," Ashley said with a small smile.

"God, yeah" was all Jay could say. Damn right he wanted to love on one of them in particular. And pretty damn soon.

Jay was restless. Bundled up in his coat and with blankets across his legs, he curled up on the porch chair and stared out into the Montana night. Here there was no light pollution—just miles and miles of endless ebony sky and scattered stars that shone brightly against the black. He knew nothing about the heavens, just that he had a Virgo star sign and somewhere up there, the stars that made up the constellation sat in a neat pattern.

Ashley had sat with him when he first came outside. They drank hot chocolate in companionable silence for a while until she complained it was too cold and wandered indoors.

Jay was amazed at how easy he had slipped into the rhythm of this new place. He loved his office, his independence, and that he was looking at marketing from an entirely new perspective and coming up with ideas. The buzz of it was as high as the office in the city—with a different focus. The contract he had here was open-ended, but maybe, he should consider whether there was enough here for him to stay in Montana. There was prestige in working for one of the big-city companies, but there he was always a small cog in a very big machine. Here on the ranch it was different.

The noise of hooves on the graveled path over the bridge had him wondering if maybe the enigmatic Nate was on his way here on his beloved Juno. They could be taking a ride in the evening as they appeared to do every night, then decided to go by Jay's place. The hoof noises grew closer, then stopped altogether. From guesswork,

Jay had the horse and rider unmoving and at the front of the cabin. A few moments later, the noise began again, and Juno appeared around the side of the house with her nose pointed up to the tourist cabins. Nate wasn't looking at the back porch—he could have no way of knowing that Jay was here, and this was the perfect opportunity for Jay to stay hidden and enjoy his peace. Only... he didn't want to.

"Evening," he called.

Nate shifted in his saddle and peered into the darkness of the porch before guiding Juno to the wooden surround. "Hey."

"Hey, yourself. Good date?" Jay knew damn well it hadn't been a date that Nate had prettied himself up for. He'd not only seen the three Todd brothers arrive back in the car, but Josh had told him before bed that Luke had a parent-teacher conference. Appeared that Nate and Gabe took a keen interest in their brother's education.

"It wasn't a date," Nate's voice rumbled. He dismounted and laid the reins on a wooden post. "I wanted to talk to you."

Jay indicated the chair next to him, then realized Nate might not be able to see the gesture. "There's a free chair here."

Nate took the steps to the porch and settled himself into the chair. Plainly the small amount of moonlight on this side of the cabin was enough for Nate to make his way there and sit without falling on his ass.

There was silence for a while, and the expectation of whatever the hell it was that Nate wanted to say was a heavy weight on Jay. In the end he dived in with conversation. "Is everything okay? Did you get my message about the website?"

Jay was particularly proud that he'd mastered some pretty hairy web code and fixed an issue with the ranch's ancient and unwieldy website so that it at least worked until the new one came online. That would go live as soon as they had the logo finalized.

"I did," Nate said simply. "It wasn't what I wanted to talk about."

"It's Henry, isn't it?" Jay asked immediately. Maybe he wouldn't have to talk about the one man he had issues with on the ranch—Nate had apparently picked up on the need to talk. "I realize we didn't get to talk about him before, and there's stuff I think you need to know."

Nate narrowed his gaze and sighed. "No, I wasn't here to talk about Henry either, but now that I am here, tell me what the problem is."

Nate settled back in the chair and propped his booted feet up on the porch surround, and for a second Jay lost his tongue. *What a photo. A cowboy silhouette with the quarter moon and the stars. Perfect.*

"It's not an easy thing to start explaining," Jay began. "You remember I was talking to the old visitors, getting feedback, and you recall I told you that everything was good, apart from the cabins being a little tired? They loved the experience and the horses, the roundups, the food at Branches, the atmosphere, the river…." Jay stopped as he realized he was simply repeating a lot of what Nate already knew. The thing was, he needed to soften the blow of the one thing that was causing an issue. Henry was a liability, but from talking to Sophie and Gabe, Jay was well aware that Henry was part of the furniture—a thirty-year employee at Crooked Tree.

"Yep."

"There was a common denominator in some of the conversations that had become more like complaints. Henry."

"Hmm," Nate hummed softly.

Jay sensed that Nate wasn't agreeing or disagreeing, just throwing out a noncommittal noise. *Going great so far. Not.*

"What do you mean by 'hmm'?" Jay asked pointedly.

"Henry. A bit of a loose cannon. Says what he wants and to hell with the consequences. Ornery and close to retiring. I don't think he's that tolerant of the guests."

"You could say that. You had a couple here for their honeymoon—a gay couple."

"The McAllisters? Yeah, I remember them."

"Seems like Henry had some things to say on the matter. Then another family with two special needs kids, from last August?"

"Bryan and Tommy, loved the horses, both on the autistic spectrum. Tommy has Asperger's, I recall."

"Do you remember everything about the guests?" Jay changed direction quickly.

"Mostly I think of what they were like with the horses, but that isn't the point," Nate replied. "What about Bryan and Tommy?"

"The parents said they were dismayed by Henry's use of the word 'retard' in their hearing."

"Why didn't they come tell anyone?"

"That is the next problem, Nate. Turns out they did, along with the McAllisters who registered their concern. They spoke to Marcus and followed it up with letters of complaint. When I dug out the paperwork, it looked to me like Marcus gave the standard reply, assuring them of the ranch's stance on both matters and how you didn't tolerate things like that. I'm not seeing any follow-up on the files, though, and believe me, those files are kind of thick for the last five years of issues. All it needs is for either one of those families to tell their friends, and suddenly Crooked Tree gets a reputation for being homophobic and intolerant."

Nate sighed and leaned his head against the back of the chair. "I'll deal with it," he said. "That guy is the bane of my life, but he's been here thirty years and is one of Marcus's close friends."

"Then you could get Marcus to talk to him."

"Marcus will tell you the same thing—that Henry is pretty much a permanent fixture around here."

Jay had a sudden unsettled feeling in his stomach about the dynamic between Nate and Marcus. He had thought Marcus was a figurehead and Nate was the one who really ran things. Was he wrong? Seemed like Marcus was the one pulling all the strings if Nate wasn't willing to cross the line and cut out the rot.

"He can't be permanent," Jay said quickly. "If you want to move Crooked Tree forward, then you need to think about letting the guy go."

"That's a bit harsh, Jay. He's a mostly harmless guy close to retiring."

Jay frowned. "You don't believe he's harmless. I can hear it in your voice."

"I said I'll deal with it."

"I'll hold you to that." That would have to do. Nate wasn't offering solutions, he was offering to handle the issue. That was sexy and at the same time kind of irritating. Jay pulled his thoughts back to whatever was the original reason Nate sat on his porch. "So, what did you want to see me about?"

"Oh, that. I'm going to Carter's tomorrow. It's Friday night and a good night to be there. I'll swing by and pick you up at ten if you want in?"

Want in? Of course, I want in. Far too many months had passed since he'd had the warmth of another guy anywhere near him. Jay considered what kind of guy might go to a biker bar. He wasn't 100 percent into the leather look, but there were bound to be cowboys there. Cowboys like Nate. Tall and strong and muscled and cut from the Montana mountains.... suddenly Jay had an image of a cowboy bending over for him and his cock stiffened under the blanket. Thank fuck for the bunched material and the dark. The thought of prepping and fucking and—jeez, that there was the sum of every single fantasy he'd used to get off this week.

He was fucked when he realized the cowboy had Nate's features.

"Tomorrow?" he asked weakly.

"If you want to come visit the place." Nate stood up and brushed the seat of his pants.

Looming over Jay, he blocked out any available moonlight, and suddenly Jay had a moment of clarity. He wanted Nate closer. *Way* closer. He scrambled to stand but still clutched the blanket over his groin. Was this actually Nate offering some kind of date? Or if not a date, an opportunity to exchange something other than this skirting around the issue they were doing.

"Yeah," Jay said eagerly. Was this going to be dancing and drinking and ending up getting some mutual satisfaction with the sexy cowboy?

Nate chuckled, leaned in, and Jay found himself mimicking the motion until not much space separated them. Anticipation curled inside Jay.

Nate whispered, "Take your own lube and condoms for whomever you hook up with. I always do." He stepped back, and with an economy of movement, he was up in the saddle and riding away.

For a second Jay stood with his mouth hanging open. He'd thought they would be going together... then... *shit*. Had he had the tables turned on him?

A smile curved his lips as he listened to the receding hoof beats and watched as the dark swallowed Nate.

Fucker.

CHAPTER FOURTEEN

True to his word, Nate was ready at quarter to ten and had the car warmed and ready to go at exactly ten o'clock. He was going to give it five minutes, then leave whether or not Jay got to the car. At two minutes after, the passenger door opened and Jay was there with an expectant look on his face. The interior light showed Nate enough to know that Jay was looking for trouble tonight. He was walking sin in a close-fitting T-shirt and jeans so tight the groin pulled. Wasn't he cold? Where was his thick down jacket? Nate saw that Jay was carrying the coat and wished to hell he'd put it on. Anything to hide his body. Added to that he was clean-shaven and smelled like heaven.

"Get in," Nate ordered gruffly. "Shut the freaking door."

Jay scrambled in and did as he was told, the scent of him enveloped Nate's senses. He couldn't damn well breathe without smelling whatever cologne or shit Jay was wearing.

"What is that smell?" he snapped irritably.

Jay cast a quick glance his way. "Hugo Boss. Present from Ashley and the kids."

"It's girly," Nate observed.

Jay turned fully in his seat, a frown pasted on his face. "It's an eighty-dollar bottle that they saved for a year to buy me, and I happen to like it."

"And what the hell are you wearing?"

Jay looked down at his lap and back up. "Clothes," he said.

Was it just Nate, or was there a hint of irritation in Jay's voice? "Put your coat on."

"We're in a car," Jay replied reasonably.

"Fuck. They'll eat you alive," Nate snapped. "This is a biker bar. For fuck's sake, go back and change into something looser and less—" He indicated with his hand the tight jeans and T-shirt. "—whatever."

"Nope." Jay leaned closer to Nate. "I happen to want to be eaten alive."

"Jesus fuck," Nate cursed. "You one of those slut gays who sleep with everyone?"

The interior light switched off on the timer and suddenly the two men were in darkness. Nate cursed the timing—he wished he could see Jay's expression in response to the last question. The thought of one of the guys in the bar getting handsy with Jay was suddenly a very pressing problem for Nate.

"Says the man who told me he takes lube and condoms to the bar every time he goes," Jay deadpanned.

Nate took the car out of park and crossed the bridge to the main road. He wanted to have last say on this. "Don't blame me when some leather bear decides to strap you to his bike and kidnap you."

Next to him in the dark, Jay chuckled. "Well, that would be one fantasy off the list."

Nate gripped the steering wheel tighter and gritted his teeth. Damn the man and his quick, clever responses. The journey was long enough for Nate to work up a head of steam, although he couldn't get to the core of what was pissing him off. Was it the thought of Jay sleeping with an indiscriminate numbers of guys? *Or not sleeping.* Was it maybe because Jay apparently had fantasies about leather and bikers and didn't mention cowboys once? Or was it just that he realized he would never be the fantasy guy Jay had suggested he lusted after? Whatever the answer was, it certainly wasn't coming to him on this journey, and all too soon they reached the bar.

Carter's looked busy, a row of bikes to either side of the door and loud music. Outside it looked like a biker's place, but inside the clientele was as varied as it could be. Couples, singles, gay or not—this was the place to come for a casual hookup or a drink in a space where no one judged you. Saul, who owned Carter's, was ex-Army, and no one argued with the fifty-year-old and his supply of registered guns, so any tensions were dealt with summarily. Added to that he was one of five siblings and the only one who wasn't a cop. Links to the force were kind of handy. Nate loved that inside was peace and security.

They walked to the door, and worry consumed Nate. What would happen in there? The guys at this place expected certain types of visitors—bikers, cowboys, some passing trade, but not much. In all the years of coming here, he'd never seen someone as pretty and fresh as Jay. He hadn't been joking when he said they would eat Jay alive. Steeling himself for a reaction from whoever was inside, Nate pushed through the door.

At first no one paid any attention, then someone noticed Jay and the talk traveled fast. The noise didn't disappear altogether, but it diminished noticeably. Next to Nate, Jay grinned, then forged a path to the bar.

Nate followed helplessly. Why the hell take the payback this far and actually carry through on taking Jay anywhere near other available gay men? He'd never expected Jay to take him up on the offer, and now he was stuck babysitting the naive city boy and watching anyone who came anywhere near him.

Nate sat on the stool next to Jay and was relieved when the chatter resumed its normal level against the sound of the music.

"Beer," Jay called out.

The guy behind the bar—a new one that Nate hadn't seen before—did a complete comedic double-take when he looked at Jay. Without saying a word, he retrieved a beer, removed the cap, and pushed the bottle over the bar. With a wink and a very obvious come-on stance, the guy smiled at Jay. "On me, gorgeous," he said.

Nate fought the desire to punch him. He didn't look much over twenty-one, and there was no way Jay was going to be falling for the barkeep's charms—not on Nate's watch.

"I'll have a Coke," Nate said forcefully.

The barkeep winced at the tone and glanced at him apologetically. Great, the guy thought Jay and Nate were an item. Nate pushed the money over in exchange for the Coke. The barkeep recovered quickly. If anything, the invitation oozed from him a little more thickly.

"Hell, cowboy, I'll pay for your drink as well," the barkeep said. "I'm Mike, and I'm off at one if you two want to play."

The barkeep waited for a response, and Nate was stunned. Playing in a threesome wasn't something he had personally tried, and for some reason the idea of him and Jay and another was something he found hard to swallow. He opened his mouth to speak, but Jay beat him to it.

"Him and me?" Jay asked with a smirk. "In the same bed? I'm lucky if I can get him in the same room and not want to kill him."

"So just you and me, then," Mike said. He flicked his blond hair away from his eyes and ran his tongue over his lips.

Christ. This was like some scene out of a porn movie or an incredibly badly written comedy.

"Maybe," Jay said, lifting the beer bottle in salute. "I want to see the rest of the menu."

He swiveled in his seat to face the sea of bodies and Nate's general level of shock rose higher. That was rude—he'd cut Mike dead. Nate glanced apologetically at Mike, then shook his head when he spotted Mike grinning and adjusting his groin. He didn't look like a man who was insulted or pissed off. He'd clearly come under Jay's spell. As did the built-like-a-brick-outhouse biker who had come to a stop in front of Jay and leaned over him to grab another beer.

"You're pretty," the biker said with a growl.

Nate's eyes widened. He looked from Jay to the muscle-bound man and back again. He knew this guy was called Hunter: built, tattooed, and with a reputation for being a bottom that went entirely against the bad-biker character he portrayed.

Is Jay interested? Is that all it takes? A man calls Jay pretty and off they go, hand in hand, to one of the back rooms?

Nate clenched his fists. Hunter may well have nearly a foot in height and many pounds on Nate, but he could take him if he had to.

Jay inclined his head, then sipped his beer. "Thank you."

Big guy indicated one of the dark corners. "I'm at the back table if you want a beer." He reached out and ran a hand from Jay's temple to his chest, circling a nipple that was erect against the silky softness of the tight T-shirt.

Nate had to hold himself back—*what the hell?*

"I'll remember that," Jay said easily.

Hunter left, and Jay didn't seem fazed at all by what had happened. In two minutes, he had been propositioned not once, but twice. When a third man stepped up beside Jay and opened his mouth to talk, Nate simply stood up in a dramatic movement and growled. He could hear himself do it. All possessive and angry, and it was enough for the new guy to slink away.

"Jesus, Nate, I can sort this for myself," Jay barked irritably. He slid off the stool. "I want to dance."

With that, he disappeared into the throng of maybe forty people—men, women, in groups, couples, or alone, all crammed into a small space made by clearing tables to one side.

Panic hit Nate when he lost sight of Jay. Perhaps bringing him here tonight was the wrong thing to do? Maybe he should have waited a bit, but all he'd wanted was to get a rise out of Jay and his infuriating calm and to get revenge for the teasing and flirting in the office. All that had happened was that he was stuck watching the sexy, sweet-smelling man writhing on the dance floor with far too many admirers. Nate forcibly unclenched his fists and stretched his fingers. He was acting like a fucking guard dog, and Jay was handling himself fine. Nate needed to relax.

At one point, when he was trying not to stare at the dancing, he spotted Liam across the room and they exchanged heated looks. Nate recalled the young guy bending over for him the last time he was here. Maybe he could get some more of that tonight. Maybe fucking Liam into the mattress would stop the irritating thought that he wanted to fuck Jay instead. Or that he wanted Jay to do the same thing to him.

Jeez.

Jay made it through three tracks of music, and when he made no sign of moving from his place alongside two men, Nate had to make a move. He sucked it up and joined the fray.

Nate was immediately swallowed into the crowd and instinctively began moving to the beat of the song as he walked closer. When he finally made it to Jay's side, he patted him on the shoulder. Jay spun on his heel and Nate held out a hand to steady him.

"Cowboy!" Jay shouted over the music.

In a sinuous movement, Jay gripped one of Nate's shoulders and shuffled closer so that very little separated them. The two men dancing with Jay drifted off to face other dancers, and suddenly it seemed like it was just Nate and Jay swaying to the music.

"You need to be careful!" Nate shouted close to his ear.

"Why?" Jay shouted back.

His breath smelled of beer and his body scent was a mix of the infuriating aftershave mingled with sweat and dust. Suddenly Jay became a four-course meal and Nate was very hungry.

"Keep your eyes open," Nate warned.

As if to make that comment mean nothing, Jay deliberately closed his eyes and moved to the beat of the music. Somewhere along the line, Jay had lost his bottle of beer, or finished it, or whatever. He had both hands free, and he used them to steady himself by gripping hard to Nate's shoulders. He had closed his eyes and was mouthing the words along with the song. Was he aware it was Nate holding him? He'd said "cowboy," they'd spoken, but there were a lot of cowboys mixed in with the bikers and the other varied clientele.

"Open your eyes, Jay," Nate shouted over the music.

Jay did as Nate had asked, and Nate was suddenly seeing brown eyes glazed with emotion. Then Jay smiled and closed his eyes again.

Instinctively Nate steadied Jay and that meant his hands rested on Jay's hips. The feel of the man beneath his touch was intoxicating and Nate held hard. Jay fit into his arms perfectly: a little shorter, a little slimmer, just the right height, and his lips, damp with sweat or beer—Nate didn't know—were what he zeroed in on. Jay swayed with the music. The move took them closer and fuck, Jay was hard. Nate gave in to the temptation and pressed them closer still until he was sure Jay could feel how hard he was as well.

All thoughts of impropriety or fears of rejection flew out the window. Nate was lost in the smile of pleasure that curved Jay's damp lips. What would he taste like? Would Jay return the kiss? Would Jay push him away? How could he risk this? He eased his hold on Jay's hips and slouched a little so that their groins aligned— suddenly they were frotting firmly and rhythmically to some Eminem mix. There was no way he could stop himself.

"Can I kiss you?" Nate said into Jay's ear.

Jay smiled at him, but it wasn't clear that he'd heard what Nate said. Hell, he should kiss Jay and stop all this delay in taking what he really wanted. Someone jostled him from behind and the movement threw him off his spiral of the pros and cons of denial. When the person who jostled them attempted to insinuate themselves between Nate and Jay, abruptly everything was clear.

"Fuck off," Nate shouted clearly to the interloper, and in a quick move, he got his first taste of the sexy city boy. The press of his lips against Jay's was intoxicating, and they kissed and swayed to the beat of the music. Their hard cocks pressed together and—finally—the kiss deepened. Jay let him in and Nate took every advantage. Fuck the fact Jay worked for the ranch, fuck that they had absolutely zero in common, forget that Jay had a degree and a life that would take him far away from Nate's world sometime soon.

Nate could ignore all that because Jay tasted good, smelled good, and the thought of taking this horizontal had him losing himself in the kiss. Jay raised his arms and wrapped his hands around the back of Nate's head, and with a groan Nate could feel in the kiss, Jay held tight and didn't let go.

One song segued into another—a faster track that blurred into the next until the press of bodies around them lessened and the kisses became nothing more than exchanged breath and a promise of wanting more.

Without words Jay released his hold around Nate's neck, and they left Carter's by the front door. The cold of the Montana night hit them. There had been no point in wearing jackets into the bar, and neither wore particularly warm clothing. Unspoken, they quickened their pace until they made it to Nate's jeep.

In the car, there was still silence. Nate gripped the wheel. *What now?*

In all his years of being gay and sexually active, Nate had never taken a lover who lasted more than one fuck.

"I'll understand if you want to…," Nate began. Although what would he understand? That Jay would be so affronted he would pack up his family and leave? Or that Jay called Nate on inappropriate advances? What?

"I brought condoms and lube," Jay said quietly. He teased, "Seems a shame to waste them."

Nate felt hope mixed with a healthy dose of lust before it hit him—he didn't want that. Not with Jay. He couldn't reconcile random sex with Jay in his head alongside what he'd done with other men at Carter's. He wanted something else—different. Very deliberately he turned in the car and willed his damn cock to settle the hell down.

"How about dinner?" he said instead.

Jay glanced at the dashboard clock. "It's 1:00 a.m."

"I don't mean tonight," Nate explained. "I mean tomorrow maybe, or another day. There's a place not far from here we could go, up the mountain. Steaks, potatoes—" He stopped talking when Jay quirked an eyebrow. Evidently Nate didn't need to list the menu.

"Like a date," Jay summed up.

Nate was relieved that Jay got the point, then waited with bated breath for the reply. He didn't know what it was like in the Big Apple when it came to relationships, and he was probably crossing all kinds of lines here, but in the three years since Carter's became more than just a bar, he'd hooked up maybe six times. Six didn't make him any kind of expert in long-term relationships or, hell, in overnight meet-ups either.

"Yeah," he said.

"Which could, in itself, lead to another date?" Jay asked thoughtfully.

"Maybe, if I don't bore you on the first one," Nate smiled.

Jay shuffled in his seat and reached out a hand to rest it on Nate's cheek. Instinctively Nate leaned into the touch.

"I'd like that," Jay said. "But does that mean we can't use the condoms tonight?"

Nate laughed lowly. "Not tonight." He was more serious. "I want to take things slow, Jay. We don't rush things 'round here."

As soon as he spouted that particular piece of nonsense, he wished he could withdraw the words.

Saying he wanted to do things slowly implied that he thought this was more than just maybe a satisfying, short-term, fuck buddy kind of thing. He was lost in the spiral of indecision, and he hated it. He wasn't that man. He was honest to a fault, normal, ordinary—nothing special. But one thing he did have going as a plus for him was that he always knew his own mind. Always. So how the hell was Jay getting under his skin and making him doubt himself?

"Do it slowly?" Jay repeated. There was a question in the three words.

Nate was suddenly on the back foot. Jay was probably looking for a one-night stand, but Nate was looking more for friends with benefits. There was something about this man and his teasing and smiling and the way he made Nate laugh.

"I like you," Nate began. "I was thinking, just for the time you're here, we could be friends."

"With benefits?"

Nate felt relief flood him. Jay got the point of what he'd been trying to say. Must be the college degree. "Yeah."

Jay hesitated momentarily, then nodded. "Okay. One thing, though—not too slow with the benefits thing because, Cowboy, I really need to get my hands on you."

Nate's cock was on board with that, but his ingrained sense of what was right fought his instinctive urges. Instead of placating Jay and giving him a timescale of when they could eventually end up in bed with each other, he turned back to face front and started the engine.

"Nope," he said with his best cowboy drawl, "won't be long."

They made the journey home in silence and left each other in the parking lot at Crooked Tree with nothing more than a lingering, soft kiss.

Nate cradled Jay's face in his hands. "Dinner. Monday night at seven. Meet you in the parking lot."

"Uh-huh," Jay whispered into the kiss.

"Are you listening to me, Jay?"

One final kiss and Jay pulled away. "I heard you, Nate. Monday."

CHAPTER FIFTEEN

Jay climbed the steps to his cabin and refused to look back at Nate, though he could feel Nate's gaze boring into his back. He pushed open his front door, closed it behind him, and only then did he slump bonelessly against the wall.

"It was good, then," Ashley said with a smile.

"Uh-huh" was about all he could come up with.

"What's he like?"

"We kissed, that's all, and it was… well, we danced as well. He's… hard… and…" He pushed himself away from the wall and made it as far as the sofa before letting gravity do its thing. He was overwhelmed and ever so slightly in shock.

"Hard," Ashley repeated. She tilted her head.

They always talked about Jay's love life—shame he couldn't get her to talk about where her energies had been focused with Lewis. Still, this was brother-sister time and he loved this part of the first date. Because, let's face it, that was what it had been.

"I'm getting the chocolate," she said.

She disappeared into the kitchen and a few minutes later, returned to the sofa with hot chocolate and cookies, and sat cross-legged next to him. It didn't matter if he got home at 2:00 a.m. or four, she was always up waiting unless he texted her and said he was staying out. Hell, he couldn't remember the last time he'd texted anything like that.

"You must have a thousand cookies in the kitchen," Jay observed. He crunched down on one and sighed at the sheer awesomeness that was chocolate and nuts. "You should take some over to Marcus and Sophie, and maybe some up to the Todd brothers."

"They're just for us," she said softly.

Jay lifted his T-shirt and patted his flat stomach. "You want a fat brother who can't land a cowboy?" he asked with a frown.

"Is that what happened? Did you and Nate...? Or was it some other random cowboy?"

Jay raised his eyebrows. "I had one focus, and Nate didn't stand a chance. I used all the plays: the flirting, the dismissal, the dancing my best moves, and finally Nate got with the plan."

"And?" She glanced at the clock on the wall pointedly. "You're home early for someone who snared Nate Todd."

Jay shrugged. "He wants to take it slow. He's asked me to go out to dinner with him."

"Wow!" Ashley smiled at him and poked his arm. "This sounds serious."

"How can it be serious? I've only known him two weeks. We're not forcing it down people's throats with all that couple stuff. It's friends with benefits. I like the guy, and for as long as we're here on the ranch, why not enjoy the time?"

He regretted his words immediately. Ashley looked sad and resignation filled her eyes.

"I'm not sure I ever want to leave Crooked Tree," she said.

"I know," was all Jay could say.

Was it Montana that called to her, or was it the ranch specifically? She had time here to be on her own, but Jay desperately wanted for his sister to connect more with the ranch. The contract he had with Crooked Tree was for the two months that Marcus had suggested, but there was an option that it would be for longer. They'd gotten places for the kids at local schools, so the move to Montana was pretty definitive.

"What will you do when it's done here?" she asked carefully.

"Onward and upward," Jay answered immediately. "This could be a permanent position as I see it, but I will find something else if I need to." Jay didn't begin to catalog the anxiety settling in the pit of his stomach at the thought of moving on. Or the worry that he might have moved his entire family to Montana only to have no work to keep a roof over their heads.

"And if you get involved with Nate and do your usual thing of backing off?"

"Harsh, sis."

"But true. Will you let it affect your job?"

Jay sat for a little while in silence. Would he let it affect his job? He sensed Nate was heading into this for the long haul with all his talk of going slow and taking time. He hoped that if things went south, both he and Nate would be professional. For a second doubts flew into his mind. Maybe Ashley was right in what she was implying. He should think about what he'd done and

182 | RJ Scott

consider he was trying to build a new life for them all. Those doubts had begun to form into something concrete when Ashley interrupted his thoughts.

"Ignore me. Nate is a good guy, and you're a good guy. It will be fine." She nodded. "So tell me more about him."

Today was the second time Jay had been on a horse, and he only needed reminding of one thing when he saddled Diablo. He was stiff and achy, and he knew he would pay for the riding. Nate told him that he had to ride every day to get his muscles in shape. Maybe he'd do what Nate said. One day when it wasn't so easy to find something he had to do first. Luckily it wasn't just him and Nate—this time Luke was with them. Or rather Luke and his camera. He guessed he'd brought the horseback ride on himself when he'd asked Luke to show him some of the most private parts of the ranch. Turned out it would be him, Luke, and the addition of Nate, who would explore the backwoods and plains of Crooked Tree.

Being up on Diablo's back was as terrifying and awe-inspiring as it had been the last time. Diablo was steady, but Jay had to push through being freaked out to settle into enjoying the scenery. He did it by focusing on what Luke and Nate were talking about. The older brother was looking fine in the saddle this morning. His shirt stretched across wide shoulders and his dark hair curled from under his hat. Jay's mouth watered at the memory of the kisses and the promise of what they could have soon. This wouldn't just be dinner—he was ready for more kissing, more touching, and to feel Nate inside him. He'd not had this need in him since he first played the romance game. Nate wasn't Mark—he was something very different. He twisted in his saddle to look back at Jay.

"You okay back there?"

Jay grimaced. He bet he didn't look as smooth and sexy as Nate did on Juno. Far too much of his ass meeting the saddle in a mismatch of trying to get into Diablo's smooth gait. "I'm good," he said quickly.

"Up here!" Luke said from the front.

Jay couldn't see the boy, but Diablo followed Juno up a steep incline through the undergrowth until the trees thinned and they were in a clearing. Nate dismounted and moved swiftly to Jay to help him off. Jay didn't exactly need help, but he could play the needy newbie if it meant some skin time with Nate. Very deliberately, he stumbled as he reached the ground and clung like a limpet to Nate's arm. Nate wasn't stupid; he smirked as he very clearly saw through what Jay was doing.

Jay forced an innocent expression on his face and waited for Nate to say something. He didn't. Instead, he stalked through a tangle of bushes, and when Jay followed him, he realized there was a rough path through the barrier. Swearing as twigs and thorns caught on him, he stumbled through until at last he was on the other side. He cursed at the line of blood from a particularly nasty thorn that had pushed through his skin where his glove didn't exactly meet his jacket sleeve and was distracted until he looked up at what Luke wanted them to see.

184 | RJ Scott

Perfect.

Crooked Tree in the distance, nestled in and around the ribbon of river that carved its way through the valley. Even the mighty Blackfoot River looked thin and quiet from here. No viewer would think of the noise of the rushing river as it journeyed through the gorge. Beyond the ranch, the rolling plains stopped suddenly at the foot of the mountains. Each peak in the range was white tipped and ice-lined against the absolute clarity of the blue sky. Green areas indicated the tree lines and the cold in the air that bit his face underlined the wintry vista.

"Oh my God," he said reverently.

"I have photos from this same spot for each season. I don't just mean the four we know, but all the in-between seasons, like when summer gives way to fall and the light changes. The rains, the snow and the cloud formations. I must have hundreds." Luke turned to Jay with a grin. "Is this what you meant when you said you wanted photos that told a story?"

Jay didn't know what to say. His brain was running a million miles a minute. A slideshow on the website, prints to sell, the brochure pages he could create with such majesty and perfection in the photos of the ranch.

"Amazing," he murmured. Stepping forward, he only stopped when Nate grabbed his arm. Stumbling to a halt, he looked down and saw that he was at the edge of a long and sudden drop.

"Watch your step," Nate said softly.

Jay was overwhelmed at the panorama before him. He didn't think he'd ever seen anything so perfect in his life. Not even the sunset from the Hudson looking at the financial district was as beautiful as the scene nature had created.

"Used to be ice flows here, millions of years back," Luke offered. He crouched down and began framing photos. "Every time I look through the lens, I think of a new image, something I missed the last time I was here."

Nate made to move, but Jay didn't want to lose the touch of them side by side. He gripped Nate's gloved hand and held him steady. At first he thought maybe Nate would pull away, but when instead he tugged Jay closer to stand in front of him, Jay couldn't be more surprised. He relaxed back against Nate and exhaled gently.

"I love it here," Nate whispered. "I remember after we lost Mom and Dad, we came up here with their ashes. We were going to scatter them in the wind in the place they loved best. But we didn't. That day was May 20—ten days after they died. It was a beautiful cloudless day, but it wasn't right. We came back at the height of summer, in the cool days of fall, and we trekked here in the deep snow of that winter and again when spring promised a new year at Crooked Tree. Every time it wasn't the right time. Not one of us could agree. We finally agreed about five years later when Luke was a few days away from fourteen."

"I remember that day," Luke said softly. "We'd been to town, and Christmas was everywhere. I remembered Mom and Dad loved Christmas. I said something, Gabe agreed, and Nate brought us up here."

Luke placed his camera carefully in its case. He crossed to an overgrown part of the overlook and gently pushed back the undergrowth to reveal a small stone cross with a single word inscribed: "Todd." Jay wanted to ask why Luke quickly covered over the cross with the plants he'd gently moved. He didn't have to.

"They're part of the ranch, hidden there where no one except the people who care will know. They'll never be moved."

"That's beautiful," Jay whispered.

Luke went back to taking photos, and Nate tightened his grip on Jay. Together they watched as clouds gathered in the blue sky, then faded as they moved away. The shadows they cast on the ground were fascinating. For a long time, Jay collected visual memories he would be able to rediscover in Luke's photography.

"Thank you," Jay said to no one in particular.

"You're welcome." Nate pushed Jay's hair aside and kissed him on the side of his neck just below his ear. "I wanted to share it with you as much as Luke did."

CHAPTER SIXTEEN

When Jay walked into the kitchen at seven the next morning only Josh and Kirsten were there. Kirsten was lounging at the breakfast bar, staring bleary-eyed into a bowl of Cheerios, but Josh was dressed and excited. Today was day one of school. A quick glance at the clock to make sure he hadn't misread the time had irritation sparking in him that Kirsten wasn't dressed.

"Gabe's picking you up in thirty," he said firmly. He waited. For the explosion, the "I'm not going," and the added qualification that Kirsten hated him. Nothing happened, and that was somehow worse. She said something under her breath as she walked back to her room but in twenty she was actually back out.

Josh was bristling with excitement and clutched his school bag close. Verwood High School and Verwood Elementary shared the same site, separated only by playing fields. Gabe and Jay had said they would share getting the kids there, which was a win for both of them. Gabe was used to driving Luke in and welcomed the company; Jay was used to the frantic rush for buses and welcomed the quieter pace—apart from the fact that Kirsten was cutting things to the limit.

"Couldn't you wear something less—" Jay stopped himself. She was a teenager who, it seemed, expressed herself through the use of black. He needed to let her do her own thing. Saying anything to her, despite it being to warn her she'd be the center of attention and for the wrong reasons, meant he was turning into his father, and he hated that.

"I didn't do my eyes," she defended snappily.

Jay peered close. She was right; she didn't look like a panda. Her beautiful eyes were highlighted with a soft pink eyeshadow and none of her usual obsidian lines. She still wore black pants, shirt, and jacket, and her hair remained ebony with mixed streaks, but the eyeliner was one win in the ongoing battle.

"They look very pretty," Ashley said from the counter.

She was making lunches and had clearly showered and made a concerted effort to be up early. Usually it was Jay who dealt with the early morning rush, simply because he was up for work and Ashley had disturbed sleep that meant she often missed the alarm. It was good to see her up and happy.

Ashley handed out lunch, and finally the Sullivan family stood en masse around Gabe's Jeep—a newer one than Nate's but just as battered and beat-up. Luke sat in the front in smart jeans and a shirt, and Josh and Kirsten took the backseat. Luke actually turned to face the two of them, and was that just Jay's imagination, or did Kirsten blush?

What was it with the Todd brothers and their magnetic appeal to his family?

"Be good," Ashley warned her children.

Josh grinned; Kirsten rolled her eyes. Stereotype perfected.

"They'll love it," Gabe said with a smile.

The smile was directed at Ashley, who didn't really notice, given her worry about her babies going to a new school.

"I should go as well," she said vaguely. "What if Josh—"

"They'll be fine," Jay interrupted. He pulled her in for a sideways hug but couldn't fail to notice the disappointment in Gabe's face at the move. He probably would have jumped at the chance of having Ashley in the car with him for the journey.

The car left, but Jay kept cuddling her. He was anxious about the changes for the kids, but Ashley was the mom and he couldn't imagine what the depth of feeling was like for her. Then inspiration hit.

"I have a meeting with Marcus and the rest. Get some cookies together and maybe some of that cake. Let's go visiting."

He didn't give her time to argue, and within half an hour, they were knocking on Marcus's door. Sophie answered with a smile and ushered them in, offering them coffee. She took the proffered cookies and cake and opened the clear container to look closer.

"May I?" she indicated the contents.

"Please," Ashley said immediately. "They're just a small thank-you and probably not the kind of thing you're used to."

They settled at the table and Marcus joined them. Sophie arranged the cookies and cake on a plate along with forks and made coffee. It was only 8:00 a.m., but no one questioned cookies and chocolate cake as a staple breakfast alternative. Jay could have kissed them for their welcome and understanding.

"Oh my God!" Sophie exclaimed through a mouthful of cake. "This is sex." Then she placed a hand over her mouth to cover her grin. "Sorry, but I know cake. What do you use?"

"Use?" Ashley appeared confused.

"There's something in here... what is it?" She poked at the cake with her fork. "Orange?"

"I always add some zest—orange or lemon." Ashley smiled.

"Cake. Coffee. Want." Gabe announced from the kitchen entrance. He threw keys on the counter and crossed to the table.

"Gabe," Ashley said quickly, "were they okay?"

"Josh went straight in happy as a pig in slop. Luke took Kirsten in, and she appeared to be okay. They're fine."

"And they have my number—" Ashley realized what she had said and blushed. Just as Jay was about to remind her that yes, the school had every contact detail available: phone numbers, emails, even a barely used old Yahoo address Ashley still kept as a backup.

"Jeez, these are heaven," Gabe said around a mouthful. "Is this a new supplier to Branches?" he asked Sophie.

Sophie shook her head. "Ashley made them."

Gabe very deliberately took another bite and spent his time chewing before swallowing. "Ashley, not only are you gorgeous, but you make cookies from heaven."

Jay looked from Ashley to Gabe and back again. He was concerned that Ashley would do her usual and run. He waited, poised and ready to move quickly. Instead Ashley simply lowered her eyes, but not before Jay saw the laughter in them.

The front door slammed open and the last person to the meeting arrived in a flurry of cold air and muttered curses. Everyone stared as Nate rounded the corner. Something had gotten to him if the number of times he used the word "fuck" was anything to go by. He looked tired—as if he hadn't slept since he and Jay had separated last night.

"Damn alarm went off at three," he muttered in explanation. "Then at four and five. Threw it against the damn wall. I will kill Luke when he gets home."

"Who said it was Luke?" Gabe asked. Nate narrowed his eyes at him, but Gabe held up his hands in defense. "Wasn't me."

The meeting was short and sweet. Nate became less grumpy in direct proportion to the amount of unsweetened black coffee he drank. Gabe and Ashley spent the whole time pretending not to look at each other. Marcus listened to everything Jay had to say with a permanently pained expression, and Sophie held Marcus's hand.

"So. Initial thoughts on the website are we need more photos and testimonials as a starter. We drop online bookings because the system you use is clunky and difficult to understand and results, it would appear, in people leaving the site altogether. I suggest we have an availability calendar that I can keep up to date, as there isn't a particular person who deals with bookings. I also suggest that you actually get someone to do that for you, or one of you volunteers—bookings and paperwork, organizing deposits, helping the visitor from the very second they visit the site to the moment they set foot on Crooked Tree, and after, maybe—like a liaison for guests."

He looked up and mulled over which of the people around the table would balk at that idea. He didn't include Ashley in that; she was here to supply the cake and cookies. She looked directly at him and surprised the hell out of him.

"I'll do it for a while." Ashley glanced at Gabe and Nate, then back at Jay. "I'm good with people and organizing. I can cover it until you find someone permanent. I don't expect money for it either. I just want to do something, and I don't have any real qualifications like Jay has, because I was only fifteen when... y'know... Kirsten was born."

Unspoken was the "this will help me." Jay concentrated on flicking through his notes, unsure of what to say. He knew what Ashley was capable of—he'd always known—but it wasn't his place to say a thing.

"If we wouldn't be taking advantage, then that is a deal," Nate said firmly. "All in favor?"

Every single person raised their hand and it was a done deal. Ashley Sullivan was the new temporary guest liaison.

"I'll show Ashley the ropes," Gabe said immediately. "I have access to the guest bookings, emails, addresses."

Jay turned to Ashley. "Ash? Is that okay?"

"Fine," she said firmly.

That was bravery that no one besides Jay could understand. He squeezed her hand.

They talked a while longer about the ideas, and Jay lifted up one of the boards he'd created for the meeting. He propped it on a chair and stood back with a flourish.

Nate peered at it and pursed his lips in concentration. "What's that?" he asked finally.

"A theme—photos, inspiration, reviews, statistics, colors, everything that will make Crooked Tree sell. This is what I do." He pointed to the new logo in the middle. The stylized drawing of Juno was bold and simple. Behind it Luke had drawn a cowboy hat and melded the two into one perfect and pleasing shape. "Luke drew this, and I'm suggesting we okay it as a logo for all marketing materials. The website, menus in Branches, business cards, staff uniforms."

"I'm not wearing a uniform," Nate said, his tone leaving no room for argument.

"A T-shirt with the logo under your normal shirt should suffice, so that if you leave your shirt unbuttoned some way you could see it," Jay said. He looked at Nate thoughtfully. "Green to go with your eyes."

Nate stiffened in his seat and Jay wished he could pull back the words. For a second an uneasy silence fell. Gabe, thank fuck, rescued them all.

"Luke's logo is brilliant," he said. "I vote yes." He raised his hand and looked around the table expectantly. One by one everyone voted yes.

"Good," Jay said. "Now, color schemes."

"Do I have to be here for that?" Nate asked.

He was clearly restless, and the blame for that fell squarely on Jay's shoulders for the eyes remark. Jay tilted his head in thought. "Unless you want the others to choose pink or lemon in your absence, then yes."

Nate muttered something under his breath, but he didn't leave, so that was a good thing, and he actually joined in the heated debate about the virtues of green and white versus blue and white. In the end they decided to go for the colors of the sky—brilliant blue, with white to highlight.

Jay passed around a sheet of paper. "The website will be live in a week. Marketing materials will take much longer. This is a schedule of where I'm at, and I also need to add in talking to Sophie and the chef guy, who I've been told arrives today at some point."

"Sam Walters," Sophie said. "I'm picking him up from the airport at three."

"So that's about it for now. Any questions?"

No one said anything but Jay saw a lot of nodding. Evidently he was going about this the right way if what he was doing was being understood and agreed on. This was the easiest meeting ever.

Until Nate opened his damn mouth.

"Not bad considering you're city to the core and have no real idea about Montana," he said with a smile.

Jay wasn't sure what made Nate say that, or what the smile was about, but the heated lust Jay had been harboring gave way to a flash of temper.

"Thank you," he bit out. Meeting over, he left immediately. If he had to sit one more minute opposite Nate and think about what was happening tonight then listen to the sarcasm, he would punch someone. He needed some air and to get his head on straight. He only got a few feet away from his office when Nate's voice called after him.

"Hang on," Nate shouted.

Jay stopped in his stride and carefully spun on his heel to face the man who was playing him like a fiddle. "What?"

Nate walked to catch up. "Still on for dinner tonight? Seven?"

Jay crossed his arms over his chest. "What if you can't get over the fact I'm *city to the core* and have *no real idea about ranching in Montana*."

Nate frowned. "I didn't mean it like it sounded."

"You were damn well smiling when you said it. Anyway, how was it supposed to sound? Was it some veiled congratulation for a job well done?"

Nate looked baffled at Jay's huffing and puffing. "To be honest, you are from the city and you don't know much about ranching."

Jay opened his mouth to argue the point about what he was learning and how marketing was about understanding the product, and were Nate's employees not happy with what he was doing so far? Instead he shook his head in disbelief. Did this cowboy really not get it?

"City or not, you need me more than I need you," Jay lied.

"All I meant was that you were doing a good job. Considering—"

"Considering what?" Jay's temper was dying down and he was angrier with himself than he was with Nate. He shouldn't let it get to him when a client qualified his experience with a passive-aggressive "well done." Not every client had a grasp of marketing. Not every client had social skills. And after all, Nate was a *client*. Not a friend or a lover—yet—and Jay should remember that. If only he hadn't connected so deeply with the man, then nothing Nate could have said would hurt as much as it did. Mentally Jay smacked himself upside the head. Who the hell had he turned into? Kirsten?

"Considering the mess we were in before you came here." Nate spoke softly and his expression was apologetic. "I was just teasing you about the Montana thing, and the... look... I don't know. I'm sorry... and I'm not good at explaining myself. Are we still on for dinner?"

Jay's resentment and anger subsided entirely along with his short stay at teenagerville. "You were teasing me?" he asked gently.

"Uh-huh."

"Then maybe I can give you some lessons about teasing," Jay whispered low enough that Nate had to lean in. "Over dinner."

With that, he turned and entered his office making sure he shut the door firmly behind him. What was it about Nate that had Jay annoyed then smiling in the same goddamn minute? *Confusing freaking man.*

He hadn't moved away from the door, however, before it pushed against his bag, and he groaned before throwing it open, ready to confront Nate.

Ashley squeaked in surprise and took a step back. "Jay!"

Jay gripped his sister's arm and guided her in. She looked pale and a little unfocused. "What's wrong, Ash?"

"What did I do, Jay? What the hell did I just volunteer for?"

CHAPTER SEVENTEEN

The drive to dinner was kind of quiet. That was okay, because for some reason this place was up in the mountains. At times the road snaked back on itself perilously, and Jay really didn't want Nate losing concentration. Instead he focused on Nate's capable hands on the wheel, the way there were calluses on each thumb and how strong the hands looked against the worn leather.

When the Jeep stopped, night had already darkened the sky. The place they were in front of sat wide and solid, backed into the mountain.

"I bet they don't get many visitors with a journey like that," Jay said. He needed to hear the sound of his own voice to settle his nerves.

"I used a shortcut. There's an easier way up from town, but it adds thirty minutes."

"Which is a lot shorter than the year I lost off my life."

Nate smiled at him. "There are worse roads around here, y'know. Some better suited to horses."

Just the thought of going up that incline and those bends on a horse made Jay grimace. "I'll pass on that."

They got out of the car and crossed to the front door. The building was made to look like a rustic log cabin—a big one—but inside it was an eyeful of white linen and candles. Each table was private and screened from others' views, and the guy who came to seat them was dressed in smart jeans and a crisp blue shirt.

"Is this expensive?" Jay asked cautiously. He didn't have an enormous budget for spending on luxuries, especially considering the whole pile of books and DVDs he'd just ordered from Amazon for Josh.

"Not at all," Nate answered. "The place is owned by Saul from Carter's. Y'know the bar we went to? Good food here... you know what I mean."

Nate dipped his head and Jay lost another brain cell to lust. How could a guy with such a presence in the room look so damn cute all of a sudden?

The waiter took drink orders—Nate stuck to Pepsi and Jay chose beer—then handed over two menus. This was the best part of being out at a meal, looking at all the possibilities and deciding which one was best for the way he felt tonight. Jay was absorbed in the descriptions and when he glanced up, Nate already had his menu shut in front of him. Evidently Nate knew the choices.

"You already know what you want?" Jay asked. "What can you recommend?" He looked back down at the menu.

"Before we go any further with anything—and why I am telling you this I don't know, because it's not like you need to know if all we're going to have is a couple months of sex—but...."

Jay glanced up at Nate, who looked concerned. He sounded very serious too. What was he saying? Something about a few months of sex, *just* a few months? Jay was determined for it to last longer if they were good together. Jay was convinced he'd only heard half of it.

Something about telling Jay and whether or not he should do so. "Sorry?" he asked carefully.

Nate had the look of someone who was about to spill his guts, and Jay wasn't very good at knowing what to say in situations of high emotion.

"You remember you asked Marcus and me to fill out information and I refused to?"

Jay nodded, then waited for the rest of what Nate wanted to say.

"Well, I could have done it, but it would have taken a hell of a long time. I have dyslexia, which means my reading and writing isn't to a very high level."

"Really?" Jay looked down at the menu. "Can you not read this?"

"I could if I wanted to. I have a sheet I put over the words if I really need to see words. But I don't need to because you're right, I do know exactly what I want to order."

"Wow." Jay closed his own menu. "We think Josh has the same problem. He was fine at school when they began teaching phonetics—you know, the sound of words."

"You don't have to explain things. I can't read, but I'm not stupid."

"I didn't mean to—" Jay began, saw the teasing expression on Nate's face and shook his head. "*Ass.* Anyway, Josh had these headaches, almost migraines, and complained the letters on the page move. It's quite severe, but the school here has assured us he'll have the proper support. Do you think they will? Help Josh, I mean?"

Nate would know; he would have an idea of how the schools up here worked. According to both Josh's old and new schools, Josh was very young to be diagnosed and there was a ton of interventions and support that could be given. Jay had only yesterday ordered a whole pile of books and teaching DVDs so that he and Ashley could help him.

The kid had come back from school today with a grin on his face—ecstatically happy with the classroom, and the teacher, and the lunch place, and in fact everything. Kirsten had a faint smile, but she hadn't wanted to talk and had mostly hidden in her room. Apparently she would "talk later," which Jay knew was shorthand for "not at all." He guessed the only way he'd find out how his niece had done would be to ask Luke, which he planned to do the first chance he got to track him down.

"I don't know if they can help him."

The waiter came back at that moment, and they both ordered steaks with all the sides and trimmings. The only difference was that Nate wanted medium and Jay rare.

"I thought cowboys liked their meat on the hoof?" Jay joked as the waiter walked away.

Nate wrinkled his nose and shuddered. "Not all cowboys."

"So what do you mean you don't know? About the dyslexia thing."

Nate smiled wryly. "I spent my entire academic career avoiding school. If someone was trying to help, I'm not sure it stuck. Doesn't really matter. I do what I love, and anyway, my brothers got the brains and talent."

"That isn't true. You sound like you got nothing, but I've seen you with the horses."

"You saw me once," Nate scoffed.

"More than once," Jay argued, then watched as realization crept over Nate's face. Jay regretted there was no undo button in real life. Admitting he had been watching Nate was just this side of creepy.

Nate raised his eyebrows and smirked. "You been spying on me, Sullivan?"

Jay could make excuses at this point, about it being an accident that he'd visited on more than one occasion and seen Nate working. He decided honesty was the best policy. They were beyond games, and the line drawn in the sand that kept them looking and not touching was one Jay wanted to step over. "Cowboy, jeans, horses… what's not to like?" Jay leaned in to add the extra bit. "By the way, your ass looks damn gorgeous in those jeans."

There was the line, and Jay had well and truly crossed it. He'd made a personal statement about the man he was with and laid his intentions on the table. Nate blinked at him for a few seconds with his mouth open. After glancing left and right, he moved in the rest of the way and laid a soft kiss on Jay, who chased for more as Nate sat back. Then it was Nate's turn to say something. Jay's lips tingled with the sense memory of the kiss. What he wouldn't give for more—much more.

"Not as fine as yours," Nate muttered.

How Jay managed to concentrate on the food when it arrived, he didn't know. Thoughts of the kiss kept him on the edge. Swiftly focusing on kissing, and talking, was secondary to tasting the best steak Jay had ever eaten. The meat was soft and juicy, the fries crisp, everything perfectly seasoned.

"This chef could make a killing back home," he said through a mouthful of steak.

"I think she's fine and happy here," Nate answered immediately. His tone held a note of warning, and Jay looked up at him from his plate.

"I was joking. You think I want to steal her and take her to New York? I'm not going back there—not if you paid me."

"That's good to hear. Marcus will be pleased you're not leaving soon," Nate said quickly. In obvious embarrassment, he looked anywhere other than at Jay.

Jay reached over the table and covered Nate's hand with his own briefly. "What about you?"

Nate stared right back at him. There was open lust in his eyes. "Me too."

"Talking of Marcus, I had a question for you. You don't have to tell me, but why did Marcus's son not stay to work at Crooked Tree?"

Nate sighed and worried his lower lip with his teeth. "It's kind of a long story," he hedged.

"We have time," Jay encouraged. He got the sense something had happened, some falling-out that hung like a dark cloud over the whole of Crooked Tree. Marcus never spoke in depth about his son, and there were only a few pictures on the wall of the hallway that led to the bathroom. They were of a much younger Marcus with two boys.

"Ethan is the older of two boys. He's my best friend, but I haven't seen him since Christmas—he doesn't really visit his dad. He's six months older than me and we grew up here. The younger boy was Justin."

That explained the two boys. Jay attempted to recall if he had heard the name of the younger son before. "*Was* Justin? I haven't heard about a Justin. Does he not live around here either?"

"He's gone." Nate shuffled in his seat and ran a hand through his hair—something he did whenever he got agitated.

Not that I'm staring at him all the time.

Nate continued. "He left Crooked Tree in two thousand four when he was fifteen. He disappeared with another boy, Adam Strachan."

"The third family at Crooked Tree," Jay said with sudden realization. "The empty house is the Strachan house—Marcus briefed me on the absent partner."

"Oliver Strachan left a couple of years after Adam and Justin disappeared. His son Cole and Cole's wife, Mary, went with him. I don't think he could face the loss of his son, any more than Marcus could. They've never found Justin or Adam."

"Why did they leave?"

"We have no idea. One day they were here, the next gone. Henry was the last person to see them alive, up by the Silver Pond. It's a self-contained pool way up in the mountains, that's incredibly deep and long and fed by a natural stream."

"Alive?" Jay felt apprehension build inside him. He sensed this wasn't a good story. No wonder no one talked about it. "You say that like you think they're dead."

"Search parties went for days without seeing a thing. They dredged the pool as best they could, given the small access to the land and the water itself, but found nothing—no sign of the boys. Henry said he saw them swimming, and when he left they were alive and playing around. His words, not mine. I think that's why Marcus is so easy on him, like Henry is the last connection to his son."

"Shit."

"Yeah. There's never been anything to track. They didn't use their phones, or cards, or anything like that. It's like they vanished completely. It's the reason Ethan switched his plans for a ranching life to become a cop. He's never stopped looking for his brother and Adam."

"I'm sorry."

Nate shrugged. "It's nearly ten years since they disappeared. I want to think of them alive and enjoying their lives, and for some reason they can't contact us. But when I'm realistic, half of me is convinced they must be dead."

"Maybe you're right? There could be a reason they can't come home," Jay offered softly.

Nate nodded in agreement. "Marcus never really recovered. His wife had died a long time before, and he was alone. When Sophie arrived, she became his crutch. I wasn't around much to help him or to be a friend to Ethan." Nate went quiet and looked expectantly at Jay.

"Do you want me to ask you why you were a bad friend? Is that where this is leading?" Jay asked. "Because I can't for one minute believe you were."

"Our mom and dad were involved in a head-on with a semi just outside of Missoula, killed outright. I wasn't even out of my teens, and all of a sudden it was me and Gabe and Luke against the world."

Jay's heart twisted. Nate gave the details so matter-of-factly, but Jay sensed there was more to this story. "Then it's understandable," he said.

Nate gave a soft smile. "I know it was. I know not being here and working the circuit for extra money was what I needed to do. I had to abandon Ethan, but much worse than that, I had to leave Gabe and Luke for long periods at a time."

"They seem pretty well adjusted to me," Jay said. "I like Gabe. I like that Gabe likes Ashley."

"That's a lot of likes."

"What can I say? You Todd brothers seem to have a good effect on us Sullivans. I've noticed that Kirsten is wearing less makeup around Luke. You three have the Sullivans all twisted up." He laughed as he said it, then realization hit. "Wait a minute. You said 'the circuit.' Are we talking rodeo?"

"Bulls, cutting, some other stuff."

"A real-life rodeo cowboy. Why did no one tell me that?" He pressed a hand to his chest. "I feel like I've won the lottery." He fluttered his eyelashes teasingly.

"Ass," Nate deadpanned. "By the way, we'd like to increase your contract to the full year."

Jay's head spun at the sudden change in the conversation. Nate's green eyes were full of expectation. Seemed as if Jay had to make a decision there and then.

"Oh," he said instead, more to buy time than actually making an observation on what Nate had said. He was still focusing on the fact that his cowboy had been in rodeo. He so needed to check the Internet for pictures of Nate at a rodeo.

"You said just now that you weren't going back to the city," Nate pointed out. "So I thought now might be a good time to tell you. Ashley certainly doesn't want to leave, and the kids will be fine. Josh already loves us, and Kirsten will come around to the idea."

"You don't need to sell it to me." Jay held a hand up to stop Nate interrupting. "I always told Marcus you needed longer than two months. I'll stay the year. But that leaves us with one problem. If we do this thing—this friends-with-benefits, random-sex thing—a whole year? That could get messy."

"What?" Nate feigned innocence. "You mean we could grow to like it? What's the worst that can happen?"

"We fall in love? Get married. Have kids. Get a divorce?"

Nate's eyes widened. "Married? Kids?"

Jay huffed a laugh. "I was joking."

That set the tone for the rest of the evening. People arrived, people left, until on a trip to the bathroom, Jay realized they were the only ones left in the restaurant. A quick look at the time showed it was only ten. Things sure emptied earlier here than they did in New York. No one was hovering waiting for them to go, but when he got back to the table, Jay suggested they look at wrapping up the meal so that the staff could go home. Nate, damn him, insisted on ordering a dessert. Something about the place having fudge sauce that was out of this world.

"It can't be better than sex," Jay protested. He knew exactly what he wanted.

Nate leaned over to whisper. "It's close."

Jay stuck to his normal eating-out choice of fruit. Living with Ashley, he could get as many home-baked desserts as he wanted, and no restaurant ever made them as well as she did. Nate went for ice cream with so much chocolate fudge sauce on it that Jay was surprised he managed to eat it. But manage it, he did. Call it cliché, but Jay wanted to lean over and lick the chocolate right off Nate's gorgeous lips. They might be sitting in a secluded spot, but Jay wasn't sure what level of PDA Nate would go for. After all, the small kiss had been very brief.

"What's wrong?" Nate asked.

"Nothing."

"Then why are you staring at my face?" Nate scooped a finger across his lips and captured the tiny amount of chocolate before sucking his finger clean.

Jay's cock, which had been half-interested all evening, went to full and hard in an instant. He squirmed in his seat. "Fucking hell," he muttered. Nate looked at him innocently, but there was a gleam in his eyes. "Get the freaking check."

Somehow they paid the check without cracking stupidly insane grins—or rather, Nate managed. Jay couldn't stop smiling.

They left the restaurant as quickly as they could. All Jay wanted was some kissing and preferably right then. Nate pushed him up against the passenger door of the Jeep, so he evidently wanted the same thing. The kissing was wild and heady and everything Jay wanted. He could forget the world when he was in an embrace like this.

Nate used his knee to widen Jay's stance, and stooped to steal more kisses as he aligned their hard cocks. He cupped Jay's face in his strong, capable hands and held him still so that he could tilt his head and deepen the kiss. Jay lifted his hands and locked them around Nate's neck to anchor himself in the here and now. Kissing was his kink, and he never got enough of it with his partners. Hell, he recalled kissing his ex the sum total of three times, and that was only when Mark was drunk. How long they stood there, Jay didn't know, but he was happy to stay until the heat of Nate's kisses and his embrace was no longer enough of a barrier against the sharp cold.

Finally they had to move. The frigid air had seeped through Jay's jacket and his ass was numb against the cold metal of the car. He shivered, and that signaled the end of the session. Nate moved back and away a little, but not far enough to move his hands from cradling Jay's face.

"The parking lot is empty," Nate said with a smile. "I think even the staff have left."

Jay looked over his shoulder. Nate's Jeep was the single vehicle left and the only real light was the moon.

He laughed at the thought that the staff had left and gone past them without Jay hearing. Nate's kisses were potent. Smiling like idiots, they climbed into the Jeep. Nate started the engine and turned on the heater. Nate cracked the window a little so that the inside was warm but fresh. He leaned over for more kisses in the dark.

Jay moved his hand from knee to thigh and finally cupped Nate's erection firmly. What he wanted then was a taste of what was inside there, and without words he scrambled until he had the buttons popped and the hardness of Nate's erection in his mouth. He wriggled until he could push his own pants down and get his hand on his dick, and he pulled himself to orgasm to the sounds Nate was making above him. Moaning, begging, cursing—Nate was everything Jay wanted as a lover. Vocal, pushy, and hot.

"You're so... hot... *Jay*."

Jay was coming too and gasping Nate's name as Nate grabbed his cock and finished himself off into his hand.

"Fuck, Cowboy, that was—" Jay didn't have the words, but he punctuated what he said with a kiss. Wiping his fingers on his pants, he watched as Nate did the same. They buttoned up and sat grinning at each other like loons. In seconds they were close in the middle of the Jeep. The center console was in the way, but they clung to each other. Neither man's breathing was all that steady.

"I'm gonna be honest here," Nate drawled softly. "This is some scary shit."

Jay nodded, then kissed Nate one final time before moving back and belting himself in. His world had been well and truly rocked. "I know. But nothing is as scary as getting down the damn mountain now."

Nate chuckled as he belted himself in. "You want me to take the long way home?"

"Hell no. I'll just keep my eyes shut and *not* enjoy the ride."

True to his word, Jay didn't open his eyes once all the way back down to the road that led to Crooked Tree and only opened them once he could sense they were on level ground and the Jeep had stopped.

Nate had pulled up under the Crooked Tree sign and put the Jeep in park. He turned in his seat. "In a week we'll have guests, and my time gets to be stretched pretty damn thin. If we do this, it won't be a secret to the family. I don't play games, but I've never had a lover living on my doorstep before. What we have needs to stay between us in front of the guests. I'll get crabby and tired and smell like horses a lot of the time, but when I'm with you, I will give you 100 percent. I haven't been tested in a while, but I don't sleep around without protection. I guess I'm more of a top, but I'm okay with switching. It's just been a while—" He paused. "—a long while. And I want us to use condoms."

Jay nodded. "We're setting the ground rules?"

"Think we should, Jay."

"Okay, so, sometimes when I'm really focused on my work, I space out when I'm concentrating and I can get all arty and hands-on and talk to you for hours about market share." He wondered what else to add. "My family knows everything about me, even Josh. I have been tested since my asshole boyfriend was fucking around on me, and I'm lucky everything's fine. I won't push you over a table in front of guests, and I am definitely a switch. Oh yeah, and yes to the condoms." He added the last bit with his hand cupping Nate's obvious erection. "Until you get tested, big guy, then all bets are off."

Nate pushed upward to the pressure of Jay's hand. "So, we're doing this thing?"

Jay huffed. "If we don't do this thing soon, I may just come in my shorts." He palmed his cock and pasted the most hopeful smile on his face that he could. He wasn't lying—he'd been hard the whole way home, and every bump and slide had his erection pressing against his jeans. He was on the edge, constantly.

"Where do you want to…?" Nate looked up the dark road. "Mine," he said with finality.

CHAPTER EIGHTEEN

They snuck into the house in the hope that Gabe and Luke would be in bed. Thankfully Luke was in bed, and Gabe took one look at them, grinned, and made a show of putting in his iPod buds before retreating to his room.

"He's an asshole," Nate murmured with no heat. "You wait until he brings his next girlfriend here." He realized what he'd said. From everything he'd seen, Gabe was interested in Ashley, which led to all kinds of awkward.

"Let's not think about that." Jay appeared to read his mind. He smiled.

"Coffee?"

"No."

"Whisky? Brandy? Beer? Nate crossed off the list of what alcohol he knew they had in the house. "Pepsi?" he added.

"You really think I want a drink?" Jay teased. His brown eyes were filled with a mix of lust and mirth. An interesting mix.

"I'm in the back bedroom," Nate said quickly.

"Show me."

Nate didn't argue. He led Jay by the hand down the long corridor that separated his room from his brothers' rooms and the main living area. As soon as they were through the door, Nate locked it—in case his brothers thought it would be fun to fuck with him somehow.

"Do you have stuff?" Jay asked.

Nate thought of what he had in his drawer. Unless Gabe had been in there, they were pretty much set for the night. "Uh-huh."

They stood for a short while in the half-light of a small bedside lamp, and Nate abruptly felt unaccountably awkward. He'd done this before, so what was going on his head? Well, when he said *before*, he'd never actually had a guy here in the house. In his room. They'd always been hookups, casual and quick and commitment-free.

"How about I take my clothes off?" Jay said in an amused tone.

The words and the teasing tone had Nate galvanizing himself into action. He pressed Jay back against the nearest wall because all he wanted was up-close-and-personal time with the man who was stealing his breath with kisses. Placing his hands firmly on Jay's hips was the only way he could stop himself from dragging him straight to bed, but when Jay wrapped his arms around Nate's neck and locked his hands together, Nate nearly lost it there and then. A smooth move and he would have Jay under him on the bed. But that would mean interrupting the kissing, and that was so not happening... not for a long while. When was the last time he'd kissed like this? Had he *ever* kissed like this before?

They broke for air, and Jay shifted a little against the hard wall.

"Are you okay?" Nate asked quietly.

"Too many clothes," Jay said with a wry smile. "I want to kiss with no clothes."

Nate smiled. He could do that. In a flurry of hands and curses, they finally stood naked, apart from their shorts, and with low laughter stumbled to the bed and fell on it. Nate attempted not to land completely on Jay, but Jay wouldn't release him. With some wriggling, Nate was at long last in the cradle of Jay's spread legs, and they went back to kissing. Nate was so hard, and Jay matched him. Each time Nate moved, their covered cocks slid together. The friction was delicious and as necessary as breathing.

Jay slid his hands under Nate's shorts and curved his grip to hold tight. "Fuck, Nate," he murmured.

Nate looked directly into Jay's eyes and watched as they closed and Jay exhaled noisily.

"Off," Jay instructed, and Nate was happy to comply. He moved to one side of Jay and wriggled out of his underwear, waiting as Jay did the same.

"Gorgeous," he mumbled.

Too many words too soon and the intimate cocoon they were creating could be destroyed. Slim was a given—Jay wasn't the biggest of guys, but he was muscled and firm and his cock was gorgeous. Thick and a handful, and Nate was only interested in one thing: getting his hands on it, followed swiftly by his mouth. He concentrated on nibbling a path of kisses from throat to navel and inhaled the scent of shower gel on warm, smooth skin. He moved to pay attention to the skin stretched across Jay's hipbones, and Jay moved restlessly under the ministrations. Nate knew he was teasing Jay. He was so close to Jay's cock that it bumped his face, and he couldn't ignore the feel of the satiny-smooth skin any longer. For a few seconds, he simply tested the weight of Jay's cock. With his fingers covering the gap between his mouth and the curly hair at the base, he settled in to taste his new lover...

He was home. Jay's taste sparked on his tongue and his delicious demands were symphony enough to bring Nate's orgasm close.

"I want yours," Jay insisted. He softened the demand with a soft "Please."

Nate didn't hesitate. Awkwardly—and how could anyone make a sixty-nine look elegant? He maneuvered until Jay had his hands on Nate's cock and his tongue laving the end of it. *Faultless. Fucking, unbelievably, perfect*, and they brought each other to the point of no return.

"I'm—" Jay was evidently trying to warn Nate, and in a scramble Nate pulled from Jay's hold and twisted himself straight so that he could grab and hold both cocks together. With fluid movement, he began jacking them off. In a single blinding flash of white, his orgasm exploded from him. Jay was with him, moaning his release and forcing a fist into his mouth to stop any further sounds. Utterly spent, Nate slumped to Jay's side and, mindless of the sticky mess between them, pulled him close. They needed a break, but fuck, he had to be inside Jay—and soon.

"That was...." Jay said.

"Yeah...."

"Want you inside me."

"Later. I promise."

Sleep pulled at Nate, and he held Jay tight. He loved to cuddle, to hold, to feel another man's heartbeat next to his. Yes, he was home.

When Nate woke, the bed was empty and Jay was nowhere to be seen. Frowning, he leaned over the side of the bed. All of Jay's clothes were there, and it was 3:00 a.m. A noise from the bathroom had him turning in bed and relief flooded him when he saw the thin sliver of light under the door. He got up and knocked—a mutual masturbation session, however satisfying, didn't mean he was ready to jump on the guy if he needed private time.

"Yeah?" Jay's voice sounded strange. A little off somehow.

"You okay?"

"I'm fine," Jay said immediately.

Then Jay moaned low in his throat and Nate knew something was wrong. Had he hurt him? Hell, he didn't know his own strength sometimes! He didn't think he'd hurt Jay, but hell, what if he had? Frustrated at his stupidity, Nate pushed open the bathroom door and was confronted by a sight he never thought he'd see in his life. Shocked eyes met his, then the shock gave way to a small amount of defiance in Jay's expression.

Jay sitting on the floor, curled with his own fingers in his ass and lube dribbling in and around him.

"Jay?"

"What?" Jay snapped. "You look like you've never seen a guy get himself ready before."

Nate didn't know where to start with that one. What surprised him more? That no, he'd never seen a lover prep himself alone in a damn bathroom. Either he'd done it, or in the case of some of the casual stuff, the guy had already been stretched open. He crouched down next to

Jay, aware he was naked and waving his stiff cock in Jay's face, and also very aware that there was confusion in Jay's eyes. Carefully he pulled Jay's fingers from his ass and wiped them on the nearest towel. He helped Jay to stand.

"I'll do that for you," he said simply. "I'll make sure that when I push inside you, you're ready for me."

"I take care of it myself," Jay said. He sounded almost distant.

Sudden realization flooded Nate. "Did someone hurt you? Before?"

Jay flushed. "I've done my time in clubs and a relationship. I look after myself, and it's not the top's responsibility to stretch me."

"Who the fuck told you that?" Nate pulled Jay close and kissed him deeply before backing out of the bathroom, pulling Jay along with him. All the time he talked: "I love getting my partner ready, getting *you* ready. I'll suck you, play with your balls, and all the time my fingers will make you ready, stretching you and loosening you so that when I push inside, I won't hurt you."

"Nate. I just need to know that—" Jay stopped and lowered his gaze momentarily. He was a mix of embarrassed and ashamed.

With a powerful adrenaline rush, Nate hated whoever had hurt Jay. "Who hurt you?" he insisted.

Jay looked up, right at him, with defiance in his eyes. "Mark," he said. "He expected me to be ready, and when I wasn't, that was when it hurt."

Nate stopped the words with a kiss, Helped Jay to the bed, arranging him on his stomach. Grabbing the other lube from his drawer, he settled himself between Jay's spread legs. He knew what he wanted to do—touch and push and make Jay ready for him.

"You're so beautiful, so strong. Why would he want to hurt you? What was his excuse when you told him?"

"I never told him," Jay said quietly.

"Why?"

"Because he wouldn't have listened."

"I'll always listen."

All too soon he had Jay twisting below him, moving to get some kind of friction for his cock against the sheets. Nate loved the sighs that left Jay's lips, the insistent press back against Nate's fingers.

"I need more," Jay near whined. "More fingers, push harder inside."

Nate almost lost it then, pinching his cock until the urge to come all over Jay's back left him. He encouraged a pliant, sexy Jay to all fours. With as much lube as Nate had on his hands, he fumbled to get a condom on. He considered asking Jay to help for all of two seconds after seeing his dazed expression as he glanced back at Nate. Finally he had a condom in place and he pushed inside, waiting for Jay to relax around him, letting him in fully.

Jay keened and arched, then pressed back until Nate was so deep inside his balls were against Jay's. He tensed his muscles and sat back on his knees, pulling Jay with him. He didn't want this to be impersonal; he wanted to be able to kiss Jay, but he wanted him to be happy and safe.

Jay fell back into his hold and Nate braced him with one hand on Jay's hip and the other across his chest.

"Touch yourself," Nate said as he moved the hand on Jay's chest to tilt Jay's face close enough that they could kiss, messy and hard, then soft and needy.

"I'm close," Jay murmured. His eyes were closed and the kisses had become shallow, a simple exchange of breath and nothing more.

"Open your eyes, Jay," Nate begged, just as he had done at the bar when they danced. He wanted to see those gorgeous eyes focused on him, but when Jay tried to concentrate, he couldn't. He was loose in Nate's hold, completely at Nate's mercy.

"I can't," Jay whispered, and He was breathing harder.

The tightness of Jay around him was intense. They kissed awkwardly, sloppily, but it was enough, and when Jay stiffened in Nate's hold and breathed through his orgasm in silence, Nate couldn't stop his own in response. He fucked deeper and they kissed and he was coming so hard that it was difficult to support Jay. He waited for a second then managed to get himself out and settle them to lie side by side on the bed.

"I think I'm falling for you too far and too fast," Jay whispered. "It scares me."

The honesty cut through Nate like a knife, and he knew he had to be truthful in return. "I know I'm falling for you," he admitted. He added brokenly, "We can be scared together."

CHAPTER NINETEEN

When Jay closed the door behind him, Ashley lay sleeping on the sofa and didn't wake at first.

Jay's ass was sore, but he was grinning from ear to ear. Nate was going to be one hell of an addiction, and Jay knew it. For however long this lasted, he would enjoy every damn minute of it. He crossed to the kitchen for a glass of water, then checked all the doors.

"Hey," Ashley said sleepily.

"I was just coming to wake you up. You should have gone to bed, sis."

"I wanted to talk to you about your date," she said with a yawn. Stretching, she swung her legs to the floor. "Also, Lewis called. He's coming to visit this weekend."

Jay's temper rose at the mention of Ashley's ex and was a sharp reminder that not everything in his world was soft and sexy and fun. "What? He just announced it? He's supposed to give notice."

Ashley held up a hand. She didn't look devastated or angry or sad—she appeared strangely Zen about the whole thing. "I suggested he come this weekend. Crooked Tree opens next week and I want it over and done with before then. I won't have him ruining Montana for us."

Jay deflated. "How do you feel?"

"Sad for me. Happy for Josh that he gets to see his dad."

"He's not staying in this house," Jay said quickly.

"He's not staying at all. He's visiting and leaving. An early flight here, a cab from the airport, and the red-eye home. Seems that's all he can spare for his son."

She stood and wrapped her arms around her middle. Vulnerability filled her eyes and tension bracketed her mouth, and Jay knew he needed to leave the discussion until the morning. He hugged her before guiding her to her bedroom. "You seem to be taking it okay."

"Gabe was here when the call came in. It helped."

Gabe was here one hell of a lot. Jay wanted to be nervous about that, but if Gabe's presence had been enough to halt Ashley's unhappiness, He shouldn't fret. "We'll deal with it when he gets here."

Ashley smiled and climbed into bed.

Feeling suddenly very protective, Jay smoothed the covers over her, kissed her on the forehead. "Everything will be fine, he'll realize it's a long way and that Josh isn't worth it, and he won't visit again."

Of course Josh was worth it. Josh was the best kid, completely beguiling and utterly perfect, and being Uncle Jay to both Josh and Kirsten was the proudest thing in his life. Not for the first time, the overwhelming wish that Lewis wasn't a part of their lives had Jay's chest tightening.

He checked in on Josh, who was lying in his usual tangle of bedclothes. There was no point sorting out the quilt or sheets tangled around him. Within minutes anything Jay tried to fix would be half on the bed and half off.

Kirsten's door was open and Jay could see her light was on. He knocked, and only went in after she said it was okay. She looked young, sitting cross-legged on her bed with her Kindle on her lap.

"It's after four in the morning" Jay wasn't lecturing, not really, but his tone was serious. He expected the usual explosion of "Don't tell me what to do!" in response. He was surprised when it was actually something very different to that.

"I know," Kirsten admitted with a sigh. "I couldn't sleep. I heard Mom crying a bit earlier, and it got me thinking about stuff." She shrugged and closed her Kindle. "It doesn't matter. You're home now."

Jay was torn. Was this the sign that she wanted him to leave, or did the rather sad tone of her voice mean she wanted him to talk? Hell if he knew anymore.

"Night, then," he said carefully and turned to leave.

"You know we talked about my dad a couple times?"

Kirsten's soft question had him turning back. "Yeah?"

"Did you like him?"

"You've asked that before," he said carefully. "I did. I always said Martin was a good guy."

She mulled over his words for a second, and Jay took the opportunity to sit on the end of her bed. He sensed she needed to talk.

"Then why didn't he want anything to do with me?"

"He was fifteen, your mom as well. He wasn't grown-up enough. We talked about this. I don't know, maybe it got to be too hard."

"He's married now. Has two kids—one of them is ten, the other eight."

"How do you know that?"

"Google, Facebook," she said dismissively. "Though you and Mom said maybe I would want to, I've never wanted to meet him, you know. Not even when he wrote to me, because I have everything I want right here. You and Mom and Josh. Who needs Martin I'm-So-Perfect Johansen. Did you know he has a degree in engineering? And a big fuck-off house in the burbs?"

"I didn't."

She pulled her knees up and wrapped her hands around them. She looked so damn young with her hair scraped back from her face and her skin devoid of any makeup.

"Sometimes I look at Mom and think if she hadn't had me, then she could have gone to college or got a job that wasn't based around being a mom. And maybe you would have got higher grades in school if you weren't babysitting me."

"You do?" Jay was shocked. Kirsten had never said anything like this before. They'd talked about the absent-father thing when Martin had written to her for her tenth birthday, then again on her thirteenth. Jay had no idea that she worried about his damn school grades or how being here may have affected Ashley.

"Yeah."

"Is this your emo side talking?" As soon as the words left Jay's mouth, he wished them back. That was about as appropriate as asking her if she was on her damn period.

He was relieved when all she did was grin at him. "Yeah, I'm pulling all my best teenager moves," she said.

"I shouldn't have said that. I'm sorry."

She huffed a small sound that indicated it was nothing. "I still have the letters and I reread them, and I wonder if I'll ever be able to think of him as anything like a dad."

"Maybe one day you will," Jay said softly. "There's one thing, though. You have to know that your mom and I never for one minute regretted having you in our lives. We loved you from the minute we saw the first scan. So don't go around thinking otherwise. Okay?"

"I'm going to read the letters. I thought about maybe writing him back."

"Good idea." Jay moved so he sat next to her with his back against the headboard. He opened his arms and she cuddled in for a hug. The move reminded him of when she was smaller and loved spending time cuddling with him or Ashley. He missed it.

"So Gabe was over this evening," she said softly. "I like him. He's normal. He's not a jock who wants to erase me, or abusive and wants to hurt Mom and Josh. It's like he's too normal, though."

Jay waited for more explanation. He had to wait a while.

"Uncle Jay, do you think he's pretending?"

"To like your mom?" Jay clarified.

"That, me and Josh. He played with Josh and helped me with a math assignment. So, is he pretending?"

"I've only known him a few weeks," Jay said. "But he and Nate and Luke seem like genuine guys. And if he makes your mom happy…." He deliberately ended there.

"I like Luke as well," Kirsten admitted. "He stood up for me when these two boys started in on me about my hair."

"That's cute."

Kirsten smacked him on the arm. "That is *not* cute. Seventeen-year-old boys are not *cute*." She snuggled in closer and yawned. "Are we okay for money?"

Jay thought about the small bank balance that was all he had left from his savings. He was due to be paid next week, but he had a couple thousand in reserve and no real expenses. "What makes you ask that?"

"I was thinking of getting my hair stripped of color. I'm kinda fed up with it now. Just want it blue-black, but if I do it myself, I'll ruin it."

"Jeez, Kirst, I'd take out a loan for that," he joked. "But yeah, money is cool. I'll drive us all into town on Saturday before Lewis gets here and you can get it done. Love you," he added.

"Love you too," she replied with a squeeze, then extricated herself and wriggled under the covers.

Jay smiled. He hoped that maybe this was the start of a new stage in their relationship—a more adult one where teenage tantrums and emotions settled down. He left her room and pulled the door shut.

He remembered being sixteen with great clarity. Kirsten had been two and he was still at home with Ashley and his parents, who were still in shock even two years after their daughter had a baby just before her own sixteenth. Added to that he came out as gay, and suddenly they couldn't find a place for their offspring to live fast enough. Jay had grown up quickly and in a city away from his parents with the only family he wanted.

He wondered if Nate would understand that, and how the hell he would attempt to start explaining their bond.

CHAPTER TWENTY

The next time they met was Monday, on something Nate called "the horse run."

Nate had explained to Jay that the horses he'd had been introduced to so far were only a small part of the total herd at Crooked Tree.

"But you have a lot of horses," Jay had said worriedly. Was Crooked Tree paying him to do their marketing only to blow money they didn't have on horses they didn't need? Was Nate just too soft and hadn't wanted to get rid of any horses when the ranch hit bad times?

Nate laughed that soft, low, sexy growl of a laugh that had excitement curling in Jay's belly. "We have six families booked in. On average mom, dad, and two kids, a minimum of twenty-four horses for them plus pack beasts to carry clothes, equipment, bags, and additional mounts for the inevitable strains and lameness."

"The riders hurt the horses?" Jay hated that thought.

"They don't mean to, but inexperienced riders are more likely to put horses off-balance. Add in that if you're successful with what you're doing for us and things go according to what we're planning we'll have all the cabins full, then I need to be able to cover the horses required. We schedule and plan as much as we can, but at the end of the day, along with the fishing and hiking, we have the horses as our selling point. So we have a big remuda tucked away up near the canyon where the cattle are kept, and it's shared with a couple other places."

Jay wasn't sure what he thought about that. Everyone rode the horses stabled there? "So who else rides the ones in the stables, like Diablo and Juno? Do the guests?"

"No one, 'cept the family and now you."

"So, when do you bring the horses here?"

And that question was what had led to today. The annual "bring the horses back to Crooked Tree ride," as Jay called it. Jay was on Diablo, utterly sure that this would be the end of his ass. He was already tender from the night before last and faced an hour in the saddle there and another hour back.

"You going to be okay?" Nate asked him seriously.

Jay raised a single eyebrow to indicate he was perfectly fine and that Nate should not draw attention to what they had done. Although the fact he and Nate were lovers wasn't a secret. He'd told Kirsten, and though Gabe had been more than aware, Nate had apparently talked at length about it to his brother on their way to Helena to sign contracts for the coming year.

Part of Jay wished that he and Nate had woken in each other's arms and somehow spent yesterday together. They couldn't, and Jay immediately assumed everything would be awkward.

It wasn't.

They met for dinner at nine, Nate exhausted from driving the two-hundred-mile round trip on just a few hours' sleep, and Jay equally tired from all his worrying about what things would be like. They fell into bed in each other's arms as soon as their heads hit the pillow.

Then it was morning and this ride was happening and Jay was abruptly thrust into the whole horses and roundup issue. Ashley was meeting them with the kids at the remuda, which could be reached by Jeep, but Jay was way too proud to join them that way. *I will do this.*

The roundup was a sight to behold. Most of the mounts were happy to see them. The wrangler up there, a man who must be close to retirement, named Duncan, helped them to cut out the Crooked Tree horses to take them back down. The action, the lassoing, and the general cowboy goings-on were more than Jay could take on many occasions. What with the ache in his ass and an erection that refused to die, he wondered if his zipper would hold.

Ashley arrived with the kids, and Gabe lifted Josh up to sit in front of him on Lightning. Josh didn't hesitate, but Jay waited for Ashley to freak out. She didn't. She stared at Gabe with a look of naked longing written in her expression.

Is that how I look at Nate?

She clearly trusted Gabe with her youngest child. Even Kirsten was up on a horse.

Luke had been giving Kirsten pointers, and the two youngsters were practicing figure eights by the corral. Luke would stop every so often and take photos of the horses, of his brothers, of Jay, the kids, and a lot of Kirsten. Not for the first time did Jay consider what Luke saw in his lens when he looked at Kirsten, Was it an attraction? Friendship? Fascination? As for Kirsten, she often looked at Luke with hero worship.

230 | RJ Scott

"Look, Uncle Jay, I'm a real cowboy!" Josh called out.

Jay looked over and smiled at Josh, who was gripping hard to the reins and helping Gabe guide Lightning in his work.

They made it back to Crooked Tree as dusk began to darken the sky. Josh had insisted on riding the whole way back with Gabe, and he spent the whole time chatting about what he would need to do to become a full-time cowboy. Jay shook his head as he thought about what Josh's dad would say to that idea. Lewis was all about his boy being a tough lawyer like he said he was himself. Not that Lewis was a lawyer, given he'd been disbarred after doing jail time for a felony.

There was no way Josh was ending up anything like his father. Not if it was the last thing Jay did in this life.

Jay dismounted, and everyone encouraged the returning horses into the large corral that spread out behind Branches and up to the Todd house.

"You know, we should have a viewing area cut into the corral for casual visitors."

"That would cost money," Marcus said immediately. He'd been pretty quiet since they came back from the roundup. He hadn't gone with them, and he wore a permanent expression of worry.

"Not much," Jay insisted. "We'd cut away some of the existing fences, make a path from Branches, and build some kind of area where people from the restaurant could pat the horses."

"Pat the horses," Marcus spluttered. "They're not dogs."

"Not sure how that would work," Gabe added his dissent, although it was quieter and more reasoned. "We wouldn't want strangers here for the day feeding the horses from their plates."

Jay frowned. Gabe had a point—a valid point—but Marcus jumped on it with enough venom for Jay to turn scarlet in embarrassment.

"Jesus, kid," Marcus snapped. "You don't know nothing about horses! Look at you, all twisted and sore from two hours' riding, and you want strangers mauling the stock?"

"No, I—"

"It won't work. Just stick to computerin'."

Nate chose that moment to walk around from where he'd been tending to the horses. He stopped as he realized he'd evidently ended up in the middle of some kind of Marcus meltdown. "What?" he asked, looking first at Gabe, then Jay, then pointedly at Marcus.

"Me 'n' Gabe think City here should stick to his computerin'."

"I never said that," Gabe defended.

"What's wrong, Marcus?" Nate looked directly at Marcus and was using that placating, I-understand-everything tone.

Marcus huffed and turned his back. "Knows nothing about people or horses," he muttered.

"Jay?" Nate asked.

Jay was still open-mouthed in shock at the vitriolic attack and realized he wasn't talking, thankful when Gabe did it for him.

"Jay came up with the neat idea of building a viewing platform so casual visitors could see the horses. Go on, Jay."

Nate turned to Jay and waited.

"Well, we could make a path, cut away some of the fences, build a small platform, and close off the fence again."

Silence. Everyone stared at Nate and waited. Marcus had turned back with a confident smile on his face.

"That's a really good idea," Nate said finally. "Long as we put signs up warning not to feed them, or maybe offer feed specifically to give to the horses. We could check the insurance, and think about whether the horses could end up nippy and pushy."

"City'll—"

Nate interrupted Marcus. "I think *City* has a point. I'll cost it up and see if I can get a volunteer or two to help."

"Me," Gabe offered.

"And me," Luke said.

"I'll paint," Josh said.

"I'll make the signs," Ashley added.

Marcus looked from Nate to Jay and back again, shrugged. "I was just worried about the horses," he said to Jay and held out his hand in apology.

Jay shook it. "The horses are our priority."

After a while, everyone cleared out until it was Nate and Jay left in the horse barn, leaning with their boots on the first rung of Diablo's stall.

"Thanks," Jay murmured.

"It's a good idea. I have been listening to you, y'know."

"I don't want you agreeing to something if it's only because we... y'know."

"Slept in the same bed? Made love?" Nate offered in a matter-of-fact fashion.

Jay loved that his cowboy was so direct. Still, it didn't stop his blushing. "Yeah."

"As I told you, it's a good idea and a way to bring in some more business. You could maybe build up some words on the website about Branches, offer coffee and things like that, alongside the idea of seeing the horses in action."

"Changing the subject, you think Marcus is okay? He seemed off today."

Nate shrugged. "We're not long for Justin's birthday, or what would have been, or what is. I don't know how to explain that. He's on edge, is all."

"Losing a son must be awful." Jay didn't have the words to explain how he felt.

"Yes, it was, and it is. He's not a healthy man either. Said there's something wrong with his blood, I don't know what that means, but some days he looks pale."

"You should maybe ask him if he's okay?"

Nate nodded. "I know. I think maybe I'm scared to know there's anything wrong. What if he dies? What if... I'm left here?"

"I'm sorry, Nate."

"It is what it is." Nate straightened his shoulders. "I'll talk to Marcus or Sophie, get a real feel for what is happening to Marcus."

They stood in silence for a while, and then Jay wanted to talk about the other part of today: the horses.

Jay turned to face Nate and winced as he did so. "That was fun today."

Nate leaned in and whispered, "Doesn't look like it was fun for your ass."

Jay pressed a quick kiss to Nate's nose. "Maybe it needs a kiss better," he deadpanned.

Nate drew him up for a heated kiss, grabbing handfuls of ass and jeans. "I can do that," he promised with heat. "Let's start now."

CHAPTER TWENTY-ONE

Friday was the calm before the storm. The cabins that needed fixing were fixed, cleaned inside and out, and the cleaning crews left with the schedule in place for their return each week at changeovers. The path from Branches had been created—a rustic collection of wood and stone—and the viewing area was very much in keeping with the rest of the ranch. The website went live, and Jay found himself shut in his office for three straight hours waiting for the site to work properly. By the time he realized the problem was due to a missing backslash in the URL, he was tense and irritable.

The door opened and he didn't look up. Ashley had brought him coffee, muffins, and sandwiches, and Jay guessed she was here offering some other nice thing to take the edge off his irritation.

"Dinner is ready," Nate said from the door. He closed it and crossed to stand behind Jay. "You look tense."

"Just technical shit," Jay summarized. He leaned back into Nate and nearly melted when Nate began to massage the tension from his shoulders. "The website is live and finally working."

"That's good. You stopping now?"

Jay tilted his head back to look up at Nate. The faint smell of horses and fresh air clung to his lover's skin and he wanted nothing more than to be held and kissed. "Are you?"

"I'm done for today. Nothing more I can do. Sam cooked, and when he cooks you don't turn it down."

"I haven't met him properly yet. Be good to meet the man with the reputation that precedes him. I need to talk menus with him, and maybe promote the restaurant on the website. He could get behind publishing menus on there as well. I can't wait to meet him."

"Hmmm," Nate made a noncommittal noise. "He's a *very* good-looking guy."

Jealousy spiked in Jay at the emphasis on the word "very," and he pushed himself up and out of his chair before turning to face Nate. "You think so?"

"Dark hair, slim, gorgeous face. Yeah, he's easy on the eyes. You'll like the look of him."

"Have you and him… y'know?"

"God, no. He's so the opposite of what I like. He's all fire and temper. I like life in a guy, but Sam is *way* too much."

"Is he a cowboy?"

"A chef, I told you that—"

"Is he over six feet?"

"He's shorter than you."

"Then nope. I think I'll stick with you." Jay smirked.

Nate returned the smile with one of his own. "You'll be okay making do?"

"I'll try," Jay offered, tongue in cheek. "Now, before we go meet this short spitfire, I want a kiss."

They spent a long time exploring the taste of each other and only moved apart when the door to the office flew open and Josh was there.

"Mom says you gotta come now," he said importantly.

Jay scooped up his nephew and carried him over to Branches, holding him by the legs and dangling his head. He entered the restaurant that way and every eye turned to him, Josh, and Nate as they entered.

"You're late for my food again and I'll kick your skinny ass, Nate," a voice snapped from the left.

Jay looked that way and found the object of his and Nate's discussion. Samuel Walter, chef, was exactly as Nate had described him. Five eight or nine with a scowl on his face and temper flashing in his icy blue eyes. He narrowed said eyes at Nate, including Jay in the appraisal, and crossed his arms over his chest. He was obviously waiting for an apology, and Jay stifled the instinctive reaction to laugh. Instead he decided to go the way that smoothed the waters.

"My apologies," Jay said evenly. "I've heard a lot about your food."

"Sit," Sam added.

Jay did as he was told when Sam softened the order with a smile. Jay was opposite Nate and next to Ashley, and the conversation was easy. Gabe had taken the seat on the other side of Ashley and they were talking low and soft. Ashley had taken to her temporary role with enthusiasm, and Jay didn't need a brother's intuition to see that she was really interested in Gabe. Past interested, actually.

Jay could see the way they looked at each other. Tomorrow would be the litmus test. Lewis was arriving in less than twenty-four hours, and while Josh was visibly excited at seeing his dad, Ashley was beginning a retreat into her shell again, which would only reverse when the visit was over.

Dessert was a concoction of cake and chocolate and was nearly as good as something Ashley would make. He smiled to himself but should have known he'd be spotted.

"Something funny?" Nate asked.

"Nothing," Jay said immediately. "I'm enjoying dessert."

They grinned at each other, and Jay wondered if he could get any sappier. Next to him, Ashley's and Gabe's voices were getting a little louder. Jay's smile was replaced by a frown at the change in their conversation. More so when Ashley pushed her chair back.

"You think I don't know that?" she asked with tears in her voice. Everyone looked at her.

"Are you okay, Mom?" Kirsten asked quickly.

"I'm all right. I just need...." Her voice trailed off and she left the restaurant. Gabe followed her immediately, but Jay could see his sister was crying and he wasn't letting whatever had just happened undo the weeks of her looking happier and finding herself. He was out of the restaurant and over to the bridge as quickly as he could. Ashley and Gabe stood opposite each other and their body language spoke volumes. Gabe apparently wanted to touch Ashley, but she was having nothing to do with it. She stepped back until she was pressed against the bridge fencing. Gabe stepped forward just as Jay reached them.

"I didn't mean what I said," Gabe said. He raised his hands in defense, palms up.

Jay was between his sister and Gabe in an instant. "What's wrong?"

Gabe backed away.

"He didn't do anything," Ashley said in a monotone. "It's not his fault."

Ashley's tone, the one where she took the blame for things, was back. Jay could punch Gabe to the ground for whatever the idiot had said. Jay should have been watching this budding romance more carefully.

"What did you say?" he asked.

"I said.... Look, I'm sorry. I didn't know what else...." He stopped miserably.

"A sentence might be a good place to start," Jay demanded.

It didn't matter how miserable Gabe looked, he had upset Ashley, and that needed dealing with.

"I said if Lewis touched a hair on her head, or one of the kids, that he would know what it was like to feel fear. But I didn't mean it for real. Not like that."

"Jesus," Jay snapped. "So you're following Ashley around like a lovesick puppy and you know what happened to her and yet you still think bringing violence into her life is the best option?"

Gabe blanched. "I didn't mean it." He contradicted himself. "God, I did mean it. I'm falling for Ashley. I want to…"

Jay ignored the declaration of love which, judging by the sharp inhalation of Ashley's breath, was news to her. "Want to what?" he snapped.

"…protect her. And the kids. Josh. I want to look after her."

Gabe looked utterly broken and confused. Jay counted to ten before he continued. He had experience with what had happened to Ashley. He'd seen it unfold and he'd made mistakes with how he talked to her. This was all new to Gabe and Jay needed to take a step back and remember that. Guilt niggled at him—he should have taken Gabe to one side and talked to him, but he'd been too involved with his own sex life to remember he always put his family first.

"She *has* people looking after her," Jay said patiently. "She has me, Kirsten, and Josh. *We* are her family. She needs something different from you. For her to love you, she has to be able to tell you what it is that she does need."

Jay waited for Ashley to say something from behind him. Three words... *I want Gabe... I need Gabe...* whatever. Some indication that she felt she was in the right place to return Gabe's affection.

"I did it wrong and I'm sorry." Gabe squared his shoulders and stepped to the side of Jay so that he could see Ashley. "I can stay out of your way tomorrow. I won't cause trouble by going all protective big-man on you."

Jay turned to his sister. "Ash?" he asked gently.

"I'm all right, Jay," she said firmly.

"Talk to Gabe, then." *Don't lose everything that's changed in you over the past few weeks.*

Ashley nodded. She looked around, probably to check if Josh was in earshot. It didn't matter what she thought of Lewis, he was still Josh's father. "I wish Lewis didn't have to come. I hate him."

Jay pulled his sister into a close hug. That was the first time he'd ever heard her use such defined emotion where

Lewis was concerned. It had always been love before, suddenly there was hate. He was both pleased and terrified. Ashley didn't have the capacity to hate as he did, and how she had come to this point was hard to see.

"Are you going to be okay? I need to go back for Kirsten and Josh. Are you coming in with me?"

She shook her head, which was difficult given she was in a hug with him. "I need to talk to Gabe."

"So it's real, then?" he whispered into her ear. He felt her relax in his arms.

"Yes," she whispered back.

"You realize we're going to be dating brothers."

He heard the smile in her voice when she replied, "That'll be a first."

Jay went into the restaurant and didn't look back. He was convinced that Gabe was the first guy Ashley had been interested in who would treasure her and treat her right.

As long as he doesn't try to fix everything.

Josh and Kirsten looked up at him when he walked in.

"Are Mom and Gabe arguing?" Kirsten asked.

She apparently didn't care that she was sitting at the table with Gabe's brothers and friends. Only Jay would be able to pick up on the fear in his niece's voice.

"No," Jay said gently, and sat back down to finish his coffee. "They're good."

Enough said. He noticed that Sam had disappeared from the table. "Where's Sam? I need to talk to him about the menus."

Silence. Then a snigger from Josh. "Kirsten said Mom makes a better chocolate cake than him. He disappeared. Think he's sulkin'."

"Kirsten?"

She shrugged. "It's true," she said. "I want people to know what she can do. I'm proud of her."

"As you should be," Sam said from the doorway to the kitchen. He had a pad and a pen in his hand. "So tell me what she does differently."

The tension was broken. Apparently Kirsten hadn't pissed off the resident chef—merely stirred his interest. Everyone was back to chatting about the ranch and the last week before opening, the website, and all the other myriad bits and pieces that made this place what it was.

"Everything okay?" Nate asked Jay directly.

"It's good," Jay said.

And for the first time in a few years, he meant it.

CHAPTER TWENTY-TWO

Nate sighed; Gabe couldn't make it more obvious if he tried. His brother had set out to fix fences around the restaurant and Jay's office at the same time as Lewis was due to arrive.

Nate frowned as he contemplated exactly what trouble that could cause. "You can't stay around here," he said.

"The fences need fixing," Gabe said immediately.

"They do, but you don't have to do them today."

With a huff of defeat, Gabe dropped the post he had been wielding as if he were some kind of Highlander about to toss a caber. "Josh is so excited. You know I'm over there every evening. We were reading last night, and he's doing so well. Josh stopped the work and told me how every time his dad visits, he gets a present. I'm sitting there helping him with spelling, and he's talking about iPads."

Nate nodded. "How is his reading coming along?"

"Slowly." Gabe crossed his arms over his chest and leaned back against the older, broken post. It moved a little, but Gabe didn't seem that concerned about ending up on his ass on the ground. "Ashley and I try with him every night and do the exercises. Jay does the same thing with him. It's only been a couple weeks and we have a ways to go, but we'll get there and teach him the coping strategies he needs."

"Kirsten told me you helped her with her math homework."

Gabe shrugged and dipped his head. "Same as I would Luke."

"What about Ashley? What are you helping her with?"

Gabe punched Nate on the arm. "Nothing I'm sharing with you, big brother."

"There—you see. You have your answer. You're feeling sorry for yourself and worrying about Ashley, and you're getting all mixed up, when Lewis is only going to be here for a few hours, give his kid a present, and leave. You get the good parts—sharing Josh's successes, and Kirsten's, and you get the best chance to be in Ashley's life."

"I'll become the boring guy who does all the dad things," Gabe said quickly in response. He immediately dropped his arms to his sides and realization spread across his face. "Oh my God. I think I want to be that guy."

Nate hugged his brother. His job was done.

Lewis arrived with very little fanfare. When the cab pulled up in the parking lot, it was anticlimactic.

"That him?" Nate asked. They were standing outside the office together, and Jay was grateful for his comforting presence.

"Yeah."

"He's kind of short," Nate observed.

"You don't have to be tall to hit your wife and kid."

Jay spotted Ashley walking out to meet Lewis, and she was holding Josh by the hand. This was his cue to go join them. With a last squeeze of Nate's hand, he released the grip he'd had on him and walked briskly down to join his sister and nephew before they reached Lewis.

"Hey, Josh," Lewis called as they walked closer. The cab turned and exited the parking lot, disappearing down the road leading back to the entrance.

"Hey Dad," Josh muttered.

Lewis crouched down and held out his hands. Ashley glanced at Jay before reluctantly letting go her hold of Josh.

Josh hugged back but pulled away quickly. He hadn't seen his dad since he was little, just had the odd phone call and they'd exchanged photos.

"I have a present for you," Lewis said. He passed a suspiciously iPad-shaped box to Josh, who took it eagerly.

Poor kid was being bought, but Jay said nothing.

Josh ripped off the packaging. "Cool, Dad," he said enthusiastically.

"Go inside and charge it up," Lewis said firmly. "I need to talk to your mom. Maybe your uncle Jay could take you."

"Josh is perfectly capable of going to his new home alone." Jay waited for the comeback, but there was none.

"How are you doing, Ashley?" Lewis asked as soon as Josh was out of hearing range.

"I'm happy," she said carefully. "We're happy."

"I want you to know, Ash babe, that I changed. When I was inside, I found God and I know it was wrong what I did to you and Josh."

"Bull. Shit." Jay said and added a snort of laughter. "You found God? Where? In the bathrooms?"

Lewis stiffened in protest, but he said nothing. He simply inclined his head. Apparently he was acting the part of "new guy" and being patient was his main facade. Jay knew for a fact that behind that first layer was the real Lewis.

"It's always good to have faith," Ashley said.

"I knew you'd realize that," Lewis responded. "You always did have such a way of seeing the world. All innocence and light and forgiving nature. I didn't mean to hit you after I left jail, it was residual anger."

"Residual anger?" Jay said. He couldn't believe what Lewis was saying.

"Faith won't make me forgive you, Lewis. You drove my daughter to near enough live at her friends' houses because she was so scared, and you knocked Josh unconscious. I don't care what you did to me...." She stopped, and Jay placed a hand on her arm in support. "No," she began again, "that isn't right. I do care what you did. You ruined me, and when I actually have a chance at happiness, all I can do is mistrust the man."

"Ashley—"

"Enough, Lewis. You have three hours with Josh. You're not taking him off Crooked Tree, and he knows that. He also knows to shout if you raise a hand to him."

She turned on her heel and headed to the house. Jay spotted Gabe hovering near their home and Gabe nodded.

There was no conscious decision that one of them could keep an eye on things, but between them they would.

Jay went to his office, and Sam caught him as they passed Branches.

"You want that meeting now?" Sam asked. He was dressed in scruffy jeans that were nearly white with wear and had holes in all the strategic places. His T-shirt proclaimed "Gayer than the Volleyball Scene in Top Gun," and he carried an empty bucket.

"Not if you're busy."

Sam shook his head. "I was cleaning the kitchen from top to bottom, but I've finished now. My staff will be in on Wednesday, so I wanted it done."

"Okay, when?"

"Now? I'll get a shower and be over in twenty with coffee."

They parted ways, Jay to his office and Sam to his small apartment in the eaves above the restaurant. Jay settled at his desk with the paperwork for the brochure spread out all over. He attempted to get a feel for this final check on the main wording. Carefully he tacked each page in order up on the board and stood back to admire the work so far. Luke's photos were stunning and captured every single image Jay had in his head. He shuffled a couple of the photos and considered what was missing. The words he had already, but he had the idea to interview Nate, Gabe, Luke, Marcus, Sophie, Sam—even Henry—and the others who worked there. Quotes from those at the center of it all would be the icing on the cake.

"You want some beauty shots of food?" Sam said from behind him, causing him to jump. "Sorry, you were in a world of your own."

Jay quickly pointed out the three pages dedicated to Branches. "I have some words about Branches, but if I can I'd like to add something about you and your ethos, maybe a quote or two? I need something simple: a more elaborate dinner, maybe the range of wines you have?"

"I can get something done so you can shoot."

"I'll get Luke to talk to you about a good time to take the photos." Jay indicated the photos on the wall. "These are all by Luke."

"Wow. He's good." Sam inspected the one closest to them and nodded thoughtfully. "Talking of a Todd brother, you and Nate...." His expression was questioning.

"We are," Jay said.

Sam made a motion like writing with a pen on paper. "Crosses that one off my list," he said with a chuckle. "Is that everything you needed to talk to me about? 'Cause if it is, that was the quickest meeting on record. Don't you want to check my menus, fiddle with prices, or anything else?"

"No," Jay said directly. "I'm not here to change anything that works. You have guests coming in from outside to eat here, your reputation is top-notch, and your food is excellent. Why change something that works? I need to sell you, get the people who visit from towns locally to see Crooked Tree as not just a place to visit every so often, but somewhere to revisit for riding lessons, or lunches, or...." Jay realized Sam was staring at him with his mouth open.

"You have a lot of ideas," Sam said with a grin.

Jay returned the smile with one of his own. His initial impression of Sam as a temperamental cliché chef was being eroded every time they met up. Maybe he was snappy and bossy only when he was in work mode.

"Everything okay?" Nate joined the conversation.

Jay turned to see Nate staring questioningly between himself and Sam. Jay couldn't decipher the look. Was Nate looking at him and feeling jealous, or was he looking at Sam and cursing lost chances? Sudden inspiration hit Jay and he took the three steps to stand in front of Nate, startling him.

"This is going to be awesome," Jay said. He crossed his hands behind Nate's head and pulled him down for a heated, sexy kiss.

Behind them Sam chuckled. "I get the message, Mr. Marketing Guy." Jay heard the door shut and relaxed into the kiss. He encouraged Nate back against the door and didn't argue when Nate flipped their positions until it was Jay trapped between the wood and a hard body. He couldn't get enough of being held and pushed and kissed by Nate.

"You were on Sam's list," he managed to say between kisses.

"I was? Hell, everyone is on Sam's list. Even Gabe, and he's straight."

"Sam doesn't seem like a guy who has lists."

"He doesn't." They kissed again. "Got his heart stomped on a few years back, found us—or we found him—and he keeps to himself. He's a quiet one when he's not in chef mode."

Interesting. Not that Sam was Jay's type, and he had Nate, who was very much his type, holding him, but he wondered who would break the heart of someone so damn cute.

"Did you see Gabe?" Jay asked.

"Yeah, he's out watching Lewis and Josh from a distance. Not sure Lewis likes it much—Gabe isn't being that inconspicuous."

"Your brother rocks."

"I didn't come here to talk about Gabe."

"What did you come here for, then?"

"Are you happy that Gabe has Lewis in his sights and your sister is okay?"

"I am."

"Good." With that single word, Nate pulled Jay close and kissed him hard.

The kisses became more in the blink of an eye. They only stopped when Jay pulled away and, after a bit of maneuvering, he had Nate pushed against the door. Jay got on his knees.

"We can't," Nate protested. "What if... the window... *guh.*"

Jay loved that he could reduce his lover to making no sense at all just by taking out Nate's cock and proceeding to completely and thoroughly blow him to orgasm. When Nate came, Jay didn't pull away; he swallowed and licked Nate's cock clean before tucking it away. Palming his own hard cock, he used the wall to help him stand. Nate had his eyes closed and was breathing heavily.

"Fuck," Nate said between breaths.

A knock on the door had the two men moving apart, Nate looking spaced out and Jay felt very satisfied with what he'd done. Nate looked down at Jay's hand, pressed against his own fly.

"I didn't—"

"We couldn't."

"Later."

"Later."

The knock came again and someone tried the door. "Jay? I have some more photos."

Luke. Nate immediately moved to the pictures on the wall, leaving Jay to open the door.

"Hi, Nate," Luke said quickly. He had a broad grin on his face and looked from Jay to Nate and back again. "You two do know this place has windows, right?"

CHAPTER TWENTY-THREE

To add more stress to the already crappy day, Jay had Henry to deal with, and it was only after Nate and Luke left that he realized the interview time was soon. Marcus was absolutely steadfast in the decision that Henry was going to be here for the rest of the season and palmed off the job of talking to Henry to Jay. Helping Nate to orgasm was going to be Jay's most successful part of the day. He'd fought off his temper talking to Lewis, and next he had to settle himself into management mode to speak to Henry.

"You wanted to see me?" Henry said from the door.

Jay shuffled to one side the new photos that he'd printed in draft, and he pulled out his notebook.

"I did, Henry. Please sit. Thank you for taking the time to visit."

"I follow orders," Henry said abruptly. "This ain't no social visit. Guessin' you got things to say." He folded his arms across his chest and sat bolt upright in the chair. His lips were tight and he looked like he was expecting trouble.

"I was working with some of our previous guests in order to create a full flow of information and feedback. I wanted to know what worked and what didn't, and I had discussions with a few who mentioned your name."

Henry said nothing. He only sat as still as stone. Nothing in his expression betrayed his emotions past an apparent disdain.

Jay continued. "I understand this is your last year with us." Henry still remained silent, so Jay forged on. "It's not my position to hire or fire here, but after discussions with Marcus, it was made very clear to me that I should talk to you about a couple of incidents that stood out in my research."

"Marcus says so, He should be here," Henry snapped.

"He wanted to be, but I didn't mean to put you in the position of answering questions that may make you uncomfortable. One couple complained, on three separate occasions, that you made comments about them that were offensive. Mr. and Mr. McAllister." Jay deliberately put the two Mr.'s at the beginning so that he could bring up the same-sex issue without actually mentioning the word.

"Ain't right," Henry said with a sneer. "Marrying two men, it's against God."

"Okay." Jay tried for patience. "That is your opinion. However, it certainly isn't the view of Crooked Tree."

"Bible says one man, one woman."

Jay blinked at the words. What the hell? "I'm sorry?"

"Saw 'em kissing like it was normal. You don't see Nate kissing men in public. He knows he should keep it inside and not let anyone know. What goes on behind closed doors is their decision, but doing it in public? Wrong."

Jay bit his lip to hold back the simmering temper left over from his encounter with Lewis. "For the record, the use of any homophobic language is not tolerated at

254 | RJ Scott

Crooked Tree. Consider this your warning. Your opinions are yours and yours alone. That brings me to the Miller family. Do you recall them?"

"Can't say as I do," Henry drawled. He'd dropped his arms from being crossed on his chest and his hands were clenched into fists in his lap.

"They had two sons and a daughter. The sons, Bryan and Tommy, had special needs."

"Ah...," Henry said, "the retarded boys. I remember 'em. Didn't want the horses to scare 'em."

Jay couldn't find the words at first. "'Retard' is another word you should be keeping to yourself. Crooked Tree does not tolerate any kind of hate words or bullying. These two cases are just the tip of an iceberg."

"What can I say, then?" Henry asked. "Seems to me that these days you can't say shit."

"Get it off your chest," Jay said immediately.

Henry looked genuinely puzzled and abruptly Jay's temper died a death. Henry really didn't seem to know what he was doing wrong. Was that Henry's fault? Or was it because of his age? He'd been on the ranch a long time, and what was considered acceptable had certainly changed since he was a young man.

Jay counted back from ten. "Tell me all the words that you want to say, so you won't need to say hate words around the guests."

"Hate words?" Henry huffed. "The world ain't the same." He shook his head and lowered his gaze.

"Can you just stop and think about what you're saying?" Jay considered suggesting some kind of training course that Henry could go on. Maybe to educate him as to what was right and not. Immediately he realized it was actually up to the younger staff to set Henry right. "You have to stop because I don't want to have to ask you to move on."

"Move on where?" Henry asked. His eyes filled with horror, then sadness, and Jay sat back in his chair.

Jay didn't quite understand the question. Henry was surely at retirement age, he'd probably want to potter in his garden and read the papers? Or whatever it was retired folks did.

"To your home?" Jay suggested.

"Since Maggie died I ain't got no home." Henry's voice was thick with emotion. He straightened in his seat. "You do your worst, but if I do something that ain't sitting right, you'll be taking me off this land in a coffin when my times up, 'cause I ain't going otherwise."

Henry's words slammed into Jay with enough force to steal his breath. "Henry, I didn't mean it to sound like I was forcing you out," he said quickly. After being fired himself, he knew exactly how that felt.

"Is that all?" Henry stood up and walked to the door.

"Henry…."

Henry turned, and there was a suspicious sheen in his eyes. "I'll keep my mouth shut from now on. I only need to be told once."

"Henry. Please." Jay stood. What could he do next? The damn man had more or less said that he was thinking of suicide or something. *Christ.* Marcus needed to know this. Jay followed him out and came face to face with Josh and Lewis. *Great, no chance to pull Henry to one side and talk.* Gabe was standing by the bridge, but that was far enough away that suddenly Jay was alone and facing his nemesis. With far too many witnesses to deck the bastard.

"We'll talk later, Henry," Jay called after the retreating figure.

Henry waved a hand and ambled toward the horses.

"Problem?" Lewis asked.

He'd made it sound like he was laughing as he asked and Jay immediately tensed up.

Josh grabbed his hand. "Uncle Jay, Dad said I could go visit him in the city if I want. Isn't that great? He said we can go see the Yankees an' everything."

Jay stared right at Lewis, who smirked. Words piled up inside Jay, but he couldn't say half of it until he had some alone time with Lewis. Preferably one-on-one at the top of a mountain so that he could shove the bastard off.

"That's wonderful, Josh," Jay lied. "Go get some cookies from your mom. Sophie asked for them." Jay added another lie, and Josh, being Josh, didn't question Jay at all.

Josh ran down the path and over the bridge, and Gabe went with him. That left Lewis and Jay standing toe to toe.

"He won't be visiting you," Jay said evenly.

"He will when I've finished overturning the order."

Jay crossed his arms over his chest. "One look at the pictures of Ashley covered in bruises and Josh's hospital report, and you'll be getting nothing, you fucking bastard." Jay took a step closer and was pleased when Lewis immediately stepped back.

Lewis held a hand up, and far too soon the smug expression was back on his face. "I'll call for an inquiry. Seems to me we could look at her brother for what happened to Josh."

They hadn't called Josh as a witness; the abuse against Ashley had been enough to persuade a judge and jury that Lewis was guilty.

"All they'll do is look back at what you did to Ashley," Jay hissed. He took another step closer, his hands clenched into fists at his side. The need to wipe the smug grin from Lewis's face was overwhelming.

This time Lewis didn't move back, he stood his ground and leaned in. "You gays are all the same—pussies. It's my duty to teach my wife where she stands with me."

Jay's fist moved of its own accord, but something stopped the swing and he stared down uselessly at the tanned hand gripping his arm.

"Cool your jets," Henry murmured. He faced down Lewis. "You been hitting on a woman?"

Jay hadn't heard Henry walk up to them, but clearly he'd been standing long enough to hear Jay's words.

Lewis sneered. "Fuck off, old man," he spat. "None of your business what I do in my own house."

"You hit on Josh too?" Henry continued. "That little boy is a dream, and you caused him pain?"

Henry took a step closer and Jay held up a hand. The last thing he wanted was his two worlds colliding. Seemed as if Henry had a different idea.

"All kids need a lesson, like their mommas," Lewis said evenly.

He punctuated the words with a smile, and Jay never saw Henry move. The blur of movement ended up with Lewis sprawled on the floor, cursing loudly, and Henry rubbing one fist with his other hand.

"Seems to me nothing is sacred in this world, and hell, some adults need lessons as well."

"I'll sue you," Lewis said with a grin, then winced as the cut on his lip dribbled blood.

"What for? You can't sue a horse for backing into you."

"What horse?"

"I saw a horse back into you." Henry shrugged in punctuation. "Jay, didn't you see a horse?"

Jay nodded seriously. "I saw a horse, Henry."

Henry left as quietly as he'd arrived, walking down the same way Josh had gone. Jay looked down at Lewis, then up at the sky. He'd wanted to hit the man, but he shouldn't. If he had succeeded, it would have made everything worse. Only Henry's intervention had saved him from making things more than they should be.

Lewis stood and brushed himself down. His face creased in a snarl and he clenched his hands into fists. Jay steadied himself for a fight. He wasn't going to be the first to throw a punch, but he would certainly hold his corner. Lewis shook his head, then pivoted to walk away.

Seemed like he was happy to hit on his wife and kids, but didn't want to fight grown men.

Jay figured him for the coward he was.

CHAPTER TWENTY-FOUR

Nate watched from the broken fence as Josh said goodbye to his dad. Gabe stood by his side and said nothing, even when Lewis touched Ashley on the arm. Gabe looked tense and stressed.

"He put his hands on her," he muttered.

"That wasn't anything," Nate said, firmly in big-brother mode. "Anyway, Jay is down there with them."

"He hurt her, bullied her. He hurt Josh."

"Jay won't let that happen again."

"I want to help her."

Gabe had his hands in fists and Nate placed a settling hand on his brother's arm. They couldn't say anymore because Kirsten walked toward them and came to a halt behind Gabe.

"I hate he gets to come here," she faux whispered. "Mom hates it, and I really think Jay may kill him one day."

Nate frowned. "Jay isn't capable of killing someone."

"He was the one who got Josh to the hospital. He wanted Lewis put away for life." The single word "Lewis" was saturated with disdain. "The thing is, Lewis being a lawyer had its perks. He ended up with soft time and only four years. Look at him. He's out in three."

"Lewis was a lawyer?"

"Intimidating asshole," Kirsten muttered.

Nate glanced at her, then did a double take. This wasn't the Kirsten he knew. She was wearing black, admittedly, but her hair was all one color and shorter, in some kind of bob thing held away from her face by probably an entire can of hairspray or gel or whatever, and she wasn't wearing makeup.

"You look...." Was it appropriate to comment on a teenager and how she looked? His only real experience with teenagers was Luke, and he was a whole different ball game.

"What?" Kirsten tilted her head to punctuate the question.

"Pretty," he finished.

She dimpled prettily. "You think?" She said this with doubt in her voice. "Luke said he wanted to take some more photos, so I thought I'd... y'know." She waved a hand at her fitted black shirt with thin silver stripes and her black skirt, which was short enough to reveal long slim legs.

"He'll love it."

"I wasn't doing it for him," she protested.

"I know. Nonetheless, he will love it."

Together in silence they watched Lewis leave, and as soon as the car rounded the bend, Gabe was down by Ashley and Josh. Gabe hugged Ashley and Nate smiled as Josh asked to be hugged as well. On the ground next to Josh was a box, and Nate assumed this was the iPad or whatever Lewis had bought him. Ashley scooped up the box, and together the three of them walked into the Sullivans' house.

"I like your brother, Nate," Kirsten said. "I like him a lot."

With that, she left, and Nate waited and watched as Jay stared into the distance and the direction the car had gone. Finally, Jay turned, and with a wave to Nate, he disappeared back into the office.

What had happened in the office earlier was mind-blowing. The sex they had—the *lovemaking*, he corrected himself—was intense and new and enough to make Nate weak-kneed. He'd decided he was keeping Jay. Nate simply had to make Jay see that a cowboy was exactly what he needed.

That was the hard part.

Luke ambled out of his room looking all kinds of nervous. It didn't take a genius to wonder why. He was going with Gabe down to the Sullivan place for dinner—he'd been invited by Kirsten, and that was the icing on the cake with all the Sullivans accounting for all the Todds in one fell swoop.

Nate scruffed Luke's hair, which he knew would send his brother straight back to a mirror. He was right.

"So are you girlfriend-boyfriend now?" he asked curiously when Luke came back out.

Luke blushed scarlet. "No, she's just a friend," he said quickly. A little too fast to Nate's ears.

"What about you?" Nate asked Gabe as he came into the room as well. Seemed as if Gabe had taken the same care and attention with his appearance as Luke had.

"What about me what?" Gabe grabbed a jacket and shrugged it on.

"Are you and Ashley girlfriend-boyfriend?" Nate smirked as he asked.

Gabe shook his head in despair. "What are you? Twelve?"

Luke sniggered and was first out the door. "Don't wait up, Mom," he called back at Nate.

"Ass" was the most Nate could come up with.

With both brothers gone, Nate was alone. He was expecting company, and tonight he had a lot to say to Jay. Starting from how the man wasn't allowed to leave Crooked Tree, *ever*, and ending with the truth about how Nate felt about him. He wasn't nervous, but he'd changed three times and checked and rechecked the chicken-in-a-pot thing that Sam had given him. He poked it with a fork and contemplated whether "simmering" was the odd bubble in the sauce or whether he should turn it up some. A knock at the door had him replacing the lid and hoping to hell he wasn't fucking up something Sam had prepared so nicely for him.

"I passed Gabe and Luke on the way down to ours," Jay observed, "sniggering about boyfriends like a couple of kids. Guess they're talking about us." He shrugged off his heavy coat, gloves, and hat, and laid everything on a chair near the door. His hair spiked up from the hat and Jay patted it down while sniffing appreciatively. "You cook?"

Nate was rooted to the spot. Overwhelming emotions threatened to have him on his ass on the floor. He couldn't find any words—none of the clever things he had thought to say, and sudden embarrassment flooded him. Jay stepped close; he carried the scent of outside with him. Nate shook his head mutely. How could he think of being able to put into sensible language any of what he felt for Jay? How long had it been? Three weeks? Four? Hell, he'd lost count of the days he'd spent thinking about Jay.

"Are you okay, Nate?" Jay asked seriously. He placed a hand on Nate's chest, right over his heart, and pressed gently. "You're worrying me! Did something happen?"

Nate cradled Jay's face and stared into brown eyes filled with concern and not a small amount of confusion. He wanted to explain that he'd never felt this way before, that this was new, that it felt right. He wanted desperately to have the words to use and not only resort to showing Jay how he felt by using sex. In the end he kissed Jay softly and sighed as Jay melted against him. Jay's hand on Nate's chest was trapped between them, but Jay snaked the other until he gripped tightly Nate's bicep. The kiss deepened, and Nate spent a long time tasting Jay and growing more and more restless in his skin. They separated, but Nate kept his hands cradling Jay's face.

"We have chicken," he murmured.

"Is that what you wanted to tell me?" Jay asked with a smile.

"That, and other stuff," Nate replied. He slid one hand up into Jay's dark blond hair and tamed the spikes with his fingers. "Want to eat?"

Jay's stomach rumbled and they both laughed at the sound. In minutes, they were all at the small kitchen table, forking chicken into their mouths and washing it down with a bottle of white wine that Sam had chosen for them.

"God, that was delicious," Jay commented as he scraped his plate clean.

Nate finished his. "Sam's good." The two glasses of wine had gone straight to his head, and everything had a deliciously soft glow to it. Including his head.

He pushed the plate to one side and closed a hand over one of Jay's. "So I wanted to talk."

"Okay, I'm listening."

Nate nodded. The action gave him time to gather his thoughts. "I love you," he said quietly. "I can't imagine not seeing you every day, or having you go off and learn to ride somewhere else, or sleep in another man's bed, or love anyone else." He finished and exhaled noisily, then waited for a response, but all Jay did was stare at him. "Say something," Nate prompted.

"Okay," Jay began slowly. "If you think I would even consider getting on a horse if it weren't for you making me, you're mistaken. So you can cross that off your list of worries."

Nate frowned. "All I said, and you pick up on the horse thing?"

Jay tilted his head like he was deep in thought. "I kind of like your bed. It's big and sturdy and doesn't squeak like mine does. So I think I'm pretty happy agreeing to that point."

"The bed? Really?" Nate had to believe Jay was teasing him.

"And I work here, so I'm happy to see you every day. I can't really not see you every day."

A glint of something in Jay's eyes sent relief scurrying through Nate. Jay *was* teasing him. *The fucker.*

"So that just leaves the 'love you' part." Jay leaned forward and Nate copied the movement instinctively. The table was too wide to kiss across, but they could lean close enough for Jay to whisper what he wanted to say and for Nate to hear him. "I love you too, Cowboy. So how about you give me a drawer in your room and I stay in your bed every night, you teach me how to ride Diablo, and how about we plan that I see you every day?"

"Really?"

"Really." Jay shook off Nate's hand and gathered up the plates to place in the sink. He turned on the hot tap and rinsed off the dishes before putting them in the dishwasher. All the while Nate sat exactly where he was, watching Jay organize what was left of their dinner. Finally, Jay turned and leaned back against the sink.

"I need to make sure the bed is okay, really," he said firmly.

In a flurry of motion, Nate was up and dragging Jay into his bedroom. Jay was laughing and tugging back, and the combined effort caused them to trip and tumble in a tangle of legs and arms onto the large, sturdy bed. Jay landed on Nate, and the weight of him was intoxicating. Nate was already so damn turned on, and he widened his legs so that Jay could settle between them. They kissed lazily, and Nate slipped his hands up and under Jay's T-shirt before pushing it up in a bunch under his arms. A quick shimmy from Jay and the offending item was off, with Nate's following suit.

Nate couldn't recall a single memory of making love like this. With no particular goal and the quickest way to get there in mind. What he was doing here was all about learning, taste and touch. *Intoxicating.* The kissing turned to touching, and when Jay lifted a little to reach between them, Nate flipped them so he could cage Jay beneath him. Slowly he unbuttoned Jay's jeans and kissed each inch of skin exposed by removing the worn material. Nate concentrated for a long time on the stretch of skin across Jay's hipbones, and when he had Jay pushing up toward his touch, he knew he wanted more. Very deliberately he peeled down the jeans and boxers and pulled them off with the socks until after a short time Jay lay naked on the quilt. Jay's cock was thick with need and he kept palming himself; squirming at the touch.

"Hurry up," Jay ordered.

Nate was naked in seconds and climbing back up the bed, stopping at each knee and beginning to kiss a trail from knee to groin. Each kiss had Jay sighing, and when Nate reached the prize, Jay twisted his fingers into Nate's hair and encouraged him to get with the program.

Nate didn't argue; he didn't tease; he quietly set about sending Jay high with lips and tongue as he worshiped Jay's cock and brought him to the edge.

"Close...," Jay warned with a hitch in his breathing. "Stop." He used the grip in Nate's hair to push him away. "In me."

Nate rolled off and opened the top drawer of the cabinet next to the bed. He retrieved the condoms and lube. Slowly Nate set about stretching Jay enough so that he could get inside. He sucked Jay down and pressed fingers inside him, crooking one finger and sending Jay skyward. Massaging softly, he felt Jay swell impossibly in his mouth.

"No... *God*." Jay whimpered. He arched into Nate's mouth, then down onto his fingers.

Nate couldn't wait any longer. He released Jay's cock and scrambled to a half sit. Jay made to turn over and offer his ass, but Nate stopped him and instead used his thighs to rock Jay back and spread his legs. With a press of his cock, he breached Jay, then pushed deeper as soon as Jay pleaded for him to do so. Nate checked for signs of discomfort, but all he saw in Jay's expression was obvious need.

"I love you," Nate said as he set a rhythm.

"I—I—l-love you," Jay said brokenly. He closed his eyes and it seemed like every muscle in him tensed. "So close."

"What you do to me," Nate said as he watched Jay come apart under him.

When Jay arched up and yelled his completion, Nate lost it inside him and bent to capture Jay's lips. Nate needed the connection so badly. They kissed as they fucked through the orgasm, and when they stilled, it was Jay who spoke first.

Jay patted the covers. "I think we need to test the bed again."

EPILOGUE

Jay could not be prouder of his sister. Somehow she had made the liaison job her own. Guests arrived happy and informed, and Ashley was there to help them in any way possible. After discussions with Nate, she'd taken over booking the rides. She argued it gave her an overview of the kinds of events she could offer to guests. The system worked. Nate gave an indication of available days and Ashley organized everything else. The ranch had been open to paying guests for two weeks by then, and the first proof of the brochure sat on his desk, unopened.

Something was stopping him. The website was working, traffic increasing, and Jay had optimized it for visibility and managed to visit businesses close by to feature local links. As stupid as it sounded in his head, the website was a constant work in progress, but the brochure was a defined goal that he had achieved. He had the PDF on disc. In a matter of minutes, he could have the file up on the website for everyone to see.

Jay picked up the envelope and turned it over. He'd received marketing material proofs before. He knew it was perfect. At this stage, if it was his decision, he'd only reject it for printing errors. So why was this so damn awkward?

Jay left the office with the package under his arm, then made his way up past Marcus's house. Marcus and

Sophie sitting on the front step holding hands. Jay didn't stop, he just waved and they both waved back, albeit not enthusiastically. They seemed to be discussing important things, and Jay wondered if Nate had talked to Marcus about this blood thing. He added it to his list of questions, but almost forgot it as he focused back on the package in his hands.

Jay walked on, past the abandoned, empty Strachan place and finally made it to the Todd house. There were no signs of anyone inside, and Jay almost turned around and left there and then.

Until he heard laughter.

All three Todd brothers sat on chairs on the porch. Jay knew from the schedule that Nate had been on a trail ride today with two families. Five hours of riding, exploring and picnicking wasn't Jay's idea of fun.

He settled down next to Nate and coughed to get his attention.

"I heard you coming up the hill," Nate murmured.

"You done for the day?"

"Yep. You?"

Gabriel coughed, then wondered away, with Luke trailing him, likely giving Jay and Nate space.

Jay looked at his watch: 6:00 p.m. and he was all finished for the day. Apart from the damn brochure burning a hole under his arm. "I have something to show you." He waited until Nate sat upright, then passed him the envelope.

"What is it?"

"The brochure. The proof, so we can do final checks."

Nate turned it over in his hands. "It's still sealed."

"I wanted you to see it first. See if it's right."

Nate nodded and slid a finger under the seal. He pulled the full brochure out and placed it on his lap. The front was a view from the outcrop where the older Todds' ashes were buried. Luke had captured the change in season from spring to summer, and the Montana sky was sapphire blue.

Jay looked at the cover through Nate's eyes. Nerves assailed him. "Maybe I shouldn't have used the view from such a special place for you?" He second-guessed himself.

"Why not? It's stunning." Page by page Nate looked at the content. Every so often he commented on a photo and he paused for a long while on the picture of him and Gabe with their boots up on the lower rung of the corral fence. With his finger, he traced the shape of Juno, who was standing next to them in the photo. Finally, he closed the brochure and examined the back. The logo repeated on each page, and the story of the logo with simple words and illustrations faded behind one sentence in bold. Jay read out each page as Nate turned them.

"And there's a tag line with every use of the logo," Jay said. "For your family, from our family."

Nate reached out and curled a hand around the back of Jay's neck. Tenderly he kissed him. Jay assumed this was a good reaction. When they pulled back, they stared into each other's eyes, and something profound passed between them.

"I love you," Nate said. "I love what you have done here, what your family has done. I want this forever."

Nate tapped the brochure with a single finger, and Jay felt himself blushing bright red. He'd never had quite this reaction to a completed job before.

"What do you say to that?" Nate asked.

"I love you, Nathaniel Todd," Jay said immediately.

"And the 'forever' part?"

Jay huffed a laugh and stole a kiss. "Forever? That's a given."

THE END

THE RANCHER'S SON

Montana 2, coming March 2016

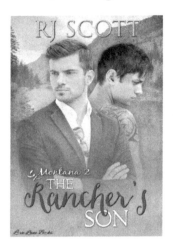

The victim of a brutal beating, John Doe, has no memories of who he is or who hurt him. The cops can find nothing to identify him and he can't remember anything to help... except the name Ethan and one recurring place from his dreams. Three words and they're not much, but it's a start. Crooked Tree Ranch.

Cop, Ethan Allens has never stopped searching for his brother, Justin, and his brother's best friend, Adam, who both vanished in 2004. When a report lands on Ethan's desk that may give new leads, he jumps at the chance to follow them up. The man he finds at the end of this new lead isn't his brother. But, could it be enough to help him discover what happened and rekindle young love?

What neither man can know is that facing the very real demons of the past could kill them both.

RJ SCOTT

RJ Scott lives just outside London. She has been writing since age six, when she was made to stay in at lunchtime for an infraction involving cookies and was told to write a story. Two sides of A4 about a trapped princess later, a lover of writing was born. She loves reading anything from thrillers to sci-fi to horror; however, her first real love will always be the world of romance. Her goal is to write stories with a heart of romance, a troubled road to reach happiness, and more than a hint of happily ever after.

Email: rj@rjscott.co.uk

Webpage: www.rjscott.co.uk

Facebook: facebook.com/author.rjscott

Twitter: twitter.com/rjscott_author

Made in the USA
Columbia, SC
08 March 2018